Chinese Lolita

Lisa Zhang Wharton

Chinese Lolita

Lisa Zhang Wharton

Cover design: Ceri Clark (original design) and Kate Leibfried

Printed in the United States of America
ISBN-13: 979-8730325302
ISBN-10: 8730325302

A project by Click Clack Writing, LLC
www.ClickClackWriting.com

Table of Contents

Disclaimer

Though several of the enclosed stories were inspired by true events, many were fictionalized to some degree or were entirely the product of the author's imagination. In several cases, names have been changed or characters invented.

Acknowledgments

People, places, memories—all have contributed to this book. I would like to thank the environment where I came of age, the Beijing Institute of Aeronautics and Astronomy in Beijing, China. I would like to thank the various nice and nasty people I grew up with, the culture, and the good and bad times.

Thank you to my father, now in heaven, for the intelligent genes he gave me and for his work ethic. And thank you to my mother, for the colorful life she has led. Although we had our difficult moments, she presented me with a world filled with many different shapes and angles.

I would like to thank my eccentric first husband, Dr. Arnold Lande, for his encouragement and contribution to my growth as a woman, an engineer, and an American. Thank you to my husband, Eric Wharton, for his persistent and silent support. And many thanks to my son, William Wharton, for his genuine encouragement and admiration.

Thank you to my editor, Kate Leibfried, for her keen eye and insights.

Thank you to Ceri Clark, who designed the original cover. It captured the heart of this book perfectly.

Many thanks to the *Paris Transcontinental* magazine for publishing my first story "My Uncle" and awarding me the second prize in their WICE competition.

Many thanks to *Great River Review* for publishing my story "Lolita II: A Chinese Student's Story."

Prologue

People often say I smile too much. To that, I answer, "What is there to cry about?" I am truly happy now, though I haven't always had much to be happy about. Given my family history and where I grew up, it is frankly astonishing that I am still alive and breathing. Because of that, I do not take my days for granted and I see no reason to live in misery. I choose happiness.

Was I happy growing up? Yes. To be sad was to waste time, I reasoned. But I was not always happy. I was unhappy when my mom brought boyfriends home right in front of my father. I was unhappy when my father threatened to kill my mother with a cleaver. I was unhappy when my father threw a shoe at me and injured my nose. Despite it all, I imagined my life would be much better than that of my parents. Some considered me a fantastical dreamer, but I knew I had the smarts and determination to achieve anything. And I was right. After years of diligently studying at school, I eventually won a scholarship to come to America. That scholarship was my ticket to leave the suffocation of Communist China and my dysfunctional and abusive family. I thought I was cleansed. But, that society and the crazy family I left behind are forever imprinted on my body, no matter how much I try to hide them.

Trial

Mother was arrested. They locked her in the county jail as she awaited her trial.

I stood on the front steps of our apartment building, staring at the brick-paved alley. Mother's voice resounded in my mind as the three stern-faced policemen pulled her away.

"Meihua, please take care of yourself. Okay? Mom will be all right. Mom will be all right!" She looked back at me hard, her swarthy face calm. Her loose fitting, half-buttoned tan blouse billowed in the air, as though she might fly away like a balloon and the policemen had to hold her fast.

When she arrived at the door of the police jeep, she halted and turned back to me. "Meihua, please remember Mom, remember me!" Tears streamed down her face.

"Mother, Mother." I ran toward the jeep.

The police jerked her in and slammed the door. They disappeared in a cloud of dust.

"Mother, Mother!" I screamed.

Our home was a mess. The police had pushed a wooden bunkbed to the center of the living room next to my father's desk; the dining table was shoved into a corner against the wall. Paper scattered the floor everywhere. The sheets in Mother's bedroom were stripped, leaving a bare mattress. The police had taken every piece of valuable furniture, including our only tape player. Reels of magnetic tapes sprawled on the floor like broken wagon wheels.

In my room stood a bare wooden bedframe, a dusty mattress, and an empty table. They had stolen my electric guitar, the cello, and even my cheap violin. I covered my face with my hands, sobbing while listening to my father and his younger brother Xiangdong, a policeman, talking.

"Brother, don't feel too bad about this. See how much trouble this woman has caused you! How much money has she squandered on her criminal friends? She deserves to be locked up for life."

Xiangdong waved a fat hand. Wrapped tightly in the blue police outfit, Xiangdong was a gigantic man. He had a square face, a broad forehead, and a wide nose that mirrored Father's. A pair of thick, black-framed glasses sat on his nose like two camera lenses—he was constantly taking pictures of people. A purple wedge-shaped scar sat under his right eye, like an additional eye for spying. Xiangdong had worked as a police investigator for thirty years and had already intimidated me with a hand revolver and leather-sheathed sharp knife.

"God damnit!" Father had dressed up a little. He even had a pair of ironed gray trousers on. His yellowish irises were hollow, and his cracked lips drooped at the corners. His hair had turned grayer overnight.

"I know you don't feel good about it." Xiangdong slithered his heavy body forward and laid his arm on Father's shoulder.

"Shit, that goddamn woman!" Father cursed as though he had not heard Xiangdong's words.

"Don't worry. Tell them you were blind to what she had done. She cheated on you and stole from you. She was corrupted by thugs and thieves."

8

I rushed from my room to confront them. "They are not thugs and thieves."

Xiangdong's eyes widened behind thick glasses; his eyeballs were two big olives staring at me. "How can you be so sure? Do you know your mother's friend Zhuzhu stole the cello, the desk, and the tape player from his work unit?"

"She's been corrupted by that woman." Father's old eyes looked sad.

"Stealing from the government is not stealing. They bought everything with people's money." Zhuzhu had told me this once.

"Damnit, how dare you defend those thieves? They are in jail now. Have you swallowed the devil's heart?" Father pounded his fist on the desk so hard, his flowerpots danced and clattered on the wooden desk. His bloodshot eyes stared as though he did not know me.

Startled, I backed off a few steps. It is a bad time to bother Father, I told myself. He might vent his anger on me.

"Big brother, calm down. Don't be too hard on yourself." Xiangdong patted Father's shoulder. "Kids don't understand. She is only fourteen. She'll grow to find out what kind of person her mother is."

"Yes." Father dropped his head. Shame stole away his courage.

"How about this," Xiangdong said, "I'll buy some wine and sausage and we can talk about how to deal with the judge."

"Wait." Father said, rummaging through the desk drawer. He found a crumpled ten-yen bill and handed it to Xiangdong, who swiveled his big body happily out the door.

"You don't understand," I murmured as I walked back to my room. "And you'll never understand Mother and me." The room felt quiet as I walked in. Just a week earlier, I had walked into live music—a sad song from *The Flower Girl*, a popular North Korean movie. Mother's friend Zhuzhu had sat in front of our old vacuum-tube radio, playing an electric guitar. His long stringy hair danced around his head and his plaid bellbottom trouser cuffs waved as he played his guitar with passionate fingers. I picked up my violin and began to play, singing along to the music. Mother smoked and watched.

On other occasions, we played cards. Sometimes Zhuzhu gave me hand-written, government-banned novels to read. Once we fired a hunting rifle at Mother's bedroom wall. I was a very good shot at two meters. Those were happy days. But they were gone, gone forever. I threw myself to the bare mattress and cried.

Father sauntered in and said, "Shame on you for crying. If you don't stop, I'm going to send you to jail, too."

The assistant judge showed us into the municipal judge's cold, bare office. A wooden desk with a few beads of paint coating the legs stood in the middle, covered with loose paper and a white, tea-stained enamel mug. On the left, a tan bookshelf held only a few volumes on the top shelf, most of which were written by Chairman Mao. A radiator sat under a screened window with a silver aluminum lunchbox perched on top. Next to it, two enamel bowls stacked together with a spoon and a pair of chopsticks in them. Toward the far side of the room, a floral metal basin rested on a wire frame, half full of brown soapy water.

We sat on two wooden stools in front of the desk, just as the judge barged in. Father stood immediately, and I followed. Father's legs were shaking. The judge, a large woman about forty years old, motioned for us to sit. Her plain appearance—an old polyester shirt and a pair of faded blue khakis—did not undermine her power. We waited until she sat on the opposite side of the desk. A huge, colored portrait of Chairman Mao hung over her head. His smooth face and graceful smile made him look like a Buddha. The assistant judge, a lanky young man wearing a loose-fitting white shirt and olive-green pants, sat next to the judge. The judge stared at us with two small, round eyes. Defeated by her stern face, Father dropped his head and folded his arms around his body as though he wanted to shrink to nothing. I glanced at the assistant judge. He was still smooth faced, probably just a hair over twenty. His eyes were exceptionally big on his small hollow-cheeked face.

"Well." The judge cleared her throat. "You know why you are here?"

"Yes, yes." Father nodded like a chicken picking grain from the ground.

"Zhang Meiling, your wife—although you may prefer not to call her your wife, if you're considering divorcing her," she cleared her throat again, "has been convicted by our great justice system for having a liaison with comrade Wang Baozhu, head of Beijing Automobile Parts Factory. She is sentenced to two years in prison. No appeals are allowed. You should be grateful our great Communist party has given her a second chance to reform herself and wash away the criminal thoughts from her mind."

"Who...who is this comrade Wang Baozhu?" Father lifted his head and glanced at the judge.

"He is the Secretary General of the Communist Party at Beijing Automobile Factory."

"Yes. But I...I didn't realize she was actually...with him," Father dropped his head again. "She just began working there two months ago."

"Two months are long enough for lots of things," smirked the judge, showing her protruding front teeth.

"But, they...they hardly know each other."

"That's the worst part." Saliva sprayed from cracks between her front teeth. "She seduces and corrupts our heads of the Communist Party with the meanest and dirtiest methods, which has even corrupted our model leader, Wang Baozhu. Comrade Wang Baozhu, who came from a poor peasant's family, joined the party at age seventeen, and was wounded during the Civil War. Pity him."

"Yes, yes." Father's body began to shiver.

I shifted on my stool, feeling as though I had a hot iron beneath me. I was so angry, like a bubble on the verge of bursting. This is ridiculous, I said to myself. Mother never liked that man and never would. I remembered she once told me how filthy and obnoxious Wang Baozhu was. He had chased her and wanted her. That was why he had used his power to transfer Mother from her old working unit to the Beijing Automobile Parts Factory.

"Okay." The judge slapped the table with her palm so loudly it woke me from my reminiscence. "Any questions?" She glanced around with her two pig eyes. "If you want to know which prison she is going to or what she might need for her stay, you may talk to my assistant." She stood.

"Yes, yes." Father nodded repeatedly. He grasped the judge's desk and pushed against it to help him stand.

"Wait!" The judge waved her fat arm. "Before you leave, I want to talk to your daughter privately."

Father followed the assistant judge out as if he were the convicted criminal.

I sat back on the stool, playing with my fingers. What had I done wrong? Maybe they found out I had spent time with my mother and her friends, and they were going to charge me with the same crime. My heart began thumping so hard it almost broke my eardrums. The judge said, "Meihua, would you come here?" She leaned against the windowsill with her back facing me. Her face was full of mock solemnity that undercut her authority. But I had to obey her. It would be foolish not to.

"What do you think of your mother's sentence?" She scanned me up and down.

"Good," I murmured, holding back tears.

"You must be happy to get rid of your terrible mother!"

I nodded and began digging dirt out of my left thumbnail.

"Has your father ever done that to you?" She turned and leaned toward me.

I did not respond.

"I mean, has he ever had sexual relations with you?"

"What?" I looked up and saw the judge's fierce face. Her front teeth stuck out like fangs. I shivered, but I could not comprehend her words.

"I mean, has your father ever raped you?" she shouted. Saliva sprayed my face.

Father rape me? What a shameful question. How could I answer her? My teeth began to chatter. I stared at the floor, face burning hot down to my neck. I shook my head.

The judge put her arm on my shoulder and said, "Calm down. Let me tell you the rules again. You should put aside your personal feelings toward your father. This is a public morality matter. You should be as honest with me as you would with Chairman Mao. Remember, you belong to your country first, and *then* to your family."

I nodded again. Yes, I will be as honest with you, as I would with Chairman Mao. I began searching through my memory. Did Father always run around at home with just his underwear on? Did Father always frown whenever I mentioned books about love or sex? It was not because he did not like those kinds of books. It was because he was guilty in his heart for thinking about the same thing.

"Don't think you can get away without telling the truth. We are going to treat you just like your mother." Her face moved closer to me, eyes popping. I could see her teeth, sharp as nails.

"Oh, yes... Father urinated in front of me." Words slipped out of my mouth.

"Congratulations. I'm glad you have finally overcome your selfish feeling toward your father and confessed to an authority." She patted my head with one of her fat hands, and I felt like spitting at her.

"Xiao Liu!" she called out.

The assistant judge showed up in an instant. I did not realize he had been standing outside the door, listening.

"Would you bring Professor Chen in?" she asked.

Father followed the assistant judge into the room. His head drooped down; his hands awkwardly folded behind his back like a prisoner ready for execution. The judge and her assistant took him to the window and let me wait by the door.

"I obtained enough evidence to prove you molested your daughter."

Father's mouth dropped. "Is...is that what she said?"

"No, she said you urinated in front of her repeatedly. This is enough evidence from a fourteen-year-old girl. She is innocent. She doesn't know how to explain sexual conduct."

"Yes, yes. I'm guilty. I'm guilty."

Mother was sent to prison. I could visit her once every six months. Father got a warning for his conduct but felt too embarrassed to visit Mother.

"I'm not going to visit a criminal. You'd better separate yourself from her activities. Otherwise, they will put you in jail, too."

I didn't want to go alone—frightened of entering a place so foreign to me—but I couldn't reject mother's plea.

Dear Meihua,

Please come visit me. I am so lonely here. When I first arrived, I spent days crying. Now, I understand I can't just cry for two years. I need to live through this and be with you again. The prison guard was sympathetic. He knew I was a wrongly accused criminal and gave me jobs that were not so physically demanding, like taking care of the stove. But I want to see you. I can't live another day without seeing you. Can you imagine I have to ask permission to use the bathroom?

Come soon. I need money and a sewing kit. Don't let them find out when you pass these things to me. They are forbidden here. What would I do without money?

Love you,
Mom

I awoke before dawn, tied a few items beneath my bicycle seat, and pedaled toward the prison. It took two hours to reach Beijing First Prison and by the time I arrived, I was dripping sweat. A female prison official met me at the small opening cut out of the heavy, metal door. She had short hair and glasses that sat on the brim of her small nose. She smiled broadly.

"Hi, Meihua. I am your mother's counselor. My job is to reform your mother and help her become a good person again. She is working on it and is making excellent progress." The woman overwhelmed me with her nice demeanor. I hadn't expected that from a prison worker.

After passing through the metal door, I followed the counselor to a large visitor's room. Mother, sitting at a table, looked up at me with her round, swarthy face. She looked healthy and had gained weight in prison.

"How are you doing," she asked with a big smile.

"Good." I nodded. Tears streamed down my face.

I spent our entire hour together crying. At the end of my visit, Mother gave me a hug, and I slipped the money and the sewing kit into her hand. I felt like a counter-revolutionary guerilla.

After she was released, Mother told me details about prison that she couldn't divulge during our short meetings.

"I met many talented people in prison who could sing and dance, and we often had concerts." We sat together on her bed, her smoking, me listening with rapt attention. "I learned that talented people are often not perfect. One prisoner was an army doctor who, with help from her boyfriend, murdered her husband. Another Xinjiang dancer liked to steal." Cigarette smoke swirled out of Mother's nose.

"The only thing I didn't like was having to ask permission to use the bathroom. But that's a small price to pay for the chance to meet a collection of brilliant individuals. Some prisoners had been arrested simply because their parents were high-ranking officials who were no longer in favor." She made the prison sound like a place where one met talented or powerful people. I began to develop sympathy toward the prisoners.

Years later, after I had moved to the United States, I saw Mother's experience in prison through a different lens. Here, prisoners were thought of as an uneducated and unattractive group of people. They were beaten, raped, and had to learn underhanded survival tricks. In the bestselling book "*White Oleander*," Ingrid tells her daughter Astrid about her roommate in prison:

Dear Astrid,

I look at the fires that burn on the horizon and I only pray they come closer, immolate me. You have proved every bit as half-witted as your school once claimed you were. You'll attach yourself to anyone who shows you the least bit of attention, won't you? I wash my hands of you. Do not remind me that it has been two years since I last lived in the world. Do you think I would forget how long it has been? How many days, hours, minutes I have sat looking at the walls of this cell, listening to women with a vocabulary of twenty-five words or less?

Great-Grandmother's Brothel

They sat on the train in silence. Great-Grandmother Weipo munched on phoenix claws (duck feet) while Great-Grandfather Weigong chewed a piece of Shuzhou roasted chicken, soft and tender with a hint of smokiness. Pearl and Jade were having boiled edamame. Looking out the window, Moon ate nothing. She cried silently and swallowed her tears. She wanted to go home, yet she knew she belonged to Weipo now, sold to the old woman by her family, who had lost everything in the flood. She had to make money to support them. Outside, a few bottomless houses floated in the flooded rice field. The train chugged along for five hours, nearing Shanghai as Shuzhou was left behind.

In Shanghai, the girls settled into the second floor of an old, shaky building on North Gong Xi Road. It sat within walking distance of the Big World; a famous entertainment center renamed People's Square after the Communists took over. All three girls were very excited to go to the Big World.

"Tomorrow, we are going shopping," declared Weipo, "but the day after tomorrow, you have to bring me back a man from the Big World."

"A man?" asked Pearl.

"Just like me," said Weigong, pointing to his own chest.

"Stop, you old geezer!" Weipo said angrily. She blew smoke from her pipe and turned to the girls. "You must earn money. You think I brought you three here to tour the city?"

Inside the shaky, wooden building, the girls occupied three rooms. A narrow, steep stairway led up to the second floor, where the big living room, master bedroom, and a smaller back bedroom were situated. The big living room and master bedroom were really the same room, divided by a folding screen. Moon, Pearl, and Jade shared the back bedroom, which also served as a lavatory, with a wooden chamber pot hidden behind a curtain. Every morning, the chamber pot was carried down the narrow stairway and emptied into the collection carts.

"Dao Ma Tong (Empty the toilet)!" people would chant in the alley. Weigong usually did the deed. The girls got up afterward and had a quiet breakfast.

"It was easy," said Pearl. She popped a piece of fried dough in her mouth and took a sip of soymilk.

"Men are easy creatures," said Weigong. He already sounded a little drunk. "You give them food, and they will come. Of course, in this case *you* are the food."

"Stop, you old geezer," Pearl imitated Weipo. Weigong was very popular with the girls, even though he was drunk half the time. He managed to be a nice man, despite his imperfections.

More than a week had passed, and Pearl was adjusting well to her new life. She laid with several men every night. Even Jade was beginning to secure regular customers. Moon, however, had not yet attracted a single man.

20

"You need to put on more makeup so you will be noticed on the street," said Pearl.

"No, you have to smile," Jade disagreed.

"Smile? She really can't smile," countered Pearl.

"She just doesn't feel like it," said Jade.

"She has to get a man tonight or she is out of here," said Weipo in her usual cold voice. Her pale face resembled a ghost; her two slanted eyes were sharp and penetrating under long, artificial eyebrows. Moon rose and ran to her makeshift room— the third bedroom located under the stairway at the mezzanine level. She fell on her bed and cried. Pearl followed her in.

"You know she didn't mean it. Her mouth is like a knife, but her heart is tofu. I will help you tonight. I bet you can find a gentleman who would like an ice queen like you. Wait here. I want to show you something." Pearl ran upstairs to her room. She brought down an embroidered silk jewelry box and opened it. A few golden rings glowed under the light.

"Look. I stole these wedding rings from my gentleman customers."

"Wow, so many already," said Moon.

"What are you girls crying about?" Weigong appeared in the doorway and handed a few sesame pancakes to the girls.

"None of your business," teased Pearl.

"Okay," he said, and went away singing.

"I want to leave this place," Moon cried again.

"Maybe you can get pregnant with someone and he'll marry you." Pearl's eyes rolled slyly.

"What if the gentleman does not want to marry me?"

"Then you get an abortion and get one month off."

"I don't think the old ghost would like it."

"No, but it's worth trying."

"Pearl and Moon, come upstairs," called Jade.

They ran up and sat around the table.

"We have guests tonight," announced Weipo. "Mr. Liu, Mr. Mao, and Mr. Xia will come to our place tonight and play Majiong. I want you three to stay and entertain these gentlemen. Put on your best clothes and be on your best behavior," Weipo commanded. "Especially you, Moon. This may be your opportunity."

They immediately went to the back room to give each other baths in the wooden basin. Pearl went downstairs to lift water with a wooden pail. Jade heated the water on the stove by the back room. Moon washed everyone's hair in the same basin of water. After washing their hair, they poured the water into a bigger basin, added more hot water, and bathed themselves. Pearl and Jade would take turns carrying the used water downstairs to pour into the alley.

After the bath, all three girls gathered in Moon's room to dress up and put on makeup. Despite its darkness, the windowless back room was quiet and private. Moon put on a yellow silk, embroidered qipao. Pearl wore a red one, while Jade wore green.

"Imperial yellow," Pearl commented. "You will have good luck tonight."

Moon flashed a smile.

With the yellow silk robe draped over her tiny frame, a golden cuff around her neck, cheeks painted pink, and lips drawn rosy red, she looked exceptionally beautiful.

The three girls sat around the table, waiting for the guests to arrive. Plate after plate of food was set on the table. The first course consisted of a cold cut sampler, with sliced pig tongues, liver, and beef, as well as jellyfish salad, radish salad, and garlic pickles. The smell of steamed crabs with ginger and garlic permeated the house. Despite the delectable smells, Moon could not pay attention to food. She was nervous, and she hoped she would like one of the gentlemen tonight. Maybe she could convince him to marry her. Then, they would have a family and a few kids. She heard footsteps approaching.

"Moon, smile. Our guests are coming." Pearl nudged Moon, bringing her back to reality.

"Welcome to our establishment. Please sit down." Smiling broadly, Weipo showed the guests their seats.

"Please enjoy some wine and cold plates. Later, we will serve freshly cooked giant lake crabs. Let me introduce my husband, Mr. Cheng, and our three beautiful daughters, Moon, Pearl, and Jade."

The three girls stood and bowed.

Two of the gentlemen wore shabby western-style suits, while the third wore a traditional Chinese long robe. This man chose a seat next to Moon.

"My name is Mr. Liu Xing. What's your name?"

"Moon." She answered immediately, but in such a low voice no one could hear it.

Weipo waved a hand. "She came from the Xiangwuo—the countryside."

Mr. Liu replied, "I, too, came from Xiangwuo a few years ago to learn how to repair watches. I finished my apprenticeship recently and started my own watch repair shop. I didn't like Shanghai when I first came here. It was too noisy and had too many crazy people, who drove me crazy, too. Now I'm just another one of them." Mr. Liu's remark made Moon laugh.

Pearl could not believe her ears. Moon laughing! She must have hit the jackpot.

Weigong nudged Pearl. "Tell Moon to have some of her favorite jellyfish."

"No. Let's not bother them." Pearl shook her head.

Moon and Mr. Liu were still talking, even after the main course arrived—red-cooked crab meat accompanied by pork steamed with rice flour. After dinner, the pair went downstairs to Moon's room. In the dim light of her cramped bedroom, Moon slipped out of her yellow qipao and gave her virginity to Mr. Liu.

After that, Mr. Liu visited almost every night, which made Weipo very happy. First, they used Moon's room. Later, after Mr. Liu's business grew and he began earning more money, they occasionally spent nights in the World Hotel in the Big World.

One day, Weipo asked Moon, "Are you in love with Mr. Liu?"

"Yes," nodded Moon.

"I thought you knew that's forbidden."

Moon was speechless.

"Okay." Weipo really liked the income from Mr. Liu. "Remember, don't get pregnant. If you do, he will abandon you."

Moon nodded, even though this was precisely her plan. She would get pregnant by Mr. Liu, he would marry her, and she would finally leave this place. She wanted a home with a flush toilet and running water. Even though Mr. Liu had not promised marriage, she somehow sensed he would. Even if he marries other women later, Moon said to herself, I still want to be his wife.

It wasn't long before she became pregnant.

"I want to keep this baby," said Moon to Weipo.

"No. You must have an abortion. You don't want to raise a child in this crazy place." Weipo was firm.

"He is a gentleman and a businessman. I am hoping he will marry me," said Moon quietly.

"A good catch! Why do you think he would marry you?" said Weipo, blowing out a smoke ring.

With decades more experience than Moon, Weipo was, of course, correct. Mr. Liu did not marry Moon, and that broke the young woman's heart. Rumor had it, Mr. Liu married a rich girl to enhance his business.

Moon had suspected that life would be difficult after her family sold her to Weipo, but she had never imagined things would turn so sour, so quickly. During her pregnancy, she rarely left her room. Another brothel had opened on the third floor, and all night long she could hear people going up and down the stairs outside her door. The constant creak of stairs put her on-edge and made her irritable. Weipo gave her no love. She refused to send her home, since she had not made much money yet and had quickly become a liability.

In 1937, when Japanese troops announced their arrival with daily bombs and artillery fire, the baby—my mother May—was born. Moon threw May on the ground and ran, screaming, into the street, wishing to die in the next bomb raid. She was sent to an insane asylum and was kept there for three months.

Weipo kept May. She grew into a young woman of extraordinary beauty. After Moon was released from the insane asylum, Weipo sold her to a different watch merchant, twenty years her senior. She became his third wife and lived a prosperous life in a lavish apartment on the opulent Nanjing Road. Her days were spent playing cards and wearing pretty dresses. With the watch merchant, she had another daughter and two sons. She rarely visited her oldest daughter, May, and she never took her back. Besides giving her the occasion article of used clothing, passed down from her other daughter, she contributed nothing.

Weipo tried to keep May away from her brothel business. She wanted her to go to college, so she locked her in the small, dark room at the mezzanine level and forced her to study. May obediently studied by the dim light of the oil lamp, only taking a break when her one friend, the neighbor boy, Xiao Dong, paid her a visit. To get to her room, he had to sneak into the house's storage room, and then crawl over the fence that separated the storage room from her room.

When May reached fifteen, Xiao Dong took her to a dance at a friend's family. The city changed a lot after the Communists gained control in 1949. Prostitution and drug use were made illegal, punishable by hefty fines or worse. Weipo closed her business. The Communist government forgave her and treated her like all other working-class people. Yet, she had lost her source of income and was forced to live off the gold and jewels she had saved over the years. May was the other investment she made to secure future income. Her hopes hinged on May and her ability to get into college. Whether May liked it or not, she was central to Weipo's plan.

Before 1949, the International Club at the Big World had been an enormous red-light district. Now, it was an entertainment center for foreign expats, mostly from the Soviet

Union, Poland, Czechoslovakia, and other Eastern Bloc nations. Operas and ballets performed there weekly.

Far from the glamor of the International Club, sixteen-year-old May sat at the dining table, sipping tea. Black pigtails hung down her shoulders, like two huge ropes. They perfectly complimented her big, dark eyes and thick eyebrows. With her high-bridged nose and high cheekbones, everyone said she resembled a Caucasian woman.

"Xiao Dong's family invited me to a dance at the Big World nightclub," said May. "I can meet many Russian and Eastern European expats there. Please Weipo, let me go."

Weipo sat silently for a while and said, "Normally, I would say no to this because I think you ought to concentrate on your studies and are too young to go dancing with men, especially foreign men. But I will make an exception, since you have been working hard and getting good grades in school."

May wrapped Weipo in a big hug. Weipo's ghostly white face looked grim.

In the nightclub, May danced with a bearded Russian. She wore makeup and a white dress that swished as she moved. Her feet effortlessly followed the movements of the Russian expat, who was apparently a very skilled dancer. He stared at her with passion. Xiao Dong watched her with envy. He told May what a star she was.

That night when May got home at midnight, Weipo rushed into her bedroom, looking angry.

"Those bearded foreigners love me," May gushed, unable to contain her excitement. "They are charming and romantic. They want to take me to operas and ballets."

"No. You can't go to that club anymore," said Weipo. Her brows knitted together. "If you do, I will lock you up day and night until you forget about them."

"Look, some of them even want to marry me and bring me back to their home countries. Isn't that nice?" She looked at Weipo with her charming, almond-shaped eyes, trying to get her approval. "I will send for you and Weigong after I get there."

"No. Men lie and they will sleep with you, get you pregnant, and abandon you, which is precisely what happened to your mother. Your father abandoned her after getting her pregnant."

"Really? Where is he?" May looked up to Weipo, eyes brimming with tears.

"Long gone. You think he would come back and give you candies? Don't be so gullible. Besides, you must study hard so you can go to college to support yourself, Weigong, and me."

May lay in bed and stared at the dark ceiling, trying to absorb this new information. Her father was not dead, as she had been told her entire life. He had abandoned them. Without wanting to repeat her mother's life, she resolved to become a stronger woman.

Not long after her talk with Weipo, the Beijing Institute of Aeronautics and Astronomy accepted her as an undergraduate student. She would study to become an engineer. Weipo soon ran out of gold and jewels, and she could no longer support May's college education. On the contrary, she needed May's help. With only one year left to complete her engineering degree, May married her professor, Professor Chen. Eighteen years her senior, this man would become my father.

Dad's Greenhouse

It was early spring. The late afternoon sun grew tired and began sliding down to meet the horizon. Father and two of his friends worked in the open field in front of our apartment building, digging and shoveling. The shovel looked strange in Father's hands—the pale, smooth hands of an intellectual. He breathed heavily and wiped his forehead with the sleeve of his old, brown sweater. His friends wore black quilted jackets and quilted hats with earflaps that waved in the air. They seemed happy, digging into the earth.

Mother and I stood in front of our three-story red brick apartment building, looking across the open space where Father was working. We had just finished shopping and held our purchases in our arms.

"What is Father building?" I asked Mother.

"He is building a home for his flowers," Mother said without enthusiasm.

"Why can't his flowers share our home with us, like they used to?"

"Our home isn't big enough. He wants to plant lots of flowers."

"Really? Will he have time?" In my mind, Father belonged in front of his desk, writing and calculating. Gardening was his weekend hobby.

"Yes, he lost his research job and became a part-time teacher."

"Why?"

"You wouldn't understand." Mother guided me up the stairs and into our apartment. Our second-floor apartment, with its one bedroom, private bath, and kitchen, was a treat reserved for professors. Most people who lived on the campus of Beijing Institute of Aeronautics and Astronomy had to fit their entire family, sometimes three generations, into an eighteen-square-meter, one-room apartment. They also had to share the bathroom and kitchen with three other families. But they never complained. "Work Hard and Live Simple!" was the slogan of the time.

Late that night, Father walked into the apartment, exhausted. His dinner had gone cold. Mother and I sat next to the dining table, waiting for him. Mother's latest knitting project fell across her lap.

"Hey, gardener, back home from work? You must be hungry," said Mother.

"What? What are you calling me? Let me tell you," Father straightened his body, arms akimbo. "I'm still a professor! I'm still a professor!"

"Professor of what?"

"Mathematics!"

"Does that mean they will send you to teach college math?" Mother raised her head from her knitting and stared at Father.

"No."

Father went to the food cabinet and retrieved a bottle of wine.

"Hey, that's for cooking."

"You can buy another tomorrow." Father poured a glass of wine and drank it straight down. His long, pale face instantly turned red.

"So, what do they want you to do?"

"Teach goddamn high school math!"

"See, I told you not to offend Mrs. Bai. She is your boss and a tough lady."

"She's a phony. A false intellectual!" Father paced the room like an angry lion. He stopped and struck the dining table with his fist.

Father gulped down more wine and fell into a stupefied silence.

After Father and his friends finished building the foundation, they began mounting the glass walls of the greenhouse.

"Father's greenhouse will be made of glass!" I had only seen transparent glass greenhouses in public parks.

"Yes, all glass," Mother said.

"Why?"

"Because glass lets the sunlight in and protects the plants from wind."

I spent several afternoons watching Father build his greenhouse. The glass came in sheets, and Father had to cut them to size with a glasscutter. At first, he cut his hands so often, they were covered with bandages.

Mother usually hollered at me to come home when it was still daylight, long before Father returned from the greenhouse project. We grew accustomed to eating without him.

"Mrs. Bai is mean," Mother said to me one day at the dinner table.

"Yes," I agreed. "Once her son Bai Gang showed me his toy airplane, but didn't even let me touch it." I always liked to agree with Mother. "And he boasts his mother is a third rank professor, even higher than father."

"That's probably true. She used to be a rank lower than your father. Since she is a Communist Party member, she gets advanced faster." Mother sighed.

"Was she Father's old boss? Did she treat him badly?"

"Yes. Your father doesn't like her because she is a woman and very tough."

"What's wrong with a woman boss, Mom?"

Mother sank into silence. I decided she was tired of me, so I rose to my feet, thinking I would go into the bedroom and play with my dolls.

The door banged open. Father had returned from his gardening. He looked like a wet dog with his thin, short hair matted to his scalp with sweat. Faded blue pants bunched up his legs, and his old, brown sweater was torn at one shoulder. He had changed into clean shoes and carried a pair of green athletic shoes caked with dirt. The gesture might have prevented a fight. Just yesterday, Mother had complained about him tracking dirt on the floor.

Father took off his sweater and pants and threw them and his shoes into the bathroom. He wiped his face with a washrag and stepped out, wearing just his underwear. The sour smell of sweat lingered in the air. He had not taken a shower in weeks. No wonder Mother did not want to sleep in the same bed with him anymore.

"Shit, why's my food cold?" Without even touching the stir fry and steamed bread, Father could tell the food had lost all warmth.

"I heated it up ten minutes ago."

"Let me tell you again." Father looked strained, ready to explode. "I'm a professor, working hard all day and earning money. It's your job to take good care of me."

"I'm sorry. I'm never sure when you are coming home."

"You damn woman! You should be sorry." He pointed at her face. "Do you think I don't know about your dirty affairs during your college years? Our marriage saved you from being notorious all over campus. In the first month of our marriage, you even let your former boyfriend back in." Shaking and backing away slightly, Father glared at Mother.

"Stop!" Mother cried. "Don't repeat rumors in front of our child. I can't take this anymore." With her face buried in her arms, she cried.

"Okay, okay!" Father gave in. He always surrendered when Mother's tears came. Sitting at the table, he pursed his lips and stared at the food. I knew he was about to say something important.

"I need money to purchase more materials for the greenhouse."

"Money? I'm not sure we have extra money this month. My grandmother in Shanghai is sick, and I had to send her extra money. And you already spent a lot on your greenhouse."

Silence. I could hear Father's chewing as he crushed bok choy between his teeth. He sat erect, staring at the dark sky out the window.

When he finished chewing, he said, "Let's sell the books."

I knew which books he meant. He kept a box of books hidden in the corner of our bedroom. They were his research books, and he had paid thousands of yen for them. The box was so precious to him, he never even let me touch it. Now, he wanted to sell the books by the pound. I asked Mother about his decision when we were in bed that night. Mother said that after Father changed his job, he was no longer allowed to do research; therefore, he had no use for the books any longer.

The next day, I could tell from Father's mood that he had sold the books. He was jubilant; he could now finish constructing his dream greenhouse.

The completed greenhouse, blazing under the summer sun, attracted the attention of many visitors. Our family had never enjoyed so much attention. People from all over campus visited our magnificent greenhouse—the only one in our university residential area. Among so much praise, Father beamed, visibly proud.

"Professor Chen, what a wonderful greenhouse!"

"Professor Chen, what an amazing achievement!"

"Professor Chen, you are so smart! You can do anything you put your mind to."

Every night, Father came home with a broad smile. Mother seemed happy, too. If it makes Father happy, she said.

Since Father spent so much time in the greenhouse, he decided to install a sink and a potbelly stove. After that, he began eating his dinner there.

In his absence, Mother and I became very close. We always slept late, since Mother had trouble getting to sleep at night. We would spend the rest of the day shopping and gossiping with other professor's wives.

Father filled his greenhouse with many new plants. He bought stacks of flowerpots and filled them with high-quality soil from a greenhouse downtown. Then, he asked his gardener friends to cut him a branch of every kind of flower in the university garden. Scraping the skin off the end of every branch, he buried them in small sand boxes or grafted them onto bigger branches in pots. After a few weeks, some of these twigs grew green buds—hopeful signs of life. That was when Father transferred them to larger pots. Not satisfied by these little plants, Father also purchased a few full-grown plants from the market, costing him between 50 and 100 yen each. One day, Father rode home with a kumquat plant tied to his bicycle seat. Its little orange fruits fascinated me. I chased Father along the road and gathered my courage to ask, "Dad, can I eat them?"

Father gladly offered me one and rode away. I put the kumquat into my mouth right away. "Yuck." It was bitter, but I still appreciated Father's offering. Maybe it was not ripe yet.

Gazing at the rows of potted plants, I started visualizing our future greenhouse. Vines grew all the way to the ceiling, weighed down by bunches of pearl-like green and red grapes. Strawberries spread like a red carpet. Orange plants, healthy and strong, produced an abundance of large, shining fruits. Among hundreds of full-bloom roses, I saw Father's face, smiling like a flower.

One day, Father started digging again. I asked him why.

"This...this afternoon," he said, breathing heavily, "a farmer is sending me a cart of chicken feces. I have to dig a storage place for them."

"What are chicken feces?" I asked.

"Chicken shit."

"Why do you need chicken shit?"

"You kids don't understand. That's the best kind of fertilizer."

"Yuck!" Suddenly, I understood why Father liked to empty my chamber pot. He must have used its contents as fertilizer.

At four o'clock, the farmer showed up. He was a little man of forty. The skin on his face was so wrinkled, I could not even tell where his eyes, nose, and mouth were. He wore a black quilted hat, a jacket, and pants and shoes that were covered with dust. One of the hat's earflaps was folded up while the other drooped down. Holding a whip in one bony hand, he guided a cart, pulled by a donkey and a mule, down the narrow brick road in front of our apartment building. He whipped them so hard, the donkey froze and yowled. Father threw his shovel and ran toward him.

"Comrade Wang!"

"Hi, Professor Chen. Call me Lao Wang." Nodding his head, he pulled his hands out of the jacket sleeves, which he used as gloves, and shook Father's hand. Smiling, he showed a mouthful of yellow teeth. Father took his dry hand as if he wanted to kiss it. Before Lao Wang could retrieve his pipe from his jacket's breast pocket, Father handed him a pack of expensive cigarettes and lit one for him. Lao Wang gladly accepted them and put the pack in his pocket.

"Good cigarette!" Lao Wang said, blowing smoke out his nose. "Hey, those bastards ain't let me in. They ain't let me ship in so much chicken shit. So, I lied. I said I saved up some natural fertilizer for the university president's garden. The guard said, 'No, even the university president ain't allowed to break the rules.' Then, I went to the other gates. Shit, no luck! Then, I tried one of my tricks. I knelt, squeezed out a few teardrops and begged. Then, holy smokes! My donkey cried. It cried really loud. Hey, this scared the shit out of the guard. He waved me right in."

Father laughed so hard, tears sprang to the corners of his eyes. They began shoveling chicken feces onto the ground, and I realized how terrible it smelled. I ran home and watched through the window. Mother joined me, "From now on, we will be living by a zoo."

That night, when Father came home triumphantly, Mother fought with him.

"Look at other people's husbands: they cook, they shop. Can you find another single one like you, tending flowers and playing with animal feces all the time?"

"You goddamn woman! I'm a breadwinner. I can do what I want! You want to tell me what to do? Who made you a god?"

"You don't respect me. You never respected me!" Mother wept.

"You dirty woman. What do you need respect for?" He stared at Mother with bloodshot eyes. His hands were shaking so hard, he spilled his cup of hot tea onto Mother's leg.

"Ahhh! How can you do this to me?" Mother pulled up her long underwear and showed her burning red skin. Just then, a knock sounded at the door. Mother arose and stumbled toward it. "Let our neighbors look at it! Let them be witnesses!"

"You're crazy. Stop embarrassing me!" Father tried to pull Mother back, but she had already opened the door. A woman stood in the entryway; a broad smile spread across her cheeks.

"Professor Chen and comrade Zhen, what a nice couple! Why do you entertain yourselves with quarreling?"

"Oh, no. Just a small matter," Father said.

"Small matter? See what he has done to me!" Mother raised her swollen leg.

"I see," the woman said. "I can help you call upon the head of the Communist party in your department. He oversees household counseling."

"No, we can handle it ourselves." Father pulled Mother inside and slammed the door.

Mother cried and told me how much she wanted to leave Father. I asked whether she was going to take me along. "Maybe," she said. That night, I had a bad dream and wet my bed.

Mother did not leave, but instead found a job in Beijing Automobile Parts Factory in downtown Beijing, while I attended kindergarten. Father always stayed away from the neighbors, avoiding eye contact like a mouse afraid of cats. Even with his not-so-sensitive ears, he knew neighbors had been gossiping about us.

Fall arrived, and our greenhouse teemed with treasures. I watched grapes grow from tiny seeds to large purple pearls. I hoped I would be the first one to taste them. One day, Father invited me to the greenhouse. I sauntered in, wondering what I had done wrong. After it was completed, Father rarely let me inside his greenhouse. He said I would make a mess. But I was not in trouble. Instead, Father explained that he had some film left after taking a picture of each flower and fruit, and he wanted to take a few snapshots of me with the flowers.

Four and a half feet tall, I stood next to the orange plant. Its thick, shining leaves served as a background, its beautiful fruit as decoration. I proudly sucked in my little belly, trying to stand up straight.

"Smile," said Father.

Click. Father cut an orange from the plant and rewarded me with half. I was so moved, I did not know how to thank him. I held the orange in my hands and beamed. Father waved me home; he wanted to continue working in the greenhouse.

After two year's hard work, Father's efforts paid off. His garden was selected as one of the university's best gardens. When we walked through the neighborhood, Mother and I felt proud. Fame, however, did not always bring Father good luck. Like the university's orchard, Father's greenhouse had become a target of greedy kids. One especially aggressive group broke in and harvested his grapes. After that, Father acted as a guard, standing watch over his plants. He moved into the greenhouse and made it his permanent home office.

Father almost disappeared from my life. He spent most of his time after work ensconced in his greenhouse, rarely bothering to come out or even acknowledge the admirers who dropped by. I visited him once a day to deliver his dinner, as if serving a prisoner. Once, when I was bringing him his meal, I saw smoke billowing from the doorway. I rushed in and found two pieces of bread burning on the potbelly stove, while Father dozed peacefully under the grapevine.

I spent most of my time after kindergarten with an unhappy mother. She gave up knitting and started tailoring. Once, Mother spent all day Sunday making a dress. When she finished, she put it on and showed me. She looked stunning. I had never seen such a beautiful dress. It had a floral print, and was long and strapless, revealing Mother's bare shoulders and the top of her full chest. She stood in front of the mirror for a long time, swiveling and laughing.

"Mom, how can you wear such a dress on the street? People will laugh at you. Only kids can wear clothes like that."

"Nonsense. This is what we wore to parties in the 1950s."

"What are parties?"

"That's when people get together, singing and dancing."

"Fun! I wish I could attend one."

Mother stared at the mirror; her face lengthened, mouth drooping into a pout. She ran to the bedroom and changed quickly. Then, she began cutting the dress into pieces.

"I don't need this. I don't need this! Nobody wears this kind of dress anymore."

"But we can put it away in our suitcase."

"No. I don't want to. I am getting older every day." She began weeping.

"You are not old, Mom." I felt guilty. I thought I made her sad.

When Father stopped by that afternoon, Mother argued with him, saying he should be sleeping at home and that he was wasting her youth. They fought again. Father beat Mother with a broomstick. From then on, Mother came home from work late at night, and I had to wait for her in the dark of the kindergarten classroom. I didn't want to make Mother and Father angry with me, so I became very quiet. Even kids in my kindergarten class teased me and called me dumb. I wished I were dumb, so wouldn't have to talk anymore. Talking to others became such a chore, I chose to only talk to myself. I began telling myself stories and daydreaming. I visualized people from my favorite movies on the kindergarten ceiling. I imagined them talking and hugging each other, and I wanted so much to become one of them.

Father's good life in the greenhouse did not last. One night, when Mother and I were sound asleep, a voice awakened us from the half-opened window.

"Oh, God damn it! Gangs have come to destroy my garden!"

I sat up and saw Mother pulling on clothes. Realizing this was not a dream, I climbed to the windowsill and looked out. Flashlight beams surrounded the greenhouse. Through the dim light, I could make out six or eight people in green uniforms with red armbands.

"Who...who are they, Mom?"

"They might be the red guards announced by the radio," she said. "Chairman Mao just started the 'Cultural Revolution,' a movement against intellectuals."

The noise grew outside. Shouts mixed with the clattering of glass.

"Please don't touch my garden!" Father shouted. I had never heard him cry so loudly. He reached out, trying to stop the Red Guards from breaking the glass greenhouse with their long sticks. "Please hit me, not the flowers! They are beautiful!" Father screamed, "Don't you think they are beautiful?"

"Beautiful? A Bourgeois idea." A young man with a soft pale face waved his fist in the air as he spoke. "Our mission is to destroy all bourgeois ideas created by people like you and pull their roots out completely! Am I right?"

"Y—yes! We support you and support Chair...man...Mao!" The rest of the Red Guards shouted.

The young man pushed Father to the ground, pulled his shirt collar up with one hand, raised the stick with the other, and hit Father's head and back.

"You are the capitalist's running dog. You are the revolutionist's enemy," the young man said. Other Red Guards, boys and girls, formed a circle around Father.

"Down with the capitalist! Down with the counter-revolutionist! Long live Chairman Mao! Long live the Cultural Revolution!" They threw their fists into the sky, to the rhythm of their shouts. Their loud, naïve voices carried through the air, powerful enough to shake the landscape and awake the nation.

The sky began to lighten. The sun emerged on the eastern horizon, casting rays of light in all directions. Another day had begun, a new day in which many people's fates had changed overnight. As the new, merciless movement grew, their lives would turn upside down.

Mother and I desperately tried to drag Father home. He awakened to our tugging, bobbing in and out of consciousness. His shirt, torn to pieces, was glued to his body with blood. His pants hung loosely around his waist. His broken nose was still dripping scarlet. The belt, used to whip him, lay curled on the ground. Blood seeped off it, nourishing the earth.

"No, I don't want to go home. I want my greenhouse! I want my greenhouse!" For the first time in my life, I watched Father cry in pure misery. Tears, mixed with blood, ran down his cheeks and dripped from his face.

There was no greenhouse left, only ruins. Broken glass spread across the ground. Flowerpots were scattered everywhere, knocked over and broken. The Red Guards had destroyed all the plants, trampling them underfoot.

Slowly, Father walked toward the ruin. His bare feet stepped on the shattered glass, but he didn't seem to notice. Stooping down, he picked up a small sandbox with a little green bud poking out from it. He put it to his nose, inhaled, and kissed it.

"It's still alive." He gave a bittersweet smile. "It's still alive!"

Before Father was sent to a labor camp, two of his former students—now in the Red Guards—came to our apartment. One was tall and skinny and wore a thin mustache. He pointed to the bottom of our bookshelf.

"Professor Chen, is that how you respect our great leader Chairman's books? By placing them on the bottom shelf on purpose. You idiot! Long live Chairman Mao! Long live the Cultural Revolution!" The young man threw his fist into the air. The other followed.

Father stared at the floor and nodded his head repeatedly like a chicken pecking on seeds. "Yes, yes," he said.

After the Red Guards left, he packed up and went to the labor camp for re-education.

I didn't cry. I came down with the hundred-day cough, so I had to stay home. Great-grandmother came from Shanghai to care for me, since Mother had to work long hours.

One day, right after my great-grandmother gave me medicine—bitter brown juice, extracted from boiled Chinese herbs—she told me the story of how our friend Dr. Liu's whole family committed suicide.

"Actually, she killed her twin boys, Xiao Gong and Xiao Dong, by injecting poison into their bodies. Then, she used the same method to kill her husband, Professor Xiu, and her mother. In the end, she did the deed to herself. How awful!"

Great-grandmother relayed the information in a calm voice, as though telling a fairytale. Dr Liu's family lived in an apartment building next to ours. The front of our building faced the back of their building. I stared at the dark, cold balcony on the third floor, unable to fathom that the cute, chubby twin boys, the kind grandmother, the fast-talking Dr. Liu, and the handsome math professor Dr. Xiu had all evaporated. I imagined them flying away like white cranes, dripping blood. I slowly sipped my bitter, brown medicine and did not know which was more bitter, the medicine or my life. I looked up at Great-grandmother, standing beside me. With her long neck, long, fake eyebrows, black clothing, and hair tied in a bun, she resembled a witch.

Until that moment, I had never thought of my life as bitter. I had been in a state of numbness, even as one bad event followed another, followed another.

In 1972, Grandmother wrote to us from Shanghai. She told us my Aunt Congying had committed suicide. She burned herself to death in a bathtub using gasoline. She went crazy because she could not stand the pressure of being a capitalistic merchant's daughter. Kids made fun of her at school. Later, she was denied entry to college because of her family's background.

I could not comprehend why she killed herself in such a brutal way. I had met her a few times during my many trips to Shanghai and remembered her as being beautiful and outgoing. I noticed she was a little eccentric. She would fight with Grandmother and cry easily.

As a professor's daughter, I experienced the same kind of brutality from my classmates at school, but I proved to be more resilient than my aunt. They would chase me and throw rocks at me when I walked home from school. They called me, "big, dumb girl," because I was the tallest student in my class—tallest among both boys and girls—and very quiet. During the school march, no one wanted to hold my hand, so I quietly followed at the end of the line, alone. This was, however, not as bad as the treatment at home.

When he returned from labor camp, Father was irritable. If he told me to do something and I did not immediately do it, he would threaten me with a spanking or a broom. Once, he threw a shoe and struck my nose. It bled a lot and swelled to a big bruise. I walked out and thought of running away but could not think of any place to go. So, I came back home and dreamed of going somewhere far away, to a place where I would be treated like a princess. Today, I often think about how my dream finally came true. I did go somewhere far away, and my life did get better. But my troubles would never truly go away.

My Aunt's
Self-Immolation

It is not the wailing. It is not the smoke, nor the gasoline smell issuing from the bathroom. It is not Grandmother's raucous screaming and days of weeping. I do not associate these things with my Aunt Congxing's self-immolation. What I think of is her singing—the songs she used to croon when she was in good mood. When I was young, I was told that Aunt Congxing's death was an accident; while taking a bath, a lamp fell into the tub and electrocuted her. Years later, I discovered she burned herself to death by pouring gasoline on her body.

Days after her death, her songs would accompany me to bed. I could see her, dressed in a black velvet traditional Chinese dress, with short curly hair and beautiful, dark eyes. She would walk toward me, grab my hands, and we would dance and swirl. Sometimes, she would wear a Charlie Chaplin costume with a little fake mustache and kiss me—a fantasy rooted in real life. When I had visited her in Shanghai many years ago, she had donned this very costume. Up to that point, the dream kiss was the most romantic moment in my young life.

She was determined in her pursuits, a woman far ahead of her time in the early 1960s and, later, during the Cultural Revolution. She was a pioneer in gay rights. But she was mercilessly steamrolled by conservative traditions.

I still remember my first visit to Grandmother's house in 1962, when I was five years old. My grandparents were wealthy then. Grandfather was a watch merchant before the Communists took over. After the establishment of the People's Republic of China, the government confiscated all his watch shops, but let them stay in their three-story apartment in Shanghai on the most opulent street, Nanjing Road. I remember the shining, dark-wood staircase, the beautifully carved red, wooden furniture, and their private, flushing toilet. We were served food on beautiful floral plates, painted with ancient Chinese legends. Grandfather had three wives, one of whom retreated to Taiwan with the Guo Ming Dang government. Grandma was his third wife, and the only wife he was allowed to have after the government outlawed polygamy. But Grandpa still visited his first wife and often brought her vegetables he purchased at the market. He had seven sons and tree daughters.

Aunt Congxing was in junior high school during my first visit. She would come home with a few classmates, boys and girls, and run wild in the apartment, playing hide and seek. Sometimes, they would include me. Then, we would walk down Hu Dong, a smaller side street, to her favorite ice cream shop and eat Bo Bin (ice-blended mung bean soup with whipped cream on top). When people at the shop made fun of my Shanghai dialect, the other kids defended me by arguing with them and threatening to go to another shop next time. But I didn't mind. I was like their little sister. Since I never had any siblings or close friends, this was as close as I could get to a childhood paradise.

Two days after Aunt Congxing's death, the funeral procession began in Hu Dong. A group of people consisting of mostly family members, very few neighbors, and a handful of friends, followed the big hearse. We wore white shirts, black pants and shoes, and a black armband on our left arms, which indicated the deceased was female. My two uncles held my grandma on each side. Her miniature frame looked so weak; she might collapse with a gust of wind. Grandpa looked serene, but the wrinkles on his face seemed to have deepened overnight. He did not go to the market that day, which was out-of-the-ordinary for him. He insisted on two daily practices to promote longevity: wake up at dawn and walk to the market *and* take a bath every day. I walked alongside Grandpa, deep in thought. I traced back everything I knew about Aunt Congxing, trying to figure out what had happened.

I returned to Shanghai in the summer of 1965, a year before the Cultural Revolution began. I was eight years old and Aunt Congxing was in high school. She would come home from school with her friend Xingzheng and, even while they played outside, they argued about China's future and how they could best serve the new China.

"I would like to go to inner Mongolia and help start a school there," said Aunt.

"Do you know how cold it is there in the winter? You will lose your fingers and toes. Your face will be so chapped, it will feel rough as a washboard."

"But they get to ride horses every day."

I looked out the window, watching them play hacky sack. Aunt waved me out to join them. Two people throw the hacky sack at the person in the middle, who could either catch the sack or dodge it. If the person in the middle was hit, they were out.

"I want to have a costume party," declared Aunt one day.

"What is a costume party?" I asked.

"It is a party where everyone dresses like someone else. Won't it be fun?" She gave me a wicked smile.

"Who are you going to be?" I had no idea whose dress style I would copy. I had always just been myself.

"I think I will be Charlie Chaplin," said Aunt proudly. She started walking like him, with feet splayed, holding an umbrella as a cane.

"I will be the homeless girl then." I remembered seeing her in the Charlie Chaplin film, *Modern Times*.

Every day, Aunt and I would practice our skit. She would dress in a black suit, baggy pants, a bowler, and a fake mustache. The part I liked best was when she fell in love with the homeless girl and kissed her. I was little shy then and not sure I wanted to perform in front of so many people. With Aunt's encouragement, I decided I could. Besides, it was a costume party, and no one would know who I was.

On the day of the party, Aunt told me that Grandma did not want her to dress like a man. So, she wore her beautiful velvet qipao, tight with slits that ran above her thighs, revealing most of her long, slender legs.

"What should we perform?" I was a little worried.

"Don't worry. We could perform *The Sound of Music*. I know the songs by heart, and you can just sing along."

50

Five people worked in the kitchen that night, preparing steamed crabs, soy sauce roast beef, jellyfish salad, and turtle soup. I helped straighten the tablecloth and set up the dishes, but Aunt soon pulled me away and told me to go play.

During the party, I never did have a chance to dance with Aunt, who was busy dancing with many handsome young men. They had to stand in line to dance with the most beautiful woman at the party. Except for a brief dance with one of my uncles, I sat and watched Aunt's elegant dancing steps and her irresistible gaze. Grandma was the proudest parent that evening, surrounded by many potential in-laws. She spent the whole evening chatting and laughing, her eyes crinkled to the size of two sunflower seeds. After a while, she stepped away from the dancing and played Mahjong until well past midnight.

After the party, I asked Aunt about the young men who had danced with her.

"They were boring. All they talked about was how big their apartments are and how influential their parents are in the Communist Party, so we could live a comfortable life in Shanghai. After I told them I wanted to go to Mongolia and live in tents, they all laughed at me. They told me I was crazy, and nobody in their right mind would want to leave Shanghai." She paused, smiled. "There was a girl who was rather interesting. She can play Pipa, and we promised to get together to play music and sing."

Every day, Aunt and her new friend Xiaoling would meet in her room, playing Pipa and singing Peking Opera. Sometimes, I would join them and sing along. Sometimes, it was just the two of them, giggling late into the afternoon with the sun streaming in through the window. If it was too hot to be indoors, we would walk to the swimming pool. The summer sun was fierce in Shanghai, and we had to use a parasol for shade. We would squeeze next to each other beneath one parasol, skipping and singing. Nanjing Road was one of the busiest streets in Shanghai, and it brimmed with shoppers, buses, and trolleys. Young people wearing the latest fashions held hands, strolled, and window shopped. Cute dogs tugged on their leashes, pulling women with huge hats down the sidewalk. Water trucks sprayed water onto streets to cool down the road. When we spotted a jewelry store, Aunt dragged us inside.

"I want to buy you a present," she said.

"Me?" I pointed to my chest, unable to hold my excitement.

"Yes. You are leaving in two days. I would like to give you a souvenir."

"I'm leaving in two days!" This simple sentence bought tears to my eyes. I didn't want to go, but school would start again soon.

I picked out a necklace with a ruby pendent. Aunt bought Xiaoling a necklace with a golden heart pendent.

After swimming, we ran home. I couldn't wait to show Grandma my new necklace.

"When you grow up, you will remember us," said Grandma with a grin.

"Yes, of course." I started crying.

Aunt thought of a way to cheer me up. "I want to have a party to see Meihua off."

"As long as you don't dress like Charlie Chaplin," said Grandma, voice tinged with worry.

"No, we are doing a Peking Opera, *Farewell to My Concubine*."

"Who will play the king?" Grandma read Aunt's mind.

"I suppose if I don't find anyone, I will have to play him myself. In Peking Opera, the men play women's roles all the time. Why can't women play men?" Aunt's argument was convincing, at least for me. Of course, to achieve the equality between men and women, we still had a long way to go.

"You are a girl, not a boy!" Grandma sounded angry.

"Just playing a man in a Peking Opera does not make me a boy. Why do you always tell me what to do?" Aunt started crying.

"Okay." Grandma hated to see Aunt cry. "Only this once. Next time you have to get a young man involved."

The party was fabulous. Our hard work had paid off. We wore our best costumes, made of fine satin. Aunt played the king, and I played the concubine. We were accompanied on stage by the strumming of Xiaoling's Pipa. Our makeup was so convincing, no one could tell the king was played by Aunt Caoxing.

After the party, I took the train home to Beijing.

The Cultural Revolution had started. The country's political situation had drastically changed. We were not allowed to wear beautiful clothes, high-heeled shoes, have parties, or sing Peking Operas, except for the ones that praised Chairman Mao and the Communist revolution. Mother cut up all her high-heeled shoes and beautiful summer dresses. Father still played the violin, but he had to close all the windows and draw the curtains whenever he practiced. Once, he invited a professional violinist to perform for us and a few friends in our bedroom. We had to stuff a layer of thick curtains around our windows and door. The violinist used a muffler to dampen the sound. While the violinist sat on the only chair in the room, playing, we sat on the edge of the bed, listening. It felt like a great adventure. Felix Mendelssohn's violin concerto brought me thousands of miles away to 19th century Vienna. Aunt and I could run wild, singing and dancing in the woods. Even though Father didn't specifically get in trouble for playing European music on his violin, he was still sent to the countryside to do hard labor for being an intellectual and teaching math at the American airbase before the Communists took over. Shortly after he was sent away, my Mother was sent to work on a farm in the Beijing suburbs because she had worked for the local government. As I had hoped, I was again sent to Shanghai to spend the summer with my grandma, grandpa, aunt, and uncles.

I cried when Mother saw me off at the train station, even though I had taken this train ride alone many times. She stood on the platform and waited until she couldn't see me anymore. The train trip took close to twenty-four hours. I occupied myself by eating sunflower seeds, reading, and knitting. Once, I spent an entire trip writing poetry.

In Shanghai, an uncle met me at the station, and we took a bus to Grandma's apartment. Because of the Cultural Revolution, Grandma's family lost half of their apartment. A young family moved into the downstairs ballroom and the room upstairs.

When I went upstairs to meet with Aunt, she was sitting on the bed looking out the window. I went to her and gave her a hug. She blinked and didn't say anything. I was told she became sick after being sent home from inner Mongolia. I didn't realize her sickness was mental, not physical. Her hair was teased into a random mess. Her eyes were unfocused. She wore a gray Mao suit and a pair of red, patent leather high-heeled shoes. Under her breath, she hummed a familiar tune. Seeing her in this state made me want to cry, but she quickly cheered me up. She gave me a few suction cup darts and showed me how to throw them to make them stick onto the window across the patio. After a while, a lady whose family lived in that room opened the window and yelled, "Stop that!! We have a baby here!" She slammed the window shut.

I ran downstairs to help Grandma prepare green beans in the kitchen, and she told me what had happened to Aunt Congxing.

"Congxing was sent to Mongolia after high school. She was very excited, and I was sad. She promised to write every week, but I still worried. She had never before been out of the house or taken care of herself. Her food had always been prepared and brought to her, her clothes always washed and folded. The only bright spot in the whole, silly plan was that her best friend Xiaoling was also going, and she was a responsible girl. At least, that's what I thought. Before they left, they were given long, quilted army coats and fur hats. We all had pictures taken at the People's Square. Since we were no longer allowed to have parties, we had one last meal together and praised Chairman Mao for giving our spoiled children an opportunity to learn from shepherds in remote inner Mongolia. So, off they went. I could not stop them from getting on the train, and I had no right to do so. They were excited. They hung out the train window, waving at me with their Chairman Mao red books."

Grandma paused and drank some tea. She wiped her old eyes with a handkerchief. "In the first few months, she painted a rosy picture of her life there. It was fun to ride horses and live in tents, she said. Even though the winter was cold, she claimed she would get used to it. Then, she stopped writing. I thought she was busy. When we did receive news, it came in the form of a letter from her boss, not from Congxing. The letter reported that your aunt had been caught in a lesbian liaison with her friend Xiaoling. We were all surprised. I knew she sometimes liked unconventional things, but I didn't think she knew anything about lesbian love. I wrote to her boss to dispute the report.

She replied, saying that she initially didn't realize Congxing and Xiaoling were in a romantic relationship, thinking that they were just close friends who snuggled together in the same tent to keep warm. But when they were caught sleeping naked together, Congxing and Xiaoling admitted they were in love. She thought that was her right. Since they were first-time offenders, they were sent home instead of sentenced to jail. Her boss went on to state that they needed to leave immediately, before they could further corrupt the rest of the team. There were no second chances, she explained. If they were caught again, they would be sent to jail. Guaranteed."

Grandma paused and looked at me. "After I read the letter, I could not stop crying," she said. "I was relieved that she was coming home, but I didn't know how she would react to all this. I knew she wanted to go to college, but she and I both know that colleges will only let in students who behaved well during their countryside service. Now, her personal file is permanently tainted. She will be lucky to find any kind of job."

Grandma's eyes dropped to her teacup. She clutched it tightly. "After she came back, she cried for three days. After that, she would sit on her bed, staring at the window and singing. Once, she disappeared for three days. I assumed she ran away with Xiaoling, but she came back. It is impossible to run away here with police everywhere. They could find you even if you decided to live with wolves."

I absorbed Grandma's story, stunned. When I was able to steal away and find some alone time, I cried and cried. I didn't know much about homosexuality, but I had heard rumors about a classmate's parents who were sent to a labor camp for being either gay or lesbian. They never came back.

Aunt Congxing grew accustomed to my presence after a few days. We would stroll through the park, with Aunt wearing her red, patent leather heels and gray Mao suit. Even though high-heeled shoes were no longer allowed, the police let Aunt go without confiscating them, because they knew she was mentally unwell. Their attention was largely wrapped up in the raucous, revolutionary activity in the streets. Young men and women wearing green army uniforms and red armbands marched on the streets, singing revolutionary songs. Sometimes, they came by the truckload.

Aunt and I would play alongside the cherry trees. We would swing in the nearby playground and sing whatever came to mind. Sometimes, we would shake off all the cherry blossoms and bury them, like the heroine Lin Daiyu in the *Dream of Red Chamber*. Sometimes, we would swing so high that it felt like flying.

"Do you want to be an angel?" Aunt asked.

"Yes. It would be great if we could fly like angels."

I knew Aunt had lost all hopes of finding a job after being labeled a lesbian. Becoming an angel was her only dream. Once, she jumped off the swing when it was high in the air. She landed on her ankle and injured it. I had to run back to Grandma's apartment and fetch one of my uncles to carry her home. She was forced to stay in bed for one month.

Uncle bought me a radio kit. I put it together, and Aunt and I listened to the Cultural Revolution news and revolutionary songs. When her ankle was mended, we sang and danced along.

I knew she missed Xiaoling. Sometimes, she would stare at the window for hours, as though she wished Xiaoling would appear on the other side of the glass.

Xiaoling did show up one night. Even though it was summer, she covered most of her face with a scarf. Grandma told her not to come in. "If the police see you, you'll both be in trouble again," she said.

"I need to come in," Xiaoling insisted. "I'm being sent to Mongolia again and might not return for a long time."

Finally, Grandma relented and led her upstairs. I followed.

We could hear the radio issuing through the cracks around Aunt's bedroom door. Grandma knocked, and Aunt opened the door. Her hair was a little messy, her mouth frowning. But as soon as she saw Xiaoling, her eyes gained focus and began to twinkle. She jumped and yelled. It was like seeing her awaken from a long nap. They hugged and kissed each other. I could see tears in both their eyes.

"Go back to your room," Grandma said to me. "Let's give them some space."

In my room, I looked out my bedroom window across the patio and tried to see them through the thin curtain of Aunt's bedroom window. Through the fog of the curtain, I saw Aunt and Xiaoling hugging and kissing slowly, like passionate lovers. I felt guilty watching their private encounter, but I couldn't look away. I was too curious.

After several more passionate kisses, Xiaoling backed away slightly and looked deeply in Aunt's soft, dark eyes. It was obvious they were deeply in love.

Feeling I was intruding on a very private moment, I tried to look away, but stayed captivated by the sight through the window across the courtyard. Night was falling, and the light from within the room brought the two figures into even sharper focus. The two girls stood close, caressing each other as the sky grew darker.

Aunt glanced out the window across the courtyard and saw me watching. She shot me a huge smile, reached over, and switched off the lamp.

In the morning, Grandma told me that Xiaoling stayed very late that night. Aunt stayed in bed for three days after that, not eating much. I brought potato cabbage soup to her and tried very hard to cheer her up by singing and dancing along with the radio and urging her to play cards with me. To show her what was going on outside, I pretended to be a truck or a bus, pantomiming their movements. Finally, she agreed to walk down Nanjing Road with me. She wanted to see the trucks that carried the Red Guards to the countryside, in hopes she might spot Xiaoling.

It was not easy to walk to the Nanjing Road from Grandma's apartment through the Hu Dong. People pointed at us and murmured. I knew that they were commenting on Aunt's strange fashion: the gray Mao suit and red high heels. I worried Aunt might be captured by the police, since nobody could wear high-heeled shoes anymore. If someone did wear heels or colorful clothing, the police would not only arrest them and confiscate the clothing, they would also put a black mark on their personal file, which would follow them forever and seriously jeopardize their professional future. But Aunt couldn't care less about her professional future, and nobody bothered her because she was considered crazy.

When we reached Nanjing Road, crowds of people were already lined up along the street, chattering. Some stood, some squatted near the road. There were people crossing the street, people on bicycles, buses crawling forward, and police zooming along on motorcycles. Truckloads of Red Guards in green uniforms began passing by. They had to move at a crawl, due to the traffic and commotion. The Red Guards sang and waved their Mao's Little Red Books. We, the bystanders, sang along. Every time Aunt saw a young woman who looked like Xiaoling, she would jump up and down, or try to squeeze to the front row to get a good look at her. We returned to Nanjing Road for several days. One day, Aunt started calling "Xiaoling," while pushing through the crowd. She ran to the road, in front of a truck. The truck screeched to a stop. Aunt said to the driver, "Take me. Can I come with you to fight the capitalist's running dog?"

"No, the truck is full. You should go with people in your district." The young man kept a straight face, unmoved by Aunt's sincerity.

Aunt blinked and started to cry. She yelled and jumped in front of the truck, lying down on the asphalt. I was so scared, I started crying and tried to pull her away, but my efforts were in vain. She was bigger than I was. The truck honked, and more and more people crowded around us. Traffic had stopped.

"Poor sister. Why can't she go if she really wants to go?" said an old lady.

"She is crazy! Can't you tell?" said a young woman holding a baby. Then she walked to Aunt. "You crazy woman. Stop disturbing the traffic and the Red Guards' troops!"

"She is not crazy! You're crazy!" I yelled back, surprised by my own courage.

Policemen dragged Aunt away by the arms. Bystanders cheered. I felt embarrassed and quickly followed the policemen and Aunt. I escorted them to our home, where they delivered Aunt, but kept her illegal red shoes.

After this incident, Aunt locked herself up in her bedroom with little food. Three times per day, I would knock on her door to deliver her food. She only opened the door half the time. I tried to coax her outside with invitations to play hacky sack, but she refused. Sometimes, I saw her in the hallway. Her hair was disheveled and her face was always smudged with tears and snot. I tried to talk to her, but she never said a thing, except for calling out "Xiaoling." Of course, I wouldn't know where to find her. One day, she went into the bathroom and didn't come out alive.

As the funeral precession went on, I felt weighed down by two hearts: my own and Xiaoling's. I didn't know whether Xiaoling would ever find out about this. I wished someday they could unite in heaven, where nobody would judge them.

I raised my head and saw two seagulls flying in the sky, squawking. They were white and pure. I wondered whether one of them was my Aunt. Finally, she was free.

My "Uncle"

It was a Sunday morning. Mother announced she was leaving for work. Father hollered, "You goddamn woman, get out of here. Go stay with your fucking boyfriend. Get out of my house!"

Father had just awakened. His eyes were still fogged. He sat on the bed, meditated a while, and then stood. Stumbling toward the door, he poked his head out of his room.

"Meihua, come back. Who said you could go?" He caught me before I slipped out the door. "Go to the kitchen and see if the garbage needs to be emptied. Goddamn shit! Why do you always have to be reminded?" Waving a filthy athletic shoe in his hand, he stared at me with half-opened, beady eyes. It seemed he might throw the shoe at my head if I did not obey. I went to the kitchen and did as I was told.

"Where are you going?" Father saw me put on my tight nylon sweater, which hugged my two small breasts. I had smeared a few dabs of blush on my round face.

"I'm going to work!" I slammed the door behind me.

The cold winter was edging into spring. The sun moved slowly from behind white clouds like a shy girl. Water from melting ice dripped from the roof. "Dita, dita." It sounded so crisp. With softening soil beneath my feet, I opened the metal buttons on my gray, down coat and unwrapped the blue woolen scarf from around my face. I breathed deeply and let the unmuffled air enter my nostrils and flow into my lungs. What a beautiful day! Everything was going exactly as planned. Father was right about Mother meeting her boyfriend. But he did not know my secret. I was going to see one of Mother's boyfriends too—a different one. I used to call him "Uncle."

It was eight years since I had last seen Uncle Weiming. I had lost track of him completely, but I was quite sure he was still working at the same place. People in China do not move until they scuff a hole deep enough to bury themselves. I was certain he'd be at the factory. Like the old saying goes, if you want to go north, follow the North Star. In this case, I followed my instinct.

Sitting on the bus, I watched the trees whip by and wished the vehicle would slow down. Questions flipped through my mind, quick as the passing trees. What was I doing? Why was I calling upon Mother's old lover—a man who had disappeared eight years ago? Was I begging a married, thirty-five-year-old man to be my father, while I was old enough to be his lover? Was I asking him to be my sister Mingming's father again, when Mingming did not even know he existed?

Ever since Mother told me he was Mingming's father, I had wanted to connect them. I knew Mingming needed some moral support, and I decided he could provide it. *But is this a good idea?* It may be as useless as picking up an old, rotten melon. I might only soil my hands.

But during the last couple of weeks, a memory kept haunting me.

64

It was 1976, a few weeks after Chairman Mao had died. One early afternoon, Uncle wandered into our one-story, red brick apartment without knocking and sat down on a chair by the dining table. Father, who was used to Mother's variety of friends, nodded stiffly and walked out the door.

"Uncle!" Having not seen him in two weeks, I was excited. Uncle looked at me and did not respond. "I'll get Mom for you!" I went to Mom's bedroom, where I found the door shut. I knocked. "Mom, Uncle is here."

I heard rustling behind the door and the sound of a male voice. "Yes, just a minute." After a while, Mother strolled out with a cigarette in her mouth. She closed the bedroom door and sat next to Uncle. They sat in silence for a while.

"Got someone new?" Uncle directed his chin toward Mother's closed bedroom.

"It's none of your business."

"You pick up fast. Let me say this, if I may. I know who he is, and he is a notorious asshole."

"Okay!" Mother stood, ran into her bedroom, and rushed back with a paper box in her hands. She opened the box, revealing stacks of photographs of Uncle and her, then she smacked the whole box of photos against Uncle's face. "Get out of here; I don't need you anymore! You'd better go back to your pretty young girlfriend!"

Uncle rose and strode out the door.

"Uncle, don't go! Uncle, come back!" I chased him and burst into tears.

From then on, laughter and happiness disappeared from my life. My heart, along with those memories, froze. I became distracted by our household's chaos. To cope with it, I grew into a quiet, hard-working girl, which pleased Mother and Father. Gradually, I took over the household chores. I cooked, shopped, and even managed the money. When Mother had a problem, she would complain to me; when Father was hungry, he would ask me to make him something to eat. I grew accustomed to this life and felt proud of my responsibilities, until I began college. Before long, my vision for life changed. I realized people laughed and joked; life was not just constant working. I felt incompetent and needed help. But who could help me? Uncle. My memories flooded with images of my long-lost Uncle. "Go see him," a voice within me urged. "Go see him."

The sun slipped behind a cloud after I exited the bus. Bicyclists, wearing tight blue jeans with red and green down coats, mingled with the slow-moving trolleybuses on the street. The riders shrugged their shoulders, attempting to shrink into their jackets to shelter themselves from the cold wind. Hanging from some of the bicycles' handlebars, bags of groceries bounced against wheels. A gust of wind skated past me. I shivered and snapped all the buttons of my down coat, pulled up the zipper, and wrapped my scarf around my face.

With every step toward the factory, my heart beat faster. What would I say? Uncle's involvement with my mother had not brought him good luck. Seven years ago, he had been sentenced to two years of community service, while Mother served two years in prison for reading western books and having an extramarital affair. Maybe he was sweeping the factory floor or cleaning bathrooms now. The new Deng Xiaoping government could not immediately resolve millions of cases like his. Besides, he was not even involved in a political case. My visit could cause him more trouble.

The muted gray factory grew steadily larger in front of me. Although it was just a one-story, flat-roofed warehouse, it seemed big as a mountain. A white board painted with the words "Beijing Automobile Parts Factory" hung on one of the pillars on the gate, glowing under the sun. I retrieved a piece of toilet paper from my pocket and wrote down the address. Yes, I have arrived, I said to myself. Cold sweat icily ran down my back.

"Hey, girl, do you need help?" Like a ghost, a little old man materialized in front of me.

"I want to...want to see Wang Meiling." I stuttered. In the panic, I told him my mother's name.

"Who?" After returning to his little station next to the factory gate, the guard glanced at me over the top of his glasses and blinked his raisin eyes.

I did not answer. Instead, I stared.

"Oh, I know who you are talking about. She's not here anymore. She...she...was arrested years ago." Then he leaned closer to me across the windowsill, widening his lids. "Hey, girl, do you know what kind of crime she committed? If it were a political crime, the new government has probably pardoned her by now. But she committed both political and sexual crimes." He extended his neck out the window to spit on the ground. "To tell the truth, I hate to dirty my mouth. I doubt if she's ever going to be pardoned. Stay away from her!"

My cheeks burned, the heat creeping past my chin and down my neck. I wanted to dig a hole in the ground and duck inside. When I was just about to flee, I caught a glimpse of several uniformed workers passing the gate. One of them resembled Uncle.

"Uncle!" I ran toward them.

"Stop! Where is your visitor's pass?" The guard jumped out of the station, arms akimbo. His eyes scanned my body. "Oh, I know who you are. You're that dirty woman's kid. I can tell from your face. Get out of here, shit!"

I turned around and ran away as fast as I could. When I got home, my heart was still pounding like a drum. The next day, I wrote a letter to Uncle at the factory.

Dear Uncle,

It has been so many years since you last saw me. I do not know whether you still remember me. If you do, would you even recognize me on the street? I am a college student now. I passed the college entrance exam and entered Peking University. I was the number one student in my high school class, and I think you would be proud of me.

Things have hardly changed since you left. Do you remember my sister Mingming? She is a very intelligent girl. If given a little push, she could become an outstanding student. However, this hasn't happened. My parents are unwilling to give her any attention.

Recently, Mother has revealed to me that you are Mingming's father. I am not surprised, but I wish you would do us a kindness and take her away.

I am approaching adulthood. There are things I do not understand when I look back on my life. Maybe you could help me.

Meihua

While enjoying the excitement of this bold adventure, I could not guess if I would receive an answer to my letter. Somehow, deep in my sixth sense, I felt confident I would. I was quietly, secretly, awaiting a reply.

The following Monday, a letter waited for me on my bed at home.

68

Dear Meihua,

I was so glad to receive your letter. I have not forgotten you. I still remember your big, beautiful eyes staring at me, trying to get me to tell you stories. I can also recall vividly our long evenings together, talking about China's future. You are one of the most beautiful memories of those turbulent years. Concerning Mingming, the issue is much more complicated than you can imagine. Societal pressures are too great. She could suddenly become the center of attention at school, and be trashed as an evil, illegitimate child.

I think maybe we should meet sometime and talk. How about next Thursday, five o'clock at the Lidou Subway Station? You can write me to say whether that suits you or not.

Fondly,

Weiming

I picked him out easily from the crowd around the subway station. His face had not changed much—high cheek bones, long straight nose, sharp eyes. His unusual curly hair made him stand out among most Chinese. Age had turned him from a pale, young man into a stout man with a slightly bulging belly and weathered skin. I ran toward him. When I neared him, I stopped short and said, "Uncle?" He smiled at me, his swarthy face glowing in the dusk. I did not want to shake hands, as the gesture felt awkward to me. A hug was even more out of the question.

Finally, I uttered, "It's nice...nice to see you." I cast my eyes down.

"It's nice to see you, too! Just like your mother, what a big girl!" He stepped forward and shook hands with me. "Oh!" I nearly cried out. His big hands crushed my fingers. Then he threw his arm around my shoulders. We walked into the subway.

"How are you?" he said in a sweet voice. Turning, he looked into my eyes.

"I'm okay."

"How is your mother?"

"As usual."

"What's new with your father, your sister?"

"As usual."

"How is the family situation in general?"

"As usual."

"What is it about all these 'as usuals?'"

"Don't you remember?" I snapped. "Don't you remember anything about them? Don't you remember how horrible it is? You walked away scot free. You walked away!" Before he could react, I bolted toward the train. He followed me. We sat next to each other on a bench as the train rattled down the track. He quietly looked at the window on the opposite side. In the reflection, I could see his solemn face. No longer able to hold them back, my tears streamed.

Uncle passed me a handkerchief. "I know life has not been easy for you, but I want you to know how lucky you are. You are in college. You should appreciate what you've got." He paused, embracing my shoulders with his arm. "I used to dream of going to college, but I never got the chance."

Uncle's father was a banker before the Communists took over. He was in high school when the Cultural Revolution began. After wandering for a few years without a job or home, he was assigned to work in the Beijing Automobile Parts Factory, which was lucky, considering that thousands of high school graduates were forced to spend their lives laboring in the countryside.

He sighed and continued. "Now it's too late for me to go to college. I'm old and have forgotten almost everything I learned in school." He gazed out the subway window. I caught a note of grief and repentance in his voice that I had never before heard from him. In my memories, he had always been happy and carefree.

By the time we left the subway station, downtown was already dark. In the lighted streets, people rushed back and forth with bicycle bells ringing. Shopkeepers were closing up their storefronts for the night.

Uncle walked me to the bus stop. As we waited, the question I had been holding back finally burst out. "Are you going to take Mingming away?"

A gust of wind blew my question past his ears. He did not respond.

"I know I shouldn't meddle, but please take her away. Please!" I snatched his coat, pulling and shaking violently. "She's twelve years old and has already started drinking and smoking."

"Meihua, your bus is here." He pushed me through the door. "Goodbye, college student! Write to me!"

The bus lunged. I did not answer him and cried all the way home.

I went back to school after winter vacation. My college life was quiet—nothing but studying. Students had become very diligent after wasting ten years on the Cultural Revolution. Besides, there wasn't much to do aside from studying. No dates or parties were permitted on campus, except on special occasions. We had to be in our dormitories before eleven o'clock every night. Because of the restrictions, I had plenty of time to satisfy Uncle's request to study hard. But I found it impossible to keep my mind on physics and mathematics twelve hours a day. Although I made myself sit in the library after class, my mind would wander miles away, fantasizing about romantic relationships.

I continued writing to Uncle from time to time. His answers were usually short and matter-of-fact, mostly describing his work and his new job in the purchasing department. He rarely mentioned his family. I was not eager to see him again. He had taken on a different image after I met him. It became difficult to connect the Uncle of reality with the Uncle of my memories. For one, he had lost some of his good looks. After years of cultivation, he had changed from a rich playboy into an ordinary working man. What's more, his disinterest toward Mingming surprised me. I had felt responsible for finding her real father, but nothing good had come of it. I would have also liked him in my life, I admitted, but not like this. I did not confide in Mother about any of this, until I received my next letter from Uncle.

It was a Sunday afternoon. After taking the outgoing mail to the mailbox, I found a letter from Uncle and tore it open.

Dear Meihua,

I have not heard from you in a while. My new job in the purchasing department is very challenging. I realize how much I must learn. Last Sunday, I visited the area where your family lived. I rode my bicycle down the street, hoping to encounter you. But I was disappointed. Then I went to the apartment building. I saw your shadow, outlined against the curtain. I tried to imagine you laughing, joking. I stood there for two hours until my hands froze and my legs numbed...

Fondly,
Weiming

The letter made me realize he was still the old romantic of eight years ago. Since I was so lonely and unhappy, this letter convinced me he was the only one who truly liked me and needed me. I folded his letter, went to the bathroom, and read it over and over, until Mother knocked on the door, asking if I was all right. I came out, red-eyed, with a face full of tears.

"What happened?" Mother asked. "Are you all right?" She spotted the letter in my hand and snatched it away. After reading it, Mother sighed and took me into her bedroom. "What's all this about?"

"I went to see Uncle Weiming, and then..." I told Mother the whole story.

"Jesus, why did you do that? He is history. He's gone!"

"Mother, I'm sorry."

"It's okay. I just don't want you to make the same mistake your mother has made. He is very good at flattering girls. If you believe his words, you are in trouble." Taking a deep drag of the cigarette, Mother sank into thought. The cigarette almost burned to the end. Ashes fell to the floor.

"He was always interested in you, you know. He didn't want to be stuck with an old married lady like me. But you were still too young." She blew out smoke slowly, as though she wanted to breath out a painful memory. Then she stubbed the cigarette butt into the ashtray, twisting it hard as if to kill it.

"Stop writing to him! Stop the whole thing! Okay? I beg you. I beg youuuuuu..." She grabbed my hands, bursting into tears.

"Look at your mother. Look at me. Am I beautiful? Am I smart? Maybe, but I used to be much prettier and smarter. Please don't waste your time on someone like him. You have much more important things to do. Study. Study hard!"

"Damnit! What are you guys yelling about?" Father tottered over and pounded his fists on Mother's half-opened bedroom door.

"We're not talking about you."

"Then don't scream and shout. You're going to wake the whole neighborhood! You don't care about your reputation. I do." He turned and added, "I know you two always talk about murdering me. Hey, I'm going to live longer than any of you!" He wobbled away.

Mother had never revealed to me that Uncle had been interested in me many years ago. I was shocked. I also felt a pang of desire. If only I had known, if only I had known...but it was too late now. He was married. But he could still be my friend, maybe even my boyfriend. Why not? Mother had done it. Having a boyfriend might solve my problems. Lately, I dreamed of being hugged and kissed by someone. I longed to be with someone who would care about me and listen to my complaints. But I did not like the young men in college. They might be good looking and good students, but they were too simple minded. Could they understand I had acted like a mother for my brother and sister when I was fifteen? Could they understand my mother's boyfriend and my father had lived under the same roof for many years? I was not normal. It was not easy to find someone who understood me.

Without telling Mother, I accepted an invitation from Uncle to visit his home.

On a Saturday morning, I took the bus, following the directions he gave in his letter.

I arrived in a newly developed area. Several gray concrete apartment buildings lined the road. Others were under construction, their naked skeletons and innards exposed and ugly.

I walked down a side street—the only old-fashioned alley left in the area. The third door on the left was Uncle's. I went through the squeaky wooden gate between two stone-lion sentinels. The house was a traditional Chinese design with a square, four-corner courtyard in the middle and rooms surrounding it on all sides. An old, grey-haired man with darting eyes brushed his teeth in front of the shared outdoor sink. He smiled at me while letting toothpaste drip from his mouth. I gave him a smirk.

I knocked on the door that I thought was Uncle's. To my surprise, a middle-aged lady appeared in the doorway.

"I am Meihua. I have come to visit Uncle Weiming."

"I am Wuhua, Weiming's wife." She took my hands. "Come in."

Uncle's wife, Wuhua, was a typical working woman. She had short, straight hair and dark skin. She wore a worn, semi-transparent polyester blouse, a pair of faded pants, and a pair of soft, dingy walking shoes.

"It's nice to see you. I remember when you were a little girl, visiting your mother in the factory." Wuhua glanced at me and smiled.

Their daughter, Qinmei, had clearly just rolled out of bed. Uncle was braiding her pigtails, which reminded me of the past.

"Could you fix your own pigtails now? Oh!" Uncle looked at my freshly trimmed short haircut and shook his head. "Do you remember what I once told you? Girls should have pigtails; boys have short hair."

I smiled quietly. Wuhua handed me a basket full of delicious Big Rabbit candies from Shanghai. After dressing Qinmei, we left for the subway station. We were going to ride around the new subway system.

Uncle carried Qinmei on his shoulders. She spun her head.

"See, Mommy, I am taller than you!"

Wuhua and I followed quietly. I stared at the ground, counting my steps. I did not know what to say to her. She worked in the same factory and knew a lot about Mother and Uncle. To my surprise, she was very nice to me. I asked myself, *what am I doing here?* Uncle had finally given up his crazy oath to "never marry in his life." He had found a wife, had a daughter, and lived like everyone else. Why shouldn't I leave him alone?

A gust of cool air swept across my face as we descended the subway station stairs. The guards, wearing heavy down coats in late spring, walked back and forth with hands shoved into their coat pockets. Their faces were shadowed, backs slightly hunched.

"Dad, tell me a story," Qinmei whispered into his ear, while we sat together on the train.

"Which story do you want to hear?"

"I want to know what happened after the 'little cloth boy' jumped out of Linlin's pocket." She stared at Uncle with wistful eyes.

"Okay. After the little cloth boy slipped out of Linlin's pocket during her primary school graduation party..."

While Uncle wove his tale, the window on the other side of the train turned into a mirror against the dark. The mirror reflected Uncle and his child, with his wife watching them.

Then the scene morphed into one that had taken place fifteen years earlier, when I was seven years old. Sitting on Uncle's lap, I listened to him tell the same story. Mother sat next to us, holding a cigarette. Outside the window, drums from one of the Cultural Revolution demonstrations clanged. The noise still rang in my ears.

Gradually, the scene shifted to my home when I was fourteen. Mother and I sat around the potbellied coal stove, listening to Uncle narrate a banned story about Mrs. Mao's illegal activities, which took place right before the fall of the Gang of Four.

The scene switched yet again to another that had occurred in the same room.

After staring at me for a while, Uncle said, "Meihua, did you know you have very beautiful eyes?"

"Thank you, Uncle." I lowered my head and nodded shyly. Mother sat next to me, smiling. "Just like Mother's," I added. I had always thought Mother was prettier than me.

"No," Uncle said. "Your mother's eyes are round like peanuts, while yours are long like almonds." He squinted, as though measuring the size of my eyes.

From then on, I looked at myself in the mirror every day, trying to comprehend Uncle's comment: you have very beautiful eyes. Although I thought my nose was too flat, my mouth too big, and my face too wide, Uncle's comments were encouraging. After all, my eyes were beautiful, even more beautiful than Mother's. After Uncle left, I became so unhappy that I intentionally messed up my eyesight by reading mounds of books and had to wear a pair of ugly glasses.

With the sad memory still floating in my mind, the scenes faded. Our trip finally drew to a close. I jumped out of the train and walked forward quietly.

"I hope you were not too cold on the train," Wuhua said.

"No," I answered. "It's the darkness that bothers me."

She nodded. I was not sure she understood what I was talking about. No one could imagine life with a mother who had both a husband and a boyfriend. It was a slow torture of the heart. It was like the subway system, an existence without sunlight.

The noontime sun struck my face. I had difficulty opening my eyes and stood, blinking, for a while.

In his house, Uncle tied an apron around his waist and became the cook. When Mother was dating Uncle, his cooking was one of my greatest joys. I still vividly remembered his delectable deep-fried pork, chicken and meatballs, varieties of stir-fried dishes, and steamed fish. He would sit in front of our coal stove, waiting for hours for the oil to get hot. Fortunately, the gas stove he now owned was much faster. Everything arrived on the little courtyard table in about an hour. We gathered around it on miniscule stools. Uncle served everyone a bowl of rice. In five minutes, three pairs of chopsticks swam in the dishes of sweet and sour pork, stir-fried green beans, hot and spicy bean curd, and chicken turnip soup.

Wuhua fed Qinmei. Busy eating, Qinmei was unusually quiet, except when requesting a certain dish from the spread.

"No, I don't want pork. I want bean curd." She pointed her fat little finger toward the table and tried to spit out her pork. The meat had stuck between her teeth, so she dislodged it with some difficulty.

The neighbors were cooking and doing laundry in the yard. The stir-fry smoke and melodies of the Peking Opera on the radio lingered in the air, like an invisible roof over the courtyard.

Uncle sat quietly through dinnertime. Unlike the others, he did not eat any rice. Instead, he drank white wine. Under the shade of trees around the house, his face was like a bronze statue, solemn and motionless. He munched on roasted peanuts and drank slowly.

"You are at Peking University. It must be an exciting place." Wuhua attempted to start a conversation.

"Not really. It's very boring." I answered.

"Boring? Why? I thought Peking University was the best university in the whole country."

"Yes, but it's also very boring. Nothing happens. We spend our days in the library, studying, studying, and studying."

"Is that right?" She looked lost.

I didn't want to stifle her attempt at conversation, so I veered into another aspect of my schooling. "But recently it's been more interesting. Local free elections turned the campus upside-down for a time. Big-letter posters about reforming our country covered the campus like a snowstorm. Candidates gave public speeches on street corners and in the cafeterias, speaking from morning till night. I went to public debates every night. Sometimes, the meeting hall was so crowded, we had to stand outside to listen. We discussed everything from the pros and cons of Communism and Capitalism to the feminist movement. For the first time in three years, I discovered friendly, interesting students at my university. At the conclusion of the election period, the citizens of Beijing West District elected one of our brightest graduate students to represent them."

Uncle and Wuhua listened quietly. Maybe it was hard for those who had wasted their youth in political movements to share my enthusiasm for the demonstrations. Maybe they didn't know how to comment on the college life they had never experienced.

After a while, Uncle stood; the shade of nearby trees dappled his face. His eyelids glistened under the spots of sunlight. He put his hand on my shoulder, looked into my eyes, and said, "I am going to lie down for a while. I'm tired. You and Wuhua can talk. Okay?"

He left quickly. Wuhua was about to help him into the bedroom. He pushed her back and said, "I can take care of myself."

Wuhua came back and sighed, "I am sorry. He is like that occasionally."

Seeing Uncle in such a bad mood, I asked myself again what I was doing here.

"Do you have to clean dishes?" Wuhua asked me, trying to put aside her worries.

"Only during weekends at home," I said, beginning to admire her.

"How lucky you are! But you'd better be prepared for it. After you get married and have children, you have to do it every day."

"I'm not sure I want to get married," I said uncertainly. In my mind, the idea of marriage seemed far, far away. Love was yet to come, let alone marriage.

"Why?" Surprise was etched across her face. "It's nice to be married and have children."

"Let me wash the dishes, please." I took a stack of dishes and walked to the outdoor sink in the center of the yard.

As I washed dishes, the old man I had met earlier approached me and asked, "Are you Wuhua's..."

"No, Weiming's niece."

"Oh, his brother's daughter?"

Nodding my head, I lied. During my youth, while Mother enjoyed her modern lifestyle, I had learned how terrible gossip could be. Gossips could chop you into pieces. Wuhua handed me more dishes and turned around, staring down the old man.

"Hey, what are you doing here? Does she bother you? Let me tell you, it's none of your business who she is! You'd better piss on the ground and admire yourself in it!" Then she grabbed the dish pan from my hands and walked back into her home.

Wuhua hung some winter jackets and blankets outside to make use of the bright sunshine.

Walking through the house alone, I noticed two books lying on top of the dresser. One was high school algebra, the other was a book on international trade. I opened the second one and started reading. The clock struck three o'clock. I wondered if I should go home. It had been an hour and a half since Uncle had gone to sleep.

I tiptoed into the bedroom. Uncle snored heavily. With his eyes half open, his rough, freckled face was red and twisted. His chest bulged. His hands were clenched into fists. It seemed he was ready to fight someone in his dream. The longer I stayed, the louder his snoring became. It resonated in my head like the humming of a primitive song. Then it stopped. Uncle was awake.

He stared at me with red, sleepy eyes. I rushed toward him. He grabbed my arms and murmured, "Meihua, Meihua, is that you?" His dry, cracked lips trembled.

"Yes, Uncle." I moved closer to him. He opened his mouth again and struggled to say something. But he sighed and dropped his head instead. "Meihua, would you go, please?" My heart, which had risen to my throat, now plunged down like an anchor deep in the sea. I quietly stood and walked toward the door.

"Meihua, wait a minute." Uncle got up quickly, opened the bottom draw of the dresser, and pulled out a beautiful pair of stonewashed blue jeans. "Please give these to Mingming." Then, he turned around. I took the jeans and paused. I wanted to call his name and give him one last hug, but I didn't. I kept walking through the yard and out the door.

The sun glared in the sky like an iron sphere convincing everyone that spring was just around the corner. Young women, wearing bright skirts and broad-brimmed hats, rode their bikes slowly and elegantly. Young men, dressed in tight blue jeans and fashionable sunglasses, wrapped their arms around young ladies' bare, smooth shoulders.

I adjusted my sight, and everything became much clearer. I walked faster, trying to catch up with the crowd.

Earthquake

In May of 1976, when I was fourteen, the largest earthquake in modern Chinese history rocked the small town of Tongshan, 120 miles northeast of Beijing. It measured 7.5 on the Richter scale.

I remember Father waking me from a deep sleep. I saw the ceiling lamp swinging back and forth. After I arose, I could feel the ground shaking beneath my feet. Everyone grabbed a chair and a blanket and ran to the main road. We sat there, waiting for the quake to end and dawn to come.

When dawn did come, the aftershocks of the quake continued. Through the institute's loudspeaker, our Communist leader told us we were not allowed to return to our apartments yet. We had to stay outside until the aftershocks ceased. The government will put up tents, we were told. We would have to sleep there.

After this announcement, torrential rain started pouring down. We retrieved raincoats from the apartment and stood under a tree, shivering. It rained continuously for three days. While we waited for the tents to arrive, we huddled together in the rain for three long days. The tents appeared magically soon after the rain stopped. They were basic setups with canvas roofs and makeshift beds, constructed of wood and bricks. For the children and even us teenagers, it was an adventure. We chased each other and played hide-and-seek. Mother refused to sleep outside. She liked the idea of having the apartment all to herself and her friend Zhuzhu.

Zhuzhu was the boyfriend who replaced "Uncle" Weiming. He was the youngest son of a purged, high-ranking Communist official, and only four years older than I was. He wore bell-bottom pants and rode a custom-made bicycle that had unusually small wheels. With his tall frame, he sometimes looked like a circus monkey on that bicycle. He could play the guitar, the cello, and the violin. Every day was a party when he was around.

One day, he told us how he got his cello. "I jumped over a high wall," he said. "It had to be at least twenty feet high. I made my way to the Communist propaganda team's practice room and nabbed the cello. I then tied the instrument to my back and climbed back up the wall. I had to skirt along the top of the wall for a while before I could jump down." As he told his story, I stared at him, mouth gaping. He was like a hero, similar to the characters in *Zorro*, my favorite childhood movie. Whenever I started staring at Zhuzhu like that, Mother always scolded me and told me to leave.

During the earthquake, I begged Mother to sleep outside. She squared her shoulders and refused. "I'm not afraid of death like your father. He wants me to die yet has no courage to kill me. He is a coward. Maybe I will die in this earthquake. Maybe I'll become a martyr. God, let me die! My life is so boring." Mother had a new, younger boyfriend about every five years. Her life was anything but boring.

That first night, I ended up lying on a bed alone in the tent, looking at the sky. An orchestra of animal sounds filled the night air—donkeys, dogs, cats, cows, buffalos, and chickens. No one could sleep following the earthquake.

On the eve of Chinese New Year in January of 1977, the wind howled and beat against the windows of our apartment. Snowflakes danced wild in the wind. Inside, the fire in our apartment's potbelly stove burned hot. Like many families, we were busy making dumplings for the New Year. Father was making the wrappers. He mixed the flour dough, rolled it into a snake, and cut the long cylinders into many pieces. After pressing them into little round pies, he rolled them into pancakes, forming the dumpling wrappers. After finishing the wrappers, he would stuff them with meat fillings, seal the two sides together, and boil them in water. My task was to help press the little round pies and fill the wrappers. Mother sat on the bed, smoking.

"Hey, slut, why don't you help?" said Father.

"I don't feel like it. I'm not hungry."

"You must be thinking about your boyfriends, those social scoundrels. Stop seeing them! You will get us all in trouble, including me."

"Get you in trouble? You only think about yourself. You blame me for having boyfriends? That's your fault. You let me do it from the start. Now, they can't marry me because you don't want to get a divorce. You *can't* do it. You are sick!"

"I'm sick? You are too hard to satisfy. You get out of here, you and your criminal friends!"

Father waved the cleaver he used to cut the dumpling dough. His face was red, partially out of anger, partially from the alcohol he drank all day.

"Kill me! I don't want to live anymore." Mother's eyes filled with tears.

"I will kill you, slut!" Father raised the cleaver over Mother's head. His face purpled.

At this moment, my body froze. I was not afraid of Mother's plea to die; that was commonplace for her. I *was* afraid of my father's actions. Lately, he had difficulty controlling himself, especially when he had been drinking.

For a moment, I was joyful about Father's threat. Father and Mother had not gotten along for many years. But neither one truly wanted a divorce. Mother needed to be associated with Father's professor title. Father felt that a divorce was embarrassing. So, they coexisted like water and oil. The only way to achieve peace would be for one of them to die. By this point in my young, turbulent life, I did not care which one died. I didn't favor one over the other. They were so different. Mother was fun, with her sense of humor and her many talented artistic friends. Most of her friends were musicians and artists. Many were troubled, high-ranking officials' sons. Father was an intellectual and a retired university professor. He was also artistic. He could draw a tiger that looked ready to spring from the page. When I was young, he often did my art homework. I never had a chance to become a great artist and could now blame my artistic shortcomings on him. Even though I did not like him after he had a few drinks, he was more predictable than Mother, which often gave me comfort.

In this moment, with Father's knife poised above Mother, I thought of last year's earthquake. I wished it would happen again and kill us all, so we could leave this misery.

Of course, an earthquake of that magnitude never came again, and the cleaver never fell on my mother's head. That New Year's Eve, like many holidays in my home, ended with Mother running away. The rest of us ate dumplings in silence.

That cleaver, however, cut a deep gash in my heart that still bled many years later.

In 1985, at age twenty-four, I passed an English exam and obtained a World Bank scholarship to attend graduate school in America. I had waited for this moment for a long, long time. I had dreamt of escaping to a faraway place. Finally, it was my time to fly.

I had never before been on an airplane, never had set foot outside China's borders. Right before I was scheduled to leave, my father was diagnosed with stomach cancer. He was immediately checked into a hospital, where a surgeon cut away most of his stomach. Many good daughters would abandon their opportunities to study abroad and stay home to care for their sick father. I decided to leave. I had worked hard to leave this toxic home, and I would not let this opportunity slip through my fingers. I left, even though I knew I might never see him again. His eyes were moist when he saw me off in front of our apartment building. Because my mother and her boyfriend had volunteered to drive me to the airport, Father stayed behind.

My father lived another ten years. When I was pregnant with my son, he finally passed from this earth. When my son was born, I looked at him and saw my father. My new son slept exactly like him, lying on his back with both hands resting above his shoulders.

A Chinese Boyfriend

I met him at my first job. After graduating from Peking University with a bachelor's degree in physics, I began work as a teaching assistant at Beijing Medical University. I loved my job. My co-workers and I often went out after work, drinking beer and playing ping-pong or badminton. I wasn't good at any of these activities, but my companions were nice enough to teach me. They knew I was a nerd from "the Harvard of China," and hadn't done much besides studying for the last few years. After a few weeks of trying, I began to enjoy beer, but I had no talent for smoking cigarettes. They always became soggy when I tried to light them. However, I was pretty good at playing badminton, especially after a few lessons from Li Xiang.

Li Xiang was a tall, handsome man in his thirties. He had small, animated eyes and a big smile with slightly protruding front teeth. He loved to tell jokes, especially self-depreciating ones about how little money his wife allowed him to have. When he told these jokes, he would jiggle the coins in the pocket of his white lab coat. As a technician in the animal lab, he was rarely without that coat.

Due to his humor and good looks, Li Xiang was quite popular—and his popularity was only amplified by his wife's poor treatment of him. His wife, Xiao Liu, was a pretty, but serious woman who worked as a military nurse. Whenever she showed up, his animated personality wilted. He would freeze whatever he was doing or saying, sometimes with his hands still mid-air. Then, he would drop his hands to the pockets of his white coat and start jingling the coins again. Sometimes Xiao Liu would simply drop off the baby and leave. Their baby girl was very cute, and everyone loved to cuddle her.

Chen Hong was a married woman in her late twenties. She also worked as a TA in the physics department. She was short and slim, with a pleasant smile. She laughed loudly at Li Xiang's jokes, and I could tell she liked him. Later, I discovered she loved him—loved him a lot.

One day after work, we gathered in our conference room/classroom. Someone brought beer and tall, plastic glasses to celebrate Li Xiang's birthday. In 1980s Beijing, there were not many restaurants, so people often had parties at work with store-bought alcohol and peanuts. We also did not have birthday cakes, so there was no blowing out candles or making wishes. Besides, in our bleak, Communist society, we didn't have high hopes for the future. What was the use of making wishes? Better to be realistic. Even the old Chinese tradition of lighting incense in front of ancient Buddhas was criticized as superstition.

On the day of Li Xiang's birthday, we sat around the table and passed a bowl of candies Chen Hong had bought. They were famous Big Rabbit candies from Shanghai, where she had grown up. Li Xiang started serving beer. When he came to me, he poured mine to the top of the glass.

"Meihua, you are an old timer now. Drink it all the way down."

People started chanting, "Drink, drink, Meihua! Drink, drink, Meihua!"

My heart sank. Did I really have to drink the whole thing down? I had heard stories about Chinese people having drinking competitions and occasionally dying from alcohol poisoning.

I wrinkled my nose and started drinking big, generous gulps. I let the glass fall to the floor, making a mess. My head spun; I began seeing the world through a dreamlike, happy lens.

Li Xiang returned to the table. Another technician named Liu Bing retrieved a cigarette, lit it, and passed it around. At that time, I had never smoked and resented cigarettes for holding my mother in their clutches. Yet, I didn't care. I kept putting the cigarette in my mouth, and it kept falling out. When I tried to light it, it was too soggy to catch fire. People laughed, but I didn't mind. For the first time in my life, I was enjoying being a clown.

Music blasted from a boombox. Chen Hong stood, grabbed Li Xiang, and pulled him to the center of the room. They started waltzing. Chen Hong was a skilled ballroom dancer. She moved her face close to Li Xiang's—so close, they appeared to be kissing. Their bodies wrapped tightly together, dancing in unison with the music. Everyone watched this pair of lovebirds showing off. Then, Liu Bing invited an older female professor to dance; they were very good together, too. I stood watching and wishing someone would take my hand and ask me to dance. But I was a nerdy young woman with thick glasses. Who would think I could dance?

To my surprise, Li Xiang approached me and asked, "Meihua, want to learn how to dance?" He bowed to me and extended a hand.

"Sure." I followed him to the dance floor.

I was clumsy at first but improved with Li's lead.

I stared into his playful eyes from behind my thick glasses. "How did you know I never learned how to dance?"

"I guessed. You can hit me if I'm wrong." He laughed.

"You were right, but I still want to hit you." I gave him weak slap on the shoulder and fell onto his chest.

"Hey, Meihua, it's fine you can't dance. You're smart as a whip. I hear you've done well in the English test for a World Bank scholarship to study in America. I'm so impressed. Can we talk about it sometime?" He sounded earnest.

"Sure." I couldn't believe my ears. This handsome, popular guy wanted to go out with me? He was married, true, but I wouldn't mind being his friend. He was charming, and I was sure I would enjoy his company.

After this first dance, Li Xiang invited me to play badminton after work. Then, we absconded to his lab. Without preamble, we fumbled for each other, intent on consummating our budding love. I removed my glasses, so we could kiss unencumbered. We made sensual, non-penetrating love on the fake-leather cover of the operating table. Even though the leather bed was cold, our pulsating bodies warmed us. I enjoyed his every kiss, touch, and sweet small talk.

After that, his lab became our regular hideaway, the operating table our bed. After one of our torrid love making sessions, we sat side-by-side on the operating table and I decided to breech a topic that had been on my mind.

"I noticed Chen Hong isn't very happy lately. Do you know why?" I suspected I knew the answer, but I wanted to hear it from him.

"Oh, I might know," he said. "She was chasing after me for a while, you know. She doesn't like her husband and wants to leave him for me. I told her I couldn't. My wife would murder me if I left her. My wife loves me, she just has a funny way of showing it. But Chen Hong wouldn't let go. I told her we should take a break, and she reluctantly agreed."

"Wow. What an intriguing love story!" I teased.

"Not as interesting as ours." He kissed me again. "People here fool around a lot, even married people. This is medical school, after all."

"What makes medical school different?" I asked.

"It's because we know physiology better," he said.

"I see. So, this is all physiology?"

"Of course not, I really love you." He embraced me and pulled me in for a long, wet kiss.

Before we finished, I heard a knock at the door and a voice call: "Li Xiang, are you here? Why aren't you home yet?"

It was Xiao Liu, Li Xiang's wife.

I fell into shock. I turned to Li Xiang with zombie-like horror on my face. Li Xiang pushed me away and threw my clothes toward me. I rushed to put them on, my head fogged as though immersed in a dream.

"Wait. I'm in the middle of a test," said Li Xiang, voice calm.

He put on his clothes lightning fast and gestured for me to hide in the far corner.

"Try to sneak out when I'm talking to her outside the door," he whispered.

I nodded, heart pounding hard and fast. *What if she sees me?* But I was out of options. The lab was on the third floor, so escaping out the window was out of the question. I readied myself to sprint out a side door.

Li Xiang opened the main door and slipped out. He tried to make himself big in the doorway to block the view of the other door.

"What's going on?" he asked.

"Nothing. I just miss you," she said sweetly.

Before she could come to the doorway and give Li Xiang a hug, I bolted out the other door and ran down the stairs as if my shoes were on fire.

I sprinted to the back of the building, where I could see the lab window on the third floor. I looked up, trying to figure out what was going on. Then, I realized I had failed to grab my glasses. They were sitting on the operating table. *What if Xiao Liu saw them?* I stood, looking up to the dark lab room and wondering what would happen tomorrow. *Would she come to the office to beat me up tomorrow morning? Should I call in sick? What happens if everyone at work finds out?* Then, I realized Xiao Liu would probably want to keep this quiet because it could damage her husband's reputation. When things like this happened, the management usually tried to separate the two parties involved. She would run the risk of her husband being transferred out of Beijing. Working at Beijing Medical University was a good job that Li Xiang's father, a high-ranking military officer, secured for him by pulling a few strings. Rumor had it, one of the reasons Xiao Liu had married Li Xiang was because of his family and his good job in Beijing.

I decided to wait in the dark and see what happened next. After about an hour, I tiptoed to the front of the building and found Li Xiang standing there, smoking. I ran to him and gave him a hug. He halfheartedly pushed me away.

"Hey, be careful," he said, voice serious.

"I can't see anyone here. But then again—" I looked around, nervous. "I left my glasses in the lab. Did she see them?"

"No." Li Xiang said. "She didn't see anything and believed everything I told her. She left."

Relief flooded through me. "Good to hear. I need to get my glasses so I can go home. Otherwise, I will fall off my bike."

"I have them." He reached into the pocket of his lab coat and handed me my glasses. We kissed goodbye.

Since Xiao Liu didn't discover us, we continued dating. He took me to the Summer Palace one day. We took many pictures together—keepsakes I could bring to America. When we were on a rowboat, he kept saying I should help him get to America as soon as I settled in. His life was miserable in Beijing. He had suffered a lot during the Cultural Revolution, he told me, due to his father's position as a high-ranking army doctor. I understood. I, too, had encountered problems stemming from my father's position when I was young. Sitting in the rowboat, I gazed at his face. Golden sunlight illuminated and warmed his features. I felt genuinely in love. He promised he would leave his wife and reunite with me in America, and I believed him. *I am lucky*, I thought, *to have such a handsome boyfriend. My future in America will be as bright as the sun.*

One day, Chen Hong walked into my shared office space. The others were not around, so she closed the door.

"I hear rumors Li Xiang is dating you, is that right?" She was on the verge of tears.

"No," I lied. "Come on, Chen Hong. He has a wife and a baby girl. He wouldn't leave his wife for anyone—not me or you."

"Don't lie. You'd better be careful not to wreck your future."

"Thank you. I will." *Yeah. I'm going to America! That's my future, and Li Xiang will follow me there.* I almost laughed out loud.

I was naïve to think America—and my future—were paved with gold. My delusions were soon obliterated.

Departure

I came from a place where the streets teemed with horse-drawn carts and chicken droppings. Our delicacies included pig's feet and pig's ears. After living in America for thirty-five years, it is hard to believe that was my reality as a young woman.

Before my flight to the United States, I couldn't sleep. I tossed and turned until I decided to arise at 5:00 a.m. and ready myself. In two hours, my mother's boyfriend, Lao Zhang, would pick me up and drive me to the Beijing airport. From there, I would board an airplane to San Francisco. August 10, 1985 was the date I would realize my long-held dream of living in America.

I was ready to go, even though I knew very little about this new country. The adventure, alone, excited me. And I had nothing to lose.

At 6:00 a.m., the small Beijing Airport was deserted. I arrived two hours early for my long trip. I had never before traveled by plane, and I ran to the locked gate where I gazed at the boarding area for China Air and looked for an airplane. All I could see was the black canvas tunnel, leading to the lobby. Questions raced through my head: Was I late? Had the plane left without me? In China, missing a connecting flight could easily mean the cancellation of the whole trip. I ached to travel to this unknown world and missing my flight would be disastrous.

My thoughts turned to the other side of the airport. Were Mother and her boyfriend still around? They had planned to take my brother and sister out to breakfast in the airport. Why didn't they take me with them? At this point, I was already behind the fence and not allowed to return to the restaurant area outside the gate. I imagined them laughing while they munched on breakfast food. For them, I was already gone.

My mind started to drift. Daydreaming had been a form of entertainment since grade school and caused me to miss large chunks of school lectures. But I always studied on my own at home. At the end of each term, I managed to get good grades in almost all subjects.

For an hour and a half, more and more people arrived at the gate, waiting to board the same plane. I was prepared to go on this big adventure alone, leaving my family behind. Secretly, I promised myself I would never come back, at least not anytime soon. Since I was so detached from my family, it was an easy promise to make. I did, however, feel a pang of regret at leaving one person: my father.

Early that morning, I bid my father farewell before climbing into Lao Zhang's car. I cried, and I could tell he was also on the verge of tears, but held them back. We didn't say anything. We hadn't had much to say to each other for years. He had stomach cancer, and we both knew we might never see one another again. My final physical departure completed the separation I had long felt from my home and my family.

My mom, Lao Zhang, and my brother and sister managed to return five minutes before the boarding call. It stung that they almost missed saying goodbye, but a sincere apology and a heartfelt send-off would have soothed my hurt feelings.

However, they spent our last few minutes together boasting about their big meal, describing the delectable food I hadn't had the opportunity to enjoy.

On the airplane, I began my dream trip by vomiting as soon as we were in the air. I was miserable from my lack of sleep and food. During the entire two-hour trip from Beijing to Shanghai, I felt so sick I wished I could jump off the airplane. After a layover in Shanghai, I magically felt better. The young lady sitting next to me offered me a pickled hot pepper. Her food choice suggested she was a southerner. I was right; she was from Hunan province, heading to the University of Iowa to study. Her name was Yan Ja. We were offered a western-style meal with a sandwich, pickle, and a square of stinky, gray cheese spread. Now that I am more familiar with cheese, I can safely say that was the worst cheese I have ever eaten. What a poor introduction to cheese for the people on that flight!

In San Francisco, Yan also had to change planes. We would spend a night at the same Chinese-owned Marriott Hotel. Later, we found out we had to share a room to save the government some money.

After checking into the hotel, we decided to take a walk to get our first impressions of America. As soon as we exited the hotel, we saw two giant women walking down the hill on a typical San Francisco street. We marveled at their size, wondering which planet we had landed on. After walking about a block and seeing a group of people bunched around a map, we decided we didn't want to get lost. We turned back and walked into a souvenir shop. The price of the clothing in the shop convinced us we could never afford a new pair of pants or a sweater with our small stipend. We walked out in disbelief. Maybe we could afford some food. We went into a restaurant and carefully ordered some Chinese dumplings. The food was delicious, but we had to add a tip.

"How much do we add?" Yan asked me.

"I don't know!" I shook my head.

"How about we leave some pennies on the table?" Yan suggested.

"What if that is not enough?" I fretted. "Maybe the shop owner will be angry with us."

We threw a few pennies on the table and dashed out of the restaurant.

The rest of the trip was not pleasant. I had to say goodbye to Yan and board my next flight alone. As soon as I was seated on my Continental Airlines flight bound for Minneapolis, I started to cry. Sitting among so many nicely dressed people with fresh makeup and foreign features made me instantly homesick. The tears flowed, and I couldn't stop them. I thought about my boyfriend, Li Xiang, in Beijing—a fresh relationship I had formed just two months earlier. I imagined him waiting to join me, anxious, even though he was married with a baby. My tears turned into none-too-quiet sobs. To my surprise, the well-dressed woman next to me wasn't at all disturbed. What was she doing, listening to her Walkman? Her nonchalance made me feel better. I needed to spill my sorrow, then I could move forward. In China, people wouldn't just let me cry on my own. They would ask why I was crying and how they could help. They would want to hear the story behind my sorrow, so they had something to gossip about. I could get used to this American attitude, I thought.

Sitting on the plane, thousands of miles from home, I realized something: My past and my history would follow me, no matter how far I strayed. I carried my home with me.

Fargo

After changing flights twice, I landed in Fargo, North Dakota. It was mid-summer, and the weather was pleasant and cool. This was quite the change from the dry, hot weather of Beijing. But, the two places did have one thing in common: mosquitoes. While coping with biting mosquitoes, I also battled terrible jetlag. For an entire week, I would wake up in the middle of the night, unable to fall back asleep. I was exhausted and didn't want to eat anything. Mostly, I lay in bed in a campus apartment located in the vast North Dakota prairie. The only living things I could see were herds of bison in a ranch behind our apartment building.

My roommate, Yiuying, was a nice young woman who had arrived a few months earlier from Beijing Agricultural University. She worked as a visiting professor in the Department of Agriculture at North Dakota State University and took her job very seriously. She left for her lab early in the morning and did not return until suppertime. An accomplished Chinese cook, Yiuying knew how to make many different dishes, including pickles without vinegar.

"Vinegar can be generated through the fermentation of sugar in water," she told me in her professorial voice. "As long as you put the cucumbers and the sugar water in a vacuum, vinegar will be produced in no time."

I still felt weak and delirious from my severe jetlag. The idea of making pickles sounded intriguing—more so than making other foods, like rice and pork. Of course, it took about a week for the pickles to ferment.

During the day, I would switch on the little nine-inch TV my roommate had purchased at a garage sale. The terrible quality of US programs surprised me. I had expected better. I didn't realize evening was the time for prime-time television. While I watched soap operas, I would occasionally glance at the pickles floating in their glass bottle. By the time they were ready to eat, I had fully recovered from my jetlag.

Because I was so turned off by daytime soap operas, I never watched TV in the evening. Besides, my work ethic prevented me from watching. I appreciated the opportunity to study in the US, even though I had to give up big-city life in Beijing in exchange for this cold, northern prairie. To amuse ourselves, my roommate and I liked to walk to a nearby ranch and sing to the bison. Sometimes, our foreign songs would frighten them, and they would gallop to the other corner of the fence. Sometimes, we tried to chase them.

Even during the winter, Yiuying and I would walk to the local supermarket, since neither of us owned or knew how to drive a car. When we needed to apply for a social security card downtown, the head of the Chinese Student Association drove us there. The short trip from campus to downtown made me carsick.

The head of the Chinese Student Association, Mr. Wu, was a forty-something PhD student in the Agricultural Department.

He had a hardworking wife and a cute five-year-old son. Like many Chinese people his age, he had suffered a lot in his youth. His father, a famous intellectual, committed suicide during the Cultural Revolution. Since he was an intellectual's son, he was presumed an enemy of the Communist Party and sent to the countryside to perform hard labor. In his thirties, he was accepted to Peking University, where he studied chemistry until the end of the Cultural Revolution. After many years of hard work and a bit of luck, he was given a chance to study in the United States. Even here, in the middle of a state famous for its snowstorms and floods, he was happy and content.

North Dakota State University had twenty Chinese students at the time. It was a close-knit society. When Mr. Wu invited me to visit his family's two-bedroom apartment suite in the married students' dormitory, I was excited. Situated on the second floor among a cluster of identical, contemporary two-story buildings, I was impressed by his apartment's sophistication. The Wu family had told their relatives in China they were living in a two-story building all by themselves which, I knew, would impress their relatives, who mostly lived in apartments with shared kitchens and bathrooms.

Mr. Wu was so enamored with his new home; he even claimed the pot-stickers were better in the US than in China. He said, "Here, the flour quality is better—good, American flour."

Raped in Fargo

My professor at North Dakota State University, Dr. Zwickey, was a tall and slender man with messy salt and pepper hair. When he wrote on the blackboard, he twisted his tall frame ninety degrees, so he could write with his left hand. He taught quantum mechanics and served as my adviser.

On my first day, he cleared a benchtop in the lab for me to use as a makeshift desk. Then, he handed me a stack of research papers on the structure of protein molecules and said, "Read up." Once I started going to the lab routinely, time flew by. Soon, snow began falling and my short bicycle commute became a long slog. I wore long underwear beneath my jeans and a down jacket I had purchased in China, but it still wasn't enough. Even with mittens, I had to bury my hands in my jacket pockets to prevent them from going numb. Instinctively, I curled up my body to preserve heat, but the cold wind cut like so many knives on my naked face. My eyelashes would freeze, and my feet cried for help. I felt inches away from morphing into a snowman. Once I returned home, I reveled in biting into steaming hot egg rolls—homemade and fresh out of the oil.

During my first quarter at NDSU, I was offered a half-time Teaching Assistant (TA) position in the physics lab. With my limited English, I did remarkably well. I used body language and my sense of humor to ease communication.

At first, the students talked too quickly for me to fully comprehend them. Yet, they were good-natured and did not mind repeating themselves when needed. Sometimes, they would mimic me and repeat their sentences in my Chinese accent. A unique chemistry developed between these pink-faced American students and me, a young Chinese transplant. At the end of the semester, I gave everyone a B or better, except two students whose lab reports were messy and illegible. They approached me, sad-faced.

"Why did you give us Cs?"

Looking at these two innocent students, my heart went out to them. I changed their lab grades to Bs and lit up inside when I saw their happy faces. Even though I had been a mostly straight-A student throughout grade school and high school, I didn't much believe in letter grades. I knew how misleading a simple and, sometimes, subjective grading system could be—my handful of Cs in college proved that.

Through student teaching, I met a young man named Mohammed. He was a new graduate student like me, but from Lebanon. He had black hair, a bushy mustache, and penetrating eyes. He loved to ask me questions. While he was asking, he would stare at me and I felt a strange sense of desire emanating from his expressive eyes. He was also rude and macho. Sometimes, he would snatch my pencil from my hand while I was doing homework.

"Hey, stop!" he would say. "Help me with this quantum mechanics homework!" Though he wasn't always the easiest student, tutoring came naturally to me. I had been an instructor at Beijing Medical University before coming to the US, and I understood the material backward and forward.

Mohammed loved driving me around in his old Chevy. However, I was busy and only had time to accompany him once or twice. He would blare rock and roll music on the radio as we drove down the quiet highway. I didn't know much about rock and roll, not even what was considered classic rock. Before I left China, I would listen to Beethoven's Third, Fifth, and Ninth Symphonies—quite a change from the Communist revolution music I had been forced to sing and listen to. I enjoyed classical musical and loved when my father played his violin when I was young. In my sheltered world, I didn't know anything about jazz, blues, or rock and roll. I was far behind in this regard, and never had much time or desire to catch up. But it didn't matter. To me, rock and roll reflected the happy, easy American culture that was so different from my difficult upbringing. I was told life was hard, and happiness was to be earned when I was young. I thought I would never understand rock and roll music.

Muhammad spoke often about his family. His parents had married young, his father fifteen and his mother twelve. He had several sisters and a nice girlfriend back home, but she "didn't want to come here."

I didn't want to date him, even though he often stared at me with wild-animal hunger. I found the attention flattering, but I did not share his feelings.

Sometimes, we studied together at night. He claimed he wanted help with his quantum or classic mechanics homework. After studying one night, he asked me to go to his apartment.

"Come on." He stared at me, eyes burning with desire.

"No," I said timidly. I wanted to go, yet I couldn't. Even though sleeping with someone who desired my body was tempting on a cold winter night, I worried about my roommate's reaction. What would she think if I returned late or not at all? Would she worry? Would she think something bad had happened to me? If she found out I had slept with a Lebanese man, would she spread it around the whole school? Deep inside me, I wanted to sleep with him, even though I was still a virgin and never had real sex with my previous boyfriends. I fantasized being kissed and caressed by a wild and sexy man. Still, I never budged. Muhammad, however, didn't give up. A few days later, he invited me to have lunch with him. He made it sound like just lunch, nothing else, and I believed him.

"Come on. Come to my apartment and I will cook for you. I can also show you some Arabic art and my family photos."

"What are you going to cook?" I asked.

"You will find out."

After he drove me to his basement apartment, I found out there were neither art nor photos. He whisked a couple of eggs and fried them in a small frying pan. During lunch, he told me about his experiences during the Lebanese war.

I was impressed by his courage. I admired people who had fought in wars, whether they were drafted or volunteered. Confronting death could entirely shift one's psyche. I listened to him with admiration.

"I was wounded once. Do you want to see my scar?" He said it earnestly, and I did not sense any of his usual animal desire. I was going to say yes. I wanted to. Before I could utter a word, he removed his pants. Apparently, he had to take off his underwear to show me the scar. Then, he quietly pulled me into the bedroom. I tried to refuse, but he was much stronger than me. He swiftly pulled down my pants and underwear and leapt on top of me. I screamed and cried, "No, no, no, no!"

It passed in a blur. Afterward, I wasn't sure what he had done to me. Blood spattered his white bed sheets. It took me another year or two before I understood I had lost my virginity that day with Muhammad. At the time, I was not convinced. It went so fast, I didn't think he had entered me at all. That was not how I had expected lovemaking to be.

I quickly gathered my things and readied myself to leave. He drove me back to my apartment.

"You never had sex before?"

"No. I want to be a virgin until I get married. I want to save my virginity for my husband."

"I thought you had a boyfriend in China."

"Yes."

"What did you do together?"

"Talk."

"I don't understand. How did you express love?"

"We kissed each other."

This was last time he invited me to his apartment. He stopped staring at me with the animal desire. Every now and then, he asked me to help him with homework. I helped him out of my duty as a TA, but conflict brooded inside me. I still liked him and found him attractive, but I could never trust him again. Even though I wished to be his girlfriend, I couldn't date a person I didn't trust. Sometimes, I saw him waiting outside the student union for someone to show up—a new girl, I guessed.

Once, I bumped into Mohammed while chatting with a group of Chinese students outside the student union. Out of courtesy, I introduced him to everyone as a fellow graduate student in the physics department. Nobody said hello. All he got were icy stares. I was relieved I hadn't shared our little episode with anyone in the Chinese community or even my roommate. My reputation would have surely suffered. They would have called me a loose woman for sleeping with someone of non-Chinese descent, especially someone from the Middle East.

After that, I didn't want a boyfriend for a long time. My experience with Mohammed had stunned me and left a bitter taste in my mouth. I decided I wanted a caring and mutual relationship, which also prompted me to break up with my boyfriend in China. As long as he was married, we would never be on an even playing field. *Someday,* I told myself, *I will find my white knight on horseback.*

The Adult Book Store

During North Dakota State University's winter break, my roommate, Yiuying, and I were bored. I went to the library to look for novels, but it was a science and engineering library and didn't contain a single work of fiction. I ended up occupying my time with a handful of computer games a professor had loaned me. Yiuying had a job, so she was a bit busier, but even she had a week off. So, we decided to join the local Chinese church group on a bus trip to Madison, Wisconsin for a meeting of the North American Christian Group. Yiuying and I were not Christian, but the organizer said that was okay. "Besides," he said, "you'll be converted by the end of the meeting."

We didn't tell the group that our true motive was simply to visit the city.

It took ten hours to drive from Fargo to Madison. We left early in the morning, and by the time we arrived, it was already dark. After settling in at a Holiday Inn by the edge of a highway, we gathered in a hotel conference room and prayed. Meeting materials were distributed. After a simple sandwich dinner, we divided into small groups. Christians would tell about their experiences of getting to know God; newcomers like us would listen and learn from them. This meeting reminded Yiuying and me of meetings we used to have in China. The Communists certainly borrowed a lot of methods from Christianity to convert people. I remembered talking about how we felt about Chairman Mao, based on our true experiences. No wonder we, students from mainland China found the Christian meeting boring. It was even more depressing when we found out we were supposed to stay in the Holiday Inn day and night, listening to constant preaching. We wouldn't have time for sightseeing at all, and we were lucky to even step outside the hotel to look at the scraggly trees by the highway.

However, we did make some friends in the group. During the break, people from the People's Republic of China often gathered around a table, complaining. There was no way we would start believing in God. We had had enough testimony and preaching about Communism in China. In the end, we had discovered that the Communists had lied to us and manipulated us to gain control. They had lived lavish lifestyles, while the ordinary Chinese people were instructed to work hard and sacrifice themselves for the party.

"We are iron chickens and will never come alive no matter what magic they use," said Yiuying.

As she was talking, I noticed a man sitting next to her. He looked to be at least forty years old, with receding thick black hair, black-framed glasses, and a full dark beard. His thick beard was rather unusual for a Chinese man. I later discovered that he hailed from Shanghai and, even though his degree was in chemistry, he had gained fame as an artist before emigrating to the US. His father had been a famous poet and committed suicide during the Cultural Revolution and, shortly afterward, the young man was sent to the countryside to perform hard labor. During those dark ten years, when he wasn't farming, he was creating thousands of paintings which portrayed his love of people and the beauty of the countryside. He had quite a one-man show in Shanghai.

"I volunteered to stay in a lighthouse so I could work on my art. It was not heated, and in the winter it became so cold that even the eggs began to crack open."

Listening to his story, staring at his beard, I simply fell in love. I told him that I, too, was doubly talented. I was a graduate student in physics and also a writer.

"Send me some writing." He gave me his address. From his eyes, I could tell that he was serious. I knew that he, too, was intrigued by me, even though we had exchanged few words.

On the second day of marathon preaching, Yiuying and I decided we needed to escape. After lunch, we stepped out the door of the Holiday Inn. But where would we go? We knew nothing about Madison, aside from the fact it housed the University of Wisconsin-Madison. Maybe we could visit the campus and find some Chinese students. But how would we get there? We decided to try hitchhiking and tramped through the deep snow, crossing beneath the highway and finding a Holiday gas station. We asked every driver in front of the gas pumps:

"Could you please take us to the University of Wisconsin? Yiuying's mom is in the hospital and she is very sick." A little lie would help, we thought.

A bearded truck driver let us into his semi-truck. We squeezed into the cab with him, eager to escape. It never crossed our minds that this old driver might take us someplace other than the University.

"Where are you from?" The driver asked.

"Fargo."

"It must be very cold up there."

People always associated North Dakota with cold weather. People in North Dakota liked to think they had other offerings besides the cold weather—art, music, the aerospace center, a multi-million-dollar hockey arena. These attractions encouraged people to visit North Dakota and stay, despite the harsh winter.

"Who are you *really* going to see?"

"My boyfriend," said Yiuying, another lie. She was married and her husband was still in China.

"Why doesn't he come pick you up?"

"He doesn't know we are coming. It's a surprise," said Yiuying. Her lie was getting better and better.

"Okay. Here's the bus stop. You can catch the #26 bus to the University." After an hour and a half of waiting, we boarded a very empty bus. The conductor told us the bus service was sporadic during weekends. By the time we got off the bus, it was almost 7:00 p.m. We wandered around campus and asked people where to find the Computer Science department. Yiuying thought she knew someone there. We ran into a Chinese student in the hallway and asked him whether he knew this person.

"No," he answered impatiently and rushed away.

Now we were both angry and hungry. Having never dined in a restaurant except for once in San Francisco, we decided we could only afford to eat at a supermarket. However, we had difficulty finding one. Finally, we found a liquor store and purchased some juice. Looking at the pitch-black sky, we both decided it was time to return to the Holiday Inn.

We found our way back to the bus stop at just past 9:00 p.m. The sign said the last bus came at 10:30.

Freezing, Yiuying and I zipped our down jackets all the way up to cover half of our faces. After half an hour, our legs started to get numb. The flimsy bus shelter was not enough to protect us from the sub-zero temperature. As the sky darkened, the wind grew fiercer. It was so cold, even the white light emitted by the street lamp looked frozen. After stamping our feet for another fifteen minutes, we didn't feel one bit warmer. On the contrary, our feet were even more frozen. Looking behind us through the foggy plastic bus shelter wall, I saw a sign that read, "Adult Bookstore." It looked warm and welcoming.

"Look, Yiuying." I bumped her with my heavily padded body.

"Adult Bookstore? What kind of bookstore is that?" Yiuying was puzzled.

"Don't know. Maybe a scientific bookstore with math and physics books." I tried to sound confident, like I had been to one before.

"And agriculture?" Yiuying asked.

"Sure."

"Should we take a look?"

"Sure." I leaped forward, eager to be in the warmth of the building.

We stayed in the bookstore for all of five minutes. For an alleged virgin from China, the store's contents shocked me to the core. I can still recall the exposed breasts, penises, and chest hair splayed across magazines and book covers. Embarrassed, I turned my gaze to the candies at the checkout counter and we rushed out.

Yiuying, being older and married, noticed more than I had.

"Did you see the rubber penis? That place even had a theater."

We tromped back to the bus stop, ready to endure another hour of frigid weather than the genitalia blizzard we had just witnessed.

An American Lunchmate

There were only seventeen or eighteen Chinese students on the campus of North Dakota State. Yet, somehow, they could not get along. Two main groups formed among the students, each with their own leader—Mr. Wu and Mr. Ding. These two groups behaved almost like America's two-party political system. These kinds of groupings were quite common during China's Cultural Revolution, with each university department dividing into at least two factions with very different viewpoints and stances. While individualism was discouraged, these schisms were actively *encouraged*, as they served to purify the Communist party.

I hated the old tradition of infighting. Pushed and pulled in two different directions, I never knew which group to join. I was too nice to disagree, yet too independent to follow either group's agenda.

When I was around thirteen years old, I would sometimes go skating with one of two girls who were competing for my attention. I couldn't go with both of them, because they would bicker constantly, and if I went with only one of them, the other would inevitably be offended. My compromise was to go with whomever asked me first. The choice was always a great dilemma for me, as I had trouble saying no to people.

In Fargo, the childish divisions continued. I cannot remember what these two groups were fighting about, but I know it had something to do with the Chinese women's national softball team's visit to campus. A young American businessman named Greg had wanted to sponsor a few young softball players to study at NDSU. Since Greg was Mr. Wu's friend, Mr. Ding was outraged and reported this activity to the Chinese Consulate in Chicago. Mr. Wu said the report was unnecessary, since Greg was just trying to help. Then, Mr. Wu started spreading rumors that Mr. Ding was a spy sent by the Chinese government to monitor student activities. What an exciting job to be a spy in such a small town! When they arrived, the Chinese women's national softball team members were locked in their dormitory and forbidden to talk to anyone local. They left Fargo immediately after their game without doing any sightseeing.

Greg was a tall, handsome young man in his late 30s. He had light brown hair, blue eyes, and a protruding nose. He drove a white Cadillac. When Greg asked me to lunch, my roommate Yiuying said, "Wow. Good for you, the great intellectual!"

"Thank you." I blushed. "What can we talk about?" I had little experience dating, barely knew the English language, and was still determined to stay a virgin until marriage. But, since I couldn't say no to people, I had said yes to Greg.

Greg picked me up from my apartment and took me to a Chinese restaurant. It was wintertime—my first winter in Fargo. Cold wind blew across my face, cutting my skin like knives. I wore my green down jacket, a scarf, and a pair of old-fashioned, metal-framed glasses to shield me from the wind. My long hair provided an additional layer of protection. Yet, when we entered the restaurant, I started shivering uncontrollably—perhaps due

120

to the cold, perhaps from nervousness. Greg pretended not to notice and asked me about the twelve animal signs on our paper placemats. Unfortunately, I didn't know much about these zodiac signs, since they were not part of my cultural upbringing in mainland China. They were considered ancient superstitions and were criticized by the Communist government. Finally, I gathered enough courage to tell him a few things about China in my broken English. I told him about getting accepted to a prestigious university in China through hard work and study. I told him how I became disappointed after realizing university life was not as exciting as I had hoped, and how I struggled to make friends, since I lacked social skills. Then, we talked about my life after college, and how I was assigned to teach at Beijing Medical University, where I learned to drink beer, play badminton, and dance. The faculty members were older, and I had found it much easier to relate to them. Again, through studying hard, I passed an English exam, obtained a scholarship provided by the World Bank, and came to the US to realize my dreams of studying abroad and leaving my dysfunctional family.

I did not think Greg comprehended much of what I told him. He had inherited his business from his father, and I doubted he could understand just how hard I had to work to achieve my goals. Besides, I had discovered that Americans tended to talk more about factual things than the deep psychological analysis I had just relayed to him. Americans often left psychoanalysis to the professionals. Still, we had a pleasant lunch. He told me he had severe type 1 diabetes and had to inject insulin daily. I said I was sorry for his illness.

After lunch, he took me to a little gift shop in the mall and bought me a carved stone elephant. Then, he asked if I wanted to visit his apartment. I was more than a little alarmed, but I didn't see anything other than a friendly invitation in his expression. There was no disturbing animal desire in his eyes, and I found him pleasant to be around. Once again, I couldn't say no, so I told him, "Yes." During the drive to his apartment, he said he was disappointed that he was not allowed to sponsor the Chinese softball players.

"They really wanted to stay and study. They are beautiful, very beautiful. "Fei Chang Piao Liang!" he said, which means "very beautiful" in Chinese.

I then taught him how to say "elephant" in Chinese.

His apartment was on the fifteenth floor of a high-rise. We stood side-by-side in the elevator.

"I have other houses," he explained. "This is just my downtown office and storage." His apartment looked like a warehouse. The solitary desk faced a window that overlooked a handful of tall buildings sitting alongside stretches of farmland, silos, and grazing animals.

"Look." I pointed at a herd in the distance.

"Bison," he said. "There are more bison than people in North Dakota."

"People must be quite lonely here."

"I think people like it that way."

He understands lonely people! In that moment, I started to like him.

Across the room, industrial bookshelves sat in neat rows, covered with stacks of documents. I did not see a bed—just a simple futon. Greg left me standing by the window, assuming I must be enjoying the view, and began searching for something. After he found what he needed, he showed me to the door. *What a gentleman,* I said to myself, relieved nothing scary had happened. Yet, part of me wished he had shown more interest in me as a woman. I wanted to tell my roommate I hadn't been just a wooden, unattractive intellectual. When he said, "Let's go," I could do nothing but follow him. He gave me a handsome smile and led me out of the apartment.

"What happened?" Yiuying asked when I returned.

"We had lunch in a Chinese restaurant and then…" I was not sure I wanted to tell her about the visit to his apartment, but I couldn't lie.

"Then…?" She stared at me with small eyes wide-open, expecting some juicy details.

"We went to his apartment."

"Woo, so fast." She looked at me with disbelief.

"No, nothing happened. He searched for some documents and I looked at the view from the window. He didn't even ask me to sit down." I knew she expected so much more and, even after weeks of repeated questioning, I could not convince her that nothing had happened. I was glad I hadn't told her about my episode with Mohammad.

"Nothing happened?" Yiuying would say. "You wooden duck, you have no seduction skills!" It would have been easier to convince her we had wild-monkey sex than otherwise.

A couple of months after our lunch, Greg gave me a call. He wanted to meet at the same Chinese restaurant. I agreed and, when I saw him, I immediately noticed how distraught and tired he seemed. His state made me less nervous.

We shook hands and sat at a table.

"How are you? You seem tired," I said.

"Xiaohong left me," he said. His eyes were unfocused and moist.

"Why? Isn't she one of the softball players? How did she manage to stay?"

"I was allowed to sponsor one player to stay and study."

"You are young and wealthy. I couldn't imagine any girl leaving you." I tried to be empathetic, but this was something I knew very little about.

"She thinks I'm too old and sick." Greg sighed.

"That's just excuse. If she loves you, she wouldn't mind your age or illness."

"You're right. She dumped me and moved in with a young Chinese man."

"You see, she didn't love you. You can't date someone because she is Fei Chang Piao Liang. You have to understand her." I sounded like an authority.

"We did have lots of fun."

"I'm guessing there is a cultural barrier between you." I looked down and started playing with my fingers. How could I help him? I didn't even know the girl. Then, I had an idea. "You should study Chinese."

"You mean Zhong Guo Hua (Chinese)?" He looked at me directly, seeming to cheer up.

"You know Chinese?"

"Just a little." He pinched his thumb and index finger.

Over lunch, we chatted—nothing much more than small talk. He asked what I had been doing, and I told him about my studies and occasional exercise. When our meal was finished, he left in a slightly better mood.

124

I never heard from Greg again. My roommate was right—I was too much of an intellectual for him and I lacked seduction skills. What she didn't know was that these were my secret weapons—weapons I yielded to keep men away from me. I had learned from Mother that men were more trouble than they were worth. Regardless, my roommate was jealous of my lunch with Greg. She was older and married, and she wanted an opportunity to date a rich American businessman. I had been given such an opportunity and let it slip through my fingers. But this episode didn't bother me much. In retrospect, Greg and I didn't have much in common anyway.

After a few months in Fargo, I grew restless. I longed for new adventures, and this small town failed to deliver. I was making good grades, my English was improving, and my TA job was becoming a breeze. Everything was too easy, and the town too quiet. When Professor Lang at the University of Houston Biomedical Engineering Program offered me a research assistant job, I grabbed it.

Molested in Houston

If the cold and snow didn't bother you, Fargo was a great place for college. The people were friendly, but the school did not satisfy my academic or personal desires. I felt like a leaf, drifting in the wind. When Dr. Lang of the University of Houston offered me a Research Assistant (RA) position in his Biomedical Engineering lab, I jumped at the opportunity. The thought of living in a warm, sunshine-filled city just two hours from the ocean, excited me. I packed and departed as soon as the offer was finalized. I even brushed aside their odd request for my photo. I was twenty-four and new to the country. Later, I would discover their odious reasons for wanting a photo of me.

The head of Professor Lang's hemodynamics lab, Mr. Gao, picked me up at the airport. He was a tall Chinese grad student who wore white-framed glasses. He told me he was originally from Hunan province and graduated from a college in southern China. He said they were looking forward to having me in the lab. Since I was equivalent to an Ivy League graduate, they were counting on me to make a substantial contribution. I nodded, even though I had never worked in a hemodynamic lab. My lab experience consisted of a college physics lab and the labs I taught at Beijing Medical University and North Dakota State University.

Professor Lang was an amiable, middle-aged man from Taiwan. He talked rapidly and had the smooth social skills of a businessman. Later, I found out he liked to gossip, especially about people's love lives.

The lab was a diverse group. There was Adam Warner, a tennis star; a Jewish American; Abdul from Lebanon; Julian from Argentina; Peng from Shanghai; and a short, blonde French girl named Yvonne. I thought I would fit right in, but I soon discovered it was not that easy.

One of my first get-togethers with the lab group was a pool party at Professor Lang's house. Like many immigrants, he was proud of his achievements and loved to show us his house in an affluent neighborhood, which he called "The Jewish Neighborhood."

His wife was a content housewife and showed me pictures of her two handsome sons, one of whom was a student at Yale. Initially, I liked her and was willing to treat her like an aunt, but I later heard her talking about going back to work if her husband left her for someone younger. I realized she was implying Professor Lang might cheat on her with me. I was appalled. As a nerd from Peking University, my dating experience included two unsuccessful formal boyfriends. I still thought of myself as a virgin, even though I had been raped in Fargo. Besides, Professor Lang was married with two sons, and he wasn't even my type.

If Professor Lang had planned on stalking me, he wasn't the only one. An incident in the lab made me realize another predator was lusting over my young, supple body. Around this time, I dreamed I was trapped in a building made of glass windows. Outside, three tigers lingered, staring at me and slavering.

In the lab, my young, male counterparts took pleasure in making fun of me. I was the only woman in the lab, and everyone found my naivete amazing. A few weeks passed before I was even allowed to touch lab equipment. One day, Mr. Gao invited me to help him with the laser visualization equipment. I gladly accepted, since I knew the laser equipment was highly sophisticated, and Professor Lang didn't let just *anyone* touch it. His request was an indication of his trust.

I followed Mr. Gao into a dark room, the only light coming from the laser beams. After switching on a table lamp, he gestured for me to sit by the bench and he lowered himself next to me. He had me look through a scope, where I saw particles suspended in clear liquid. "The laser can measure the distance between particles," he said, "and we can thus determine the viscosity of the liquid."

At first, he seemed attentive and serious. I tried to remember everything he told me. Then I felt his hands on my breasts. His tone shifted.

"Meihua, I love you. Could we date?"

"But you are married," I said innocently. I was totally dumbfounded by this turn of events and had no idea how to react. His hands started rubbing my nipples, making me squirm with discomfort. He leaned his head closer to me; I could smell garlic on his breath. I wanted to jump up, to flee.

"We could have a secret affair."

"What? But I don't love you." I couldn't tell him anything but the truth.

"Could you please try?" He attempted to kiss me.

"No." I pushed him away. Before he could protest, I rushed out of the lab.

That was last time I was allowed to see the fancy laser equipment. After the incident, Mr. Gao told Professor Lang I was unfit to work with the equipment. Not only that, Gao would also not allow me to work on the Mock Circular Loop, a circulatory system model made of silicon rubber. I occupied my time by taking classes to fulfill the requirements for my master's degree in Biomedical Engineering.

Around this time, I discovered I had to move. I had been living with two nice Chinese women in an apartment across the street from the lab. The building was situated by a canal, and I would jog alongside the water almost every day. One of my roommates, Lingling, was from Taiwan and loved to cook. When I arrived home at night, I was inevitably greeted by the pungent smell of roasted chicken. My other roommate, Xiao Pan, hailed from Beijing and had a boyfriend in Austin. She would travel there almost every weekend to see him. Eventually, Xiao Pan was accepted to the University of Texas at Austin. Around the same time, Lingling decided to return to Taiwan. I was left alone in a one-bedroom apartment that was too expensive for me to afford on my own.

I decided to look for a new roommate and began scanning the school message board. One listing was from a young Chinese student, Tao Wang, who had rented an apartment across the canal and was seeking a roommate. It was a great location, but Tao Wang happened to be a man. Could I room with a young man? Why not? I didn't foresee any problems.

"But Tao has a bad reputation," said one of my Chinese friends.

"Really? I don't care. Chinese people love to gossip."

"It's not gossips," said my friend. "He is famous for talking advantage of people."

"I would love to see it with my own eyes." In truth, I didn't believe a word she said. In fact, being hated by Chinese people made him very attractive to me. I became determined to move in with Tao. After a brief meeting, he accepted my offer. He seemed polite at first glance, and I agreed to move in after dinner on Friday.

I knocked on the door.

Tao opened it and let me in. "Let me show you the bedroom."

I followed with my small suitcase and a backpack.

The room was pitch black. Surprised, I dropped my suitcase and felt for the light switch. He grabbed my hand and pushed me down. Unzipping my jeans, he leaped on top of me. The whole thing happened so fast; I can't recall any details.

I only remember standing, taking my still-packed suitcase, and leaving without a word. I was embarrassed and humiliated.

After storming out of the building, I discovered I'd left my backpack. I doubled back and found the door still unlocked. Tao was on the phone. When I walked inside, he hung up and turned to me. He stared impassively.

"Who were you talking to?" I asked.

"My girlfriend," he said with a frown.

Without wasting another second, I retrieved my backpack and walked back into the dark Friday night.

I had to find another apartment in a hurry. Otherwise, I would be sleeping in my little, beat-up Honda—a vehicle I had purchased before I even learned how to drive.

I opened the university student paper and found a one-bedroom apartment listed at $130 per month. Without hesitation, I made the phone call and met up with a large, African-American woman with dark, braided hair. She agreed to lease the apartment to me, and I felt fortunate to find such a good deal. In the evening, after returning to the apartment from the lab, I realized why my rent was so low. This was a predominantly African-American neighborhood, and 1980s Houston was a very segregated city which tended to shunt working-class African-Americans into run-down neighborhoods. Professor Lang, who was so proud of his fancy Jewish neighborhood, was shocked by my decision.

"You're crazy," he said, "and you'll regret that decision someday."

"So what?" I answered, flippantly.

I was new in this country and wasn't tainted by its long-standing prejudice. Living in that neighborhood, I never felt unsafe. However, after I moved into a different neighborhood a few months later, I was threatened by a young man late at night while riding my bike home from the lab.

My former "roommate," Tao Wang, continued to harass me. One night, before heading to bed, I heard a knock. Puzzled, I opened the door and my mouth dropped to the floor. Tao stood in the doorframe, smiling. I didn't know what to say. Nobody had ever pursued me so persistently. Even though his eyes burned with desire, my subconscious willed me to let him in. I didn't have time to think rationally—to run the decision through my head.

He and I cooked stir-fried vegetables with sliced pork and ate it with rice. After dinner, he even washed the dishes. As I was sitting down, he grabbed me and pulled me to the bed next to the dining table. He made love to me and made me say I liked it. That night, he cuddled next to me in bed. In the middle of the night, I woke to find him on top of me, trying to penetrate me while I slept. When I was fully awake, he got his way. The sex seemed passionate. I could see his red eyes and smell his wet hair and semen.

In the morning, he cooked four eggs for his breakfast because he believed they would make up for his lost semen. That was the weirdest theory I had ever heard, but despite his strange views—and despite his predatory behavior—I decided to go out with him. The decision was questionable, at best, but I was lonely and thought it would be nice to have a boyfriend who was so attracted to me.

Going out with him was difficult because of his temperament. He was erratic and maniacal. Initially, I thought it was fun. I liked eccentric people, but soon realized his behaviors went beyond *eccentric*. He would become violent, and I was lucky to get out of some situations alive.

Tao had a small Toyota Tercel, and he liked to drive me around in it. He was new at driving, and not yet adept. One day, he got a speeding ticket and blamed me for talking too much. I apologized, yet I didn't learn the lesson. As immigrants, we tried to go to court to challenge the ticket, because we were too cash-strapped to pay for it. On the way to court, distracted by my jabbering, he got into an accident. No one was hurt, and the front of the car was only slightly smashed, but the repair would cost even more money—much more than the ticket. What's more, he didn't win his court case and would have to pay the full amount of the ticket. He was furious. On our way back from court, his anger reached a climax. Despite the rain, he drove fast, cursing as he went.

"I will kill you," he said in one breath.

I was frightened and scrambled to find a way out of the car, but it was sailing down the road at over sixty MPH. I considered pulling the emergency brake but was not sure it would work. Fortunately, we arrived at my apartment unscathed. But his anger had not subsided. If anything, it was even worse.

"I will cut you open and dissect you alive. I have gone to medical school in China. I know how." Without looking at me, he walked into my apartment. I believed the threat and had no clue what to do. I thought of running away but wasn't sure I could outrun him. He seemed to resemble my father, who would say cruel things and didn't always mean them. I crossed my fingers for that to be the case.

Inside the apartment, he pushed me onto the bed and shoved himself into me. I let him, while trying to predict what would happen next and how I could deal with it. I eyed a knife on the kitchen table and thought of grabbing it.

He got up, pulled up his pants, and left.

I locked the door behind him, fell on bed, and let out a huge sigh. *I AM SO LUCKY*, I said to myself. I didn't want to see him again, so I decided to move once more.

When I first arrived in Houston, I didn't own a car. In Fargo, I could walk anywhere I needed to go, but in sprawling Houston a car was practically a necessity. With the help of a nice young man from a local church, I bought a car. I didn't want to bother him too much, so I purchased the first car we saw, a Honda Civic that had clearly been in an accident at some point. Its right frontend was smashed in, but it was still drivable.

I quickly found a new apartment. With my car, it was easy. I rented a basement unit in a house, situated in a predominantly Latino neighborhood. The home owners were a mixed-race couple—the husband was Caucasian, while the wife was a beautiful Latina. Their hospitality made me feel safe and welcomed. I let myself forget about Tao and began a long-distance relationship with an older man I had met in Madison, Wisconsin during the North America Chinese Christian Gathering I had attended a year earlier. He had been an established artist in China and was studying chemistry at the University of Iowa. As usual, the relationship was not perfect. He was married. However, I was attracted to his talent and willing to ignore this inconvenient fact. Since our relationship spanned a thousand miles, what harm could we do? I was lonely and called him a lot. A large portion of my meager graduate student stipend was spent on long-distance calls.

When Christmas came, he asked me to visit him in Iowa, since his wife would be in Chicago. I immediately accepted the invitation.

Back in Houston, Tao eventually found me. He confronted me in the lab where I worked and put on a huge show in front of my colleagues and Professor Lang. He demanded I pay for his car repair, since I—he claimed—was the cause of the accident. I told him I didn't wish to ever see him again. My Lebanese colleague, the big and tall Abdul, had to scare him away.

Professor Lang watched Tao drive away and shook his head. "I should never believe in an unmarried woman. They can't be trusted as engineering students."

His statement made me heavy with guilt, and I felt the burden of representing an entire gender resting squarely on my shoulders.

Iowa

I met Xiaoying Wang in a North American Chinese Christian Group gathering in Madison, Wisconsin. We connected during our ten minutes of conversation because we were both science majors in graduate school with creative avocations, an artist for him and a writer for me. We both had fathers who were purged during the Cultural Revolution. He was a tall, stout Chinese man with a full beard, dressed head to toe in black. His eyes twinkled behind his black, square-framed glasses.

"My father was a famous poet and a friend of Chairman Mao. He lost favor during the Cultural Revolution. In a moment of despair, he took his own life by jumping off our three-story apartment building." He paused for a while. "After high school, it was my turn to go to the countryside to be reeducated, since my father was now a dead intellectual."

His voice mesmerized me, and I listened intently. "Was it hard work?" I asked. "I know hard work and suffering can sometimes generate great art. When I'm sad, I'm more motivated to write."

"I volunteered to stay in a lighthouse, so I could practice my art. It was not heated in the winter and the air grew so cold that an egg spontaneously cracked open." He said it as though it were part of everyday life. "I created thousands of oil paintings that

137

depicted the beautiful countryside and its people. It was an amazingly productive period for me."

I was stunned. I stared at him with my mouth open, imagining Xiaoying wearing a black quilted jacket, pants, a hat and mittens, trying to paint with dried-up, cracked paint. I could see his breath in the lighthouse's cold apartment. I could see him wipe his fogged-up glasses and rub his hands for warmth.

"All that suffering paid off." He smiled. "After ten years of hard labor, I became a celebrated artist in Shanghai. I had a very successful one-man show."

"I'm impressed." I looked at him with admiration that he obviously appreciated.

"Now I'm here and I have to start all over again." He sighed. "I'm in graduate school for chemistry."

"I'm in graduate school for physics." I mirrored his frown and made him smile.

"But no one can keep us from our art and writing, right?" he asked.

"Yes." I almost jumped. I had finally found someone who truly understood me.

"Send me some writing." He gave me his address and phone number before we returned to the Christian meeting.

I clutched his information as though it were a Bible, which was the only religious act I performed during this gathering. When I arrived back in Fargo, I wrote him a letter and enclosed a few of my short stories. He replied with a love letter and a drawing of a beautiful dove on the envelope. I gazed at the letter, feeling waves of love emitting from it. I was in love with Xiaoying and he was in love with me. The world was suddenly much brighter.

Now, when I slept in my rented basement room, I had something exciting to dream about. I had a new boyfriend, and he was a handsome Chinese artist. Whenever I had the impulse, I would pick up the phone and call him. I was so head-over-heels, I paid no attention to the cost of the long-distance phone bills. Those bills easily ate up one-third of my meager $600 per month stipend, but I didn't mind.

During Christmas of 1987, the third Christmas since I had arrived in the US, Xiaoying invited me to visit him. His wife had moved to Chicago to work in a museum, so he was now living alone. I immediately said yes.

I had just moved to Houston, Texas from Fargo, North Dakota at the invitation of a Chinese professor, Dr. Lang. Hardly settled into this new big city, my heart flew to Iowa City. I could hardly wait to see him, my handsome long-distance boyfriend. I dreamt of kissing him, and more.

When he picked me up at the airport, he showed me a white wool jacket and red wool hat. He had bought them for me at a Salvation Army store. I was moved by his gesture. As a graduate student myself, I knew how little we could afford with our stipends.

Since he didn't have a car, we took a taxi. He told me he rode his bicycle to school every day. I said I was lucky to live across the street from my professor's lab with two other roommates. After a brief ride, we arrived at his apartment in a white building next to a snow-covered corn field. Having lived in Fargo, winter in Iowa seemed mild and more picturesque.

When we entered the apartment, I froze. This was only my second time meeting with him. Our first meeting included less than fifteen minutes of talking. Yes, we had exchanged many love letters, but they were just writing and anticipation. Now that we were finally seeing each other in person, I had no idea what to do. Xiaoying was more mature. He stepped forward and gave me a long kiss.

Then he asked, "Do you want some tea?"

"Sure." Relief washed through me. I wanted to get to know him better as a person before taking our relationship to its inevitable next step.

After the tea was ready, I sat on his lap while he told stories about his life in the countryside. I had heard some of them in Madison, but he added more details. Listening to them wasn't quite as interesting the second time. Then, he started talking about his grand unification theory about the life sciences. He would quantify culture with geography and geology using math and geometry. He said a country's culture was related to its weather and temperature. As I listened, I became mesmerized by his grand theories and impressed by his intelligence. His beard had grown longer, his hair messier. To me, he was a young Einstein. In this moment, I fell in love with both his intellect and his artistic talent.

I don't remember how we ended up on his bed. He asked me whether it was my first time, and I said yes. There was no blood, of course, because I had lost my virginity to rape in Fargo. He didn't press for an explanation. The sex was okay, but not as spectacular as I had imagined. I hoped he forgave my inexperience, since I was almost a virgin.

Afterward, he cooked a popular Chinese dish called "monkey climbing the tree," which consists of cellophane noodles with ground pork. Though it's a simple dish, I thoroughly enjoyed it. Eating alongside him—a man eighteen years older than me—I felt more like his daughter than his girlfriend.

At dinner, two of his friends joined us. He tried to introduce me as his niece Helen, just like the beauty that caused the Trojan War. I was flattered but had trouble keeping it straight. I kept telling the guests my name was Meihua.

One of the young women at the dinner was also from Shanghai. She was studying chemistry at University of Iowa like Xiaoying. She was single and beautiful, and it dawned on me that I might be only one of many girlfriends. I didn't know for sure, but I had a woman's premonition.

After the party, we went to the local Chinese students' activity center to play ping-pong. I walked in and noticed a young woman with glasses. We immediately recognized each other. I had met her on my flight to the US, and we had shared a hotel room in San Francisco when we arrived.

"Meihua!" she yelled out.

"Yan Ja." I burst out her name.

It was amazing we still remembered each other's names. Yan Ja introduced me to everyone as Meihua, and Xiaoying stopped calling me Helen. People from China were accustomed to using two names—their given name and their English name—so, no one was confused by my dual identity or even questioned it.

"What are you doing here?" Yan asked.

"I'm visiting my uncle." I pointed to Xiaoying.

"I see." She didn't question my lie.

It seemed that Chinese people in the US were less curious about people's personal lives than they were back in China. Xiaoying and I played ping-pong for a while before returning to his place.

Back in his apartment, he opened a bottle of wine and motioned for me to sit on his lap. He asked, "Do you know why countries in the southern hemisphere are less well off than those in the north?" I thought he was kidding, but he looked serious.

"I know. It's because people in the south have tape worm parasites in their stomachs, which make them less motivated and, therefore, work less." I remembered that tidbit from a magazine article.

"A good explanation! The heat can also make people lethargic." He gave me a kiss. "Should I turn down the heat?"

I kissed him back. "Sure, if you want to snuggle with me under the duvet."

The second time was much better. We were becoming more comfortable with each other, and afterwards we didn't move until almost dinner time, with occasional kisses and touches.

"Let's go outside and take a walk." He sat up and dropped his legs to the floor. "My legs are getting a little numb." He smiled to indicate he didn't mind.

"Sure. I love walking in the cold," I said, feeling energized.

"Me, too," he chirped.

"I know. You were trained to persevere in the cold when you were living at the top of the lighthouse. The eggs didn't make it, but you pulled through. I guess you must enjoy the cold by now."

"Yes. That's why I live in Iowa."

"Iowa's winter is nothing," I laughed. "Try North Dakota."

"I don't want to push the envelope. I believe I have been punished enough. I have lost so many years." He sighed. "Now I'm in graduate school at age forty-four with a bunch of twenty-somethings."

"Age has made you more attractive," I said and gave him a big hug.

As we walked along the Iowa cornfield, with a few skeletal stalks rattling in the wind, Xiaoying talked about his grand unification theory. He thought climate affected people's diet which, in turn, helped shape their culture.

"I think people in southern China work harder," I said, "because their rice is harvested three every year, while in northern China it is harvested once. Thus, they must work three times harder. How do you explain that?"

"China is a big country," Xiaoying replied, "therefore it is very complicated. Shanghai, for instance, is not far south, geographically. It is in the south of China, but all of China is in the Northern Hemisphere." He said this as though he had thought about it before.

As we walked past the open fields, I thought about how Xiaoying often ended up in the countryside. He created hundreds of oil paintings while living in rural China. In Iowa, he was forming his grand unification theory. The countryside was his muse.

I left Iowa City after three days, by which time we had become very comfortable with each other, but still spontaneous. When I returned to Houston, I made a point of visiting Dr. Manny Goodman, a doctor I had dated briefly, but hadn't pursued because he was thirty years my senior. He had trained as a thoracic surgeon under Dr. C. Walton Lillehei, a pioneer in open-heart surgery. He and Dr. Lillehei invented the first commercially produced membrane oxygenator. Dr. Goodman was also the inventor of an artificial heart, an artificial lung, and an artificial kidney for continuous hemodialysis. An avid sailor (he once participated in the America's Cup with his fifty-foot sailboat), he had also designed an upside-down catamaran.

He was delighted to hear from me. I told him about my little Iowa adventure, and he patted my shoulder saying, "No matter how nice and smart he is, he is married." He took the opportunity to wink at me, trying to hint that he was available. It dawned on me that he was right. I needed a fresh start. Since Xiaoying was more than one thousand miles away, it was safe and easy to dump him.

For being so much older than me, I was surprisingly comfortable with Dr. Manny Goodman. Two years after my trip to Iowa, we were married in a small ceremony.

Lolita II: A Chinese Student's Story

Call me Lolita if you want, although I am not fourteen. Sometimes I hold his neck, whispering into his ear sweetly, "Manny, you are so cute." Sometimes, at the end of our daily run, when he mercilessly sprints past me, I will say angrily, "Yuck." My husband Manny and I run along the Mississippi River every morning and evening, in the rain, after a snowfall, under the sun, and in the wind. We have left so many pairs of invisible footprints that even the road begins to echo the cadence of our footsteps. Only in winter can we see our footsteps, outlined in the snow, his with toes pointing slightly inward, mine pointing outward.

Now, these two pairs of feet have diverged and are no longer next to each other. Two months ago, we separated.

Since then, I've not been in a hurry to gather my things from his office. I am scared of seeing him, though scared may not be the right word. Anxious? Recently, whenever I imagine being alone with him in his office, I have visions of him hitting me on the head or jabbing me with a knife. I imagine he hates me for leaving him, for ending our wonderful five-year marriage. At least *he* would call it wonderful. And, at first, it was, but things changed and so did my feelings.

I must see him today. I will show him I won't change my mind. I did leave him once before, when we were dating nearly six years ago. That time, I came back.

I was a graduate student and research assistant in the Biomedical Engineering Program at the University of Houston. Like many other Chinese students, I came to the United States to attend graduate school. I met Manny in the University's Cardiovascular Fluid Dynamics Laboratory, where he was working on a joint research project with my boss. The device from the project did not end up working, but Manny got a young Chinese girlfriend as compensation.

He initiated the relationship by teaching me how to drive. By the time I received my driver's license, we had been on many outings together—movie theaters, concerts, ballets, sailing trips. I was having a wonderful time with him. He taught me about sex, and eventually about love. Then, I disappeared from his life (*disappeared* was his term for it). I left him for my roommate, a handsome young Chinese student. Soon, I discovered the young student was only dating me out of convenience. Not only that, he was so possessive by nature that he would not let me answer Manny's phone calls.

One Saturday afternoon, I ran into Manny at my lab. He was no longer collaborating with my boss, so I knew he was not there by chance. Although I was the only one in the lab, his presence did not scare me. I appraised him for a moment. At age fifty-four, he had salt-and-pepper hair, but his face was youthful, and his body lean and trim. He was wearing jeans, a red button-down cotton shirt, and a pair of New Balance running shoes. His eyes twinkled.

"Meihua, how are you?"

"I'm...I'm fine." I did not know how to explain my disappearance. For me, going out with multiple men in a short time was something new.

"Have I hurt you?" he asked.

"No."

"Then why did you stop seeing me?"

"You...you are too old." I finally uttered the real reason.

"Okay, I had hoped I did not hurt you." He patted me on the shoulder, winked, and swiftly left.

After I broke up with my handsome roommate and my long-distance artist boyfriend in Iowa, I made a point of calling him. I simply needed someone to talk to—a friend—and I had no serious intentions in mind.

He recognized my voice right away. "Meihua, it's so nice to hear from you." Our conversation was so pleasant and sweet, I decided to try again with him.

On my birthday, he took me to a nice seafood restaurant along the Gulf coast, where we enjoyed fresh oysters and shrimp. Then, we returned to his house and swam in his pool.

After we dried ourselves with towels, he grabbed me and held me tight against his naked chest. The gesture felt friendly, rather than sexual.

"Meihua, I don't want to lose you again," he said. Although he did not cry, I sensed the deep emotion hidden behind his bony, tan chest.

These words grabbed me deeply, the gospel of my life. I could not deny him. We had passionate sex that night, and a year later, we were married.

After five years of marriage, I am certain I am immune to his pleading. Things change, situations change, I tell myself. I am no longer that young, naïve Chinese girl he swept off her feet.

He has taken my car and I must now commute to work by bus, but I still feel free. Today, I am driving my boyfriend's car, and I feel relaxed. I know I will run into people I used to see every day in the hospital—nurses, volunteers, custodians, cafeteria workers. They grew accustomed to seeing Manny and me, the odd couple, arriving at work together, eating lunch together.

Despite the eventual erosion of our relationship, there were many reasons for us to marry. And there were many more reasons for us to not marry. What finally forced us to make a decision was quite simple: I became pregnant.

The pivotal event happened on a visit to Minnesota, when I was still a graduate student at the University of Houston. It's hard to say whose fault it was: Maybe mine, for not taking the pill, maybe his, for not giving me any input when I asked whether or not I should take them. When we learned I was pregnant, I became nervous. He was proud. His daughter said, "Shit!" She suggested an abortion (something he revealed to me much later), because she did not think the marriage would last. Manny insisted I make the decision myself.

While I was in Houston, he called me one day from Minnesota. "Meihua, we need to decide whether or not we want to keep this baby."

"Why?" The statement surprised me. So far, we had only talked about having this child. We had even discussed names for the baby: Elizabeth for a girl, Walton for a boy.

"Well, we've only been married for a short time. Maybe we should enjoy each other's company for a while. What if we want to travel or sail around the world? That would be much easier without a child."

"You want me to have an abortion," I said. "But I'm afraid..." I almost cried. In my mind, any kind of surgery was associated with pain and horror.

"You can decide for yourself. Abortions are very safe nowadays."

"But I'm approaching the end of my first trimester. Can I still have one?"

"I think so. They just have to put you to sleep. Again, you can decide whether we will keep this child or not. We can have it if you want. I'm not against it. I just wanted you to know you have options."

I hung up, unsure if his verbal ambiguity meant he would truly support whichever decision I ultimately made, or if he just wanted to distance himself from the whole thing.

At this point, Manny was already uninvolved with many aspects of our life together and had relocated to Minneapolis. The fear of having a child alone and raising it by myself in Houston was so great, I ultimately chose to have the abortion. Although it was a scary experience, I made it through without any complications. After three weeks, I had completely recovered. I did not think I had any regrets. If I had decided to have our child, my life would be a completely different story.

After that, when we drove to work together at the Fairview Southdale Hospital, we often did not arrive until mid-morning. He worked as a house physician in the hospital from about ten in the morning until six in the afternoon. When we arrived, we would bump into other doctors in the parking lot who had just finished their early rounds. The ones who knew Manny would greet him and comment on how they envied his easy schedule (what they didn't say—but what I understood from their glances—was that they also envied the fact that he was accompanied by a pretty, young wife). I was usually silent or gave them a nice smile. But internally, I seethed. *I have my own work to do and I'm not just accompanying him. But you wouldn't understand, because I'm just a writer.* Maybe these daily unspoken scorns evolved into one of the reasons I left Manny.

After tunneling through the crowded hospital corridors, we arrived at our reclusive office. Our old office was located on the third floor near the noisy Human Resources office and a string of patient's rooms. It was a very public place, and I would often encounter questions about our relationship. Our new office was stationed in a quiet part of the hospital, away from whispers and probing eyes. The nurses did not talk to us much.

One day, I needed to make photocopies at one of the nursing stations. As usual, I rushed through the entrance and ignored everyone. Everyone knew my face, and they never questioned my use of the copy machine.

"Hi, are you working for your father?" asked a middle-aged nurse, trying to be friendly.

"No," I explained calmly, "my father is in China. That's my husband."

"Oh." She left without saying anything more. Maybe she was satisfied with my answer. Maybe she was too startled to react. Maybe she did not want to have anything to do with a young woman who was married to a man old enough to be her father.

Whatever the reason, her clipped answer left me angry. I hated to admit that her judgment affected me, but it did.

After that first encounter, I saw that nurse almost every day. Eventually, she seemed to get used to thinking of us as a couple, instead of father and daughter. She even began to smile at us, because we appeared to be so happy. The day I returned for my things, I was apprehensive that I would bump into her.

He is waiting at the office door. He has changed the lock, and my key no longer works. I'm sure that's significant. He waited three weeks before deciding to change the lock, and I could have retrieved my belongings during that time without seeing him. But I was busy—too busy with my new life, too busy being in love.

I met my new boyfriend, Byron, at the University Club on a Friday night. That weekend, Manny was on a rowing regatta trip, and I hadn't been invited.

While he was away, I was itching to go out, so I called up a girlfriend and the two of us went to the University Club. There, I ran into Byron, a quiet man whom I had met a year earlier through the club's Great Books Discussion Group.

That evening, he behaved differently around me than he had in the past. He smiled and his face glowed. He talked about the beauty and ecstasy of piano music and, for the first time, I realized that this quiet, reserved person had secret feelings and passions. A deep understanding began to develop between us.

The next day, we attended a play together while Manny was still away. After Manny returned, I continued to occasionally meet with him in secret. It was easy to do. Manny was so obsessed with rowing that he spent nearly every evening on the river, rarely caring about my whereabouts. Instead of swimming in the University Club, as I told Manny, I spent my evenings with Byron in restaurants, in the Club, and in his apartment. We talked about art and literature, he wrote me poems and read them aloud, and we exchanged romantic feelings. In just three weeks, I asked to move in with him, and he said yes.

For the next three months, life became a real-life fantasy. I discovered that quiet, reserved people can be just as passionate in bed and in life as extroverted ones. They are more patient, more sensual, because they channel their feelings into beautiful poetry instead of wasting them on mundane conversation. After I moved in, we began eating dinner regularly together, but our collaborative cooking was often interrupted by our desire to take off each other's clothes. Sometimes, things would start in the kitchen, continue on the staircase, and end in the bedroom. We would not come down until midnight, exhausted and hungry, and find the unprepared food we had abandoned on the counter. One Friday night, we made love until two in the morning. When we woke up, we would roll over and do it again. Even routine tasks were disrupted by love making—ironing clothes could turn into passionate sex by the ironing board. Sometimes, we would kiss on the floor of the bathtub, holding each other tight until the hot water ran out and turned ice-cold. I lost track of dates, I lost track of time, and I lost the desire to do any form of outdoor exercise.

I also lost weight, which was Manny's primary complaint about me. The easiest way to resolve that issue, I knew, was to leave Manny.

At the office door, he appears robust, red-cheeked. He is even smiling, not the usual wink though. From his dry, hardened cheeks and slightly swollen eyes, I can tell he has been through a lot. His face is so drawn, that even his dimples have disappeared. He has stopped dying his hair and eyebrows and has let them go gray. He has always been a restless sleeper, and now I imagine him waking up at midnight, reading and typing up grant proposals.

I used to hate when he rushed to get a proposal out just before the deadline. He would work overnight for a few days, forgetting about sleep, food, and me. I hated his total devotion to work, and his willingness to ignore me. He had these projects—the total artificial heart, the artificial kidney, the artificial heart and lung, and the disposable heart-lung machine—and dreamed of bringing them to the market. Twenty years ago, he had been a well-respected pioneer for the mass-produced membrane oxygenator, and a star researcher and surgical resident under the famous surgeon, Dr. C. Walton Lillehai. But his methods were no longer fashionable. In the last ten years, mechanical devices were losing ground to molecular and genetic science. Human organs could be grown in laboratories and implanted in bodies instead of made with titanium and silicon rubber. Federal funding was cut for his type of work, resulting in fierce fights over the limited funds. Oftentimes, large, powerful universities were awarded whatever funds were available.

Manny's stubborn pursuit of his creative ideas was considered madness by most of his former colleagues and friends. Without federal funding, he pursued his inventions with our own limited resources. He wanted to attract a rich patron, but that Santa Claus never showed up at our chimney. With no real path forward, he devolved into madness. Since my mother was crazy and my father eccentric, perhaps I was initially attracted to Manny's instability. Maybe. But our marriage lasted for five years, which was longer than most people had expected.

Now, whenever I think of him writing a proposal alone at his desk at midnight, I feel sorry for him. After more than ten failed attempts to apply for research money from the NIH small business administration, even he admits he will never get any government funds. But he always tries again—the very definition of madness. I know his habit of diverting attention toward work during hardship.

"Hi!" He greets me as though nothing has happened. He even waves at Doctor Peterson, who passes by.

I follow him down the hallway toward his office and laugh at myself for imagining him hitting me on the head. Now, I am here with him alone and I feel safe.

"Come on in. Take your time." He opens the office door for me. The office lab still looks the same. A sink is on the left, behind the door. A multi-purpose EKG machine sits in the corner, dusty and untouched. We bought it from the hospital for his scientific experiments two years ago, but we have not yet designed an experiment which needs to use it. A small desk, emptier without my books, is framed by two filing cabinets.

154

His inventions used to excite me. I would spend every afternoon working in the hospital's electronic shop, designing a circuit board for his artificial kidney project or calibrating the EKG machine. I always had to work alone in the electronic shop, and only after the regular workers left. I would page the security guard, and he would open the door for me. The man was tall and stuffy, with a meaty face and lusty eyes.

"How are you?" He would say, touching my chin with his fat hand and cornering me against the counter.

"Not bad."

I abhorred him, but needed him to continue opening the door for me.

"How old is your husband?" he said once, leaning over me.

Silence. I did not want to tell him.

"Forty, forty-five?"

I nodded, and did not care which one he thought it was.

"Are you working here alone?"

"Yes." I indicated I was not interested in talking anymore.

"Okay, have fun!"

After he left, I immediately locked the door.

I was left alone. As a graduate student, I often worked alone in the lab, but here, in this crowded hospital, it seemed strange. Manny would stop by sometimes to see if I was working on something interesting, but he had little understanding of my projects. Sometimes, he would construct something out of a piece of plastic and try it out in the food service sink across hall. Gradually I grew tired of my amateurish science projects, which would never come to fruition. I spent more time writing, first secretly, and then I was honest with Manny and told him I wanted to write. He agreed to let me pursue my interests. At least I could do something meaningful during my solitary hours—I could write.

On the floor, the usual bag of rowing clothes, shoes, and a bag of old, unread mail lie against the wall. But today, a basketball sits among them.

He notices me staring at it. "I picked it up from the road in the neighborhood. I may use it today after work if it is too windy for rowing."

"You play basketball? I never knew you could," I say.

"I was always too small to play, but never too old to learn."

Manny and I were runners. We were both addicted to exercise, and we would run at least twice every day, swim together in the summer, and ski in the winter. At the end of every run, Manny would speed up and pass me, and a victor's smile would cross his face. When I would finally catch him, he would wrap his arm around my shoulder as I caught my breath. The spring I moved from Texas to Minnesota, I joined the Minneapolis Rowing Club with him, which is where we did our summer exercise. Although rowing was hard work, we used the club daily. The motion, the challenge of it, made us feel invigorated. When we had to choose between watching a movie and rowing, we chose rowing. It became as essential as eating. We rowed every day until I became addicted to writing.

"I hope you become more involved with rowing," said Manny after I no longer regularly accompanied him to the rowing club.

"I don't have time."

"Nonsense. You have the whole day to yourself."

"I have to write. Don't you understand? That's my future. I don't see my future in rowing."

"But it's good for you."

"I know. But I can't spend all my life on something which only makes me feel good."

That was Manny. He rowed because it made him feel good. He invented medical devices, even if they weren't practical, because the work made him feel good. He had grown into a less responsible man as he became older and chose to do things just for fun. In college, he and his best friend swore a pledge that they would never grow up. He told me about it, saying that if he ever stopped learning he would break that pledge and become mature. Maybe that explained his entire mindset.

"Okay, let's talk about something more interesting. I have just handed in the yogurt-maker grant proposal to the State Agriculture Utilization Agency."

I should have known he would switch to his favorite subject.

"They are very positive about it."

He always says so.

"The only thing they need is some literature to prove there is a big enough market to make it worthwhile. I am working day and night on the artificial kidney patent. Without you discouraging me all the time, I can work much more efficiently."

"Manny, I never agreed we should get a patent for that project so early in the game."

"You don't understand! If I don't have a patent, I can't show it to anybody."

He is too possessive of his ideas and constantly afraid someone may steal them.

I frown at him. "How can you write a good patent without doing any experiments and collecting data?"

"Data, data. The fucking data!"

He has never thought data is important in scientific experiments. "And you get ripped off by patent lawyers," I say. "We have spent ten thousand dollars for nothing."

"Stop! Fortunately, it is no longer your business."

"Okay." I lower my head and keep collecting my books.

When we were newly married, he was not making much money and we had few arguments about finances. It was useless to talk about money when we did not have much. Only lately, when he was making more than one hundred thousand dollars each year, did we argue over money. I wanted to save more, since he was not going to make that kind of money forever and we did not have much in savings. He wanted to spend it on his invention, because he considered it an investment. I told him I did not think he spent it wisely and it was a very risky investment...and so on and so forth.

After a long pause, he said, "By the way, before you leave, could you show me how to copy a file onto a disk?" Pause. "It's not urgent. But it would be nice if you could help me."

"Sure." I stand up and go to the computer, which rests on a raised bedside table, meant for patients. Manny likes standing up and working. He falls asleep if he sits down.

I was always amazed how someone with such habits made it through medical school and a long cardiovascular surgery residency that wrapped up when he was forty-two. At the same time, his first wife developed a mental illness, and he had to raise their daughter by himself. And, if that weren't enough, he also invented the first commercially produced membrane oxygenator. At the end of the residency, instead of buying a house, he bought a fifty-foot sailboat and spent some time at sea. Eventually, he realized maintaining the sailboat was a full-time job and gave up his seafaring life. That was Manny. He worked hard, and at the same time, never missed a chance to have fun.

A picture that used to hang in our bedroom depicted Manny standing at the edge of his boat, holding on and leaning toward the sea. That was his personality—a risk-taker. Trying to build the world's most advanced artificial heart, kidney, heart, and lung was a challenge. Trying to maintain a marriage with a much younger woman was also a challenge, especially when he tried to do them both at the same time. Manny said he always tried to take on more things than he could handle. I agreed. That was why I had to leave.

I agree to help him copy the disc. I don't know why I am so softhearted today. Ever since he took away my car, I have been trying to hate him. I thought of stealing his car, destroying his precious paintings. But I have done nothing.

I used to be his computer consultant. He depended on me and even refused to learn when I tried to teach him something. Now, he must learn. I wish him luck.

He belongs to a generation that sees computers as nightmares or aliens from Mars. Given their late-in-life introduction to these machines, it's almost impossible for them to become computer literate.

"Is this what you should do?" He shows me a DOS reference book. I am surprised he has found one.

"Yes, but you can do it in WordPerfect directly. Like this.

"Slow down, damnit! You're too fast."

"Okay, do this first."

"Wait a minute. Let me write it down." He goes to the desk and picks up a message pad.

"See, it's easy."

He nods, then shifts his eyes from the computer screen to me. He hugs me and buries his head in my chest. "Meihua, what happened? It's so sad. We did not even try counseling, you know."

Tears stream down my face.

"I'm sorry, I'm sorry, Manny." I say repeatedly. "I just needed someone younger, but more mature. Next time, don't find someone so young."

"Oh, nonsense! I'm younger than you are."

"No, it's not true. You are crazy, Manny."

When he's rowing, sometimes he thinks he is as young as twenty-five—the average age of the college crews he rows with.

"It's too bad. We had five wonderful years of marriage," says Manny. I can tell he is on the verge of crying.

"It's human weakness. I'm sorry." I go back to the corner to pack my books again. I am still sobbing.

Yes, it is the human weakness. Is that it? Of course not. It is a factor, but there are other reasons for our separation.

Think about our declining sex life just before I left. He had trouble concentrating during intercourse, which could be contributed to our unsolvable differences—I was no longer

160

interested in his research, and he was *only* interested in his research.

A month before I left, he had an upset stomach for an excruciating two weeks and only subsisted on chicken broth. The illness was self-induced, brought about by a late-night incident.

That night, I was sleeping lightly because I was mad at him for another failed attempt at sex. He bumped against me, and I opened my eyes to find him reading by the bed.

"Can't you sleep?" I asked.

"No. Do you want to know why?"

"Why?"

"I have been thinking about us."

"Manny, why? Why can't we make love anymore? I don't understand. Can't you give me a reason? Can't you tell me?"

"Meihua, I didn't want to tell you, but after mulling it over for three hours, I have decided it's best to tell you the truth. You are getting fat. You are no longer my beautiful young wife. Lately, you've been eating too much and hardly doing any rowing. I can't stand a fat wife."

Nonsense! Although I might have gained a few pounds in the last year or so, I was by no means *fat*. I ran six miles every day and hardly ate any meat. If I had gained weight, it was healthy weight. After that incident, he was upset. He felt so bad, he made himself sick for two weeks. I had seen him with upset stomachs before, but this was the worst one yet. Even so, he did not realize how upset I was. That was the tipping point. I decided to leave him.

By the time I finish packing, my face is too messy to walk out. I stand there, facing the wall.

"There's no hurry. You can stay as long as you want."

I used to come here every day. Spend eight hours here every day.

"No," I say. "I have a dental appointment soon." I tell myself I must get out. Now. If I don't, I may never escape. If Manny cannot keep me here, this place will.

"Can I at least help you carry your bag to the bus station?"

"I drove."

"I see. Let's go." He takes my bookbag in his hand.

"Okay." Another stream of tears run down my face. I wipe them with the back of my hand and wonder how I can possibly face all those people in the hospital hallway with my smudged face.

"You don't really have to leave," Manny says, seeing me hesitate.

What does he mean? Does he really want to keep me here? No way! But what am I crying for?

I am the one who decided to leave, and now I'm being so sentimental. But I am not a quitter. I wipe my face again and walk out the door.

It's a bright, sunny day. Manny and I used to walk together and chat when the weather was nice, but today we have nothing to say. The hot sun has a soothing effect. I stop crying. We come to the parking lot and unlock the car door. I start the engine.

"Meihua, don't be so practical." That is his last desperate attempt to get me back. I know it will get me. I cry again.

"If that old guy is too old for you, give me a call."

Tears burst forth again. "He is not old! He is forty-two."

"He sounds pretty old-spirited."

I do not argue. I shift the car into gear and drive away. Thank God I do not have to argue with him anymore. Yes, Manny is mentally younger. But that's his problem. At age sixty, he has the mind of a twenty-year-old, and he wanted a young wife to match. It is safe to say, he has lived up to his college promise of never growing up. The trouble is, I have grown older, while he has grown younger. We do not match each other anymore.

Hanging in Two Pieces

The airplane wobbles in the air. It is windy, stormy weather. The cold air blows through the window and makes me shiver. My heart is like a tide pummeling the shore, up and down. Manny and I are on our way to New York City to attend a conference. This is also a chance to see my former boyfriend, Wang Ming, and I am excited.

I've changed a lot in the past three years. Now, I walk with my American husband shoulder to shoulder, not dragging three steps behind. I speak in a loud, aggressive way, sounding just like most American girls. Today, I wear a spiral perm, makeup, gold earrings, and a necklace. I've put on a miniskirt and an oversized sweater for the flight.

I am not really missing Wang Ming. My motivation for reconciliation is rooted in my desire to heal the wound between us, which was caused when we broke up three years ago. My friends think Wang Ming is a victim of our love affair, because I was the one who left.

I have carried the emotional burden of our breakup over these past three years. Since we broke up, whenever I've had a new boyfriend, I can't help but compare him with Wang Ming—his looks, his taste, his attitude toward woman, his knowledge about art.

Manny cannot understand why I am so eager to see my Chinese friends. During our two years together, he's rarely known me to mingle with other Chinese people. Whenever I meet one, I always complain about how little they understand me. Manny is unperturbed by my complaints, instead he is proud of transitioning me from a Chinese woman to a good American. Yet, I want to tell him Wang Ming is different. Like a lot of Peking University graduates, he understands and appreciates western art. When we were friends, we would go to museums, ballets, operas, and concerts, and talk about poetry and Impressionism. Despite our commonalities, I am not sure what will happen this time. It is a brave act on my part. After I left him, he fell into a terrible depression, which lasted two years. If he points a gun at me this time, I will not be surprised.

Manny nudges me. Looking out the window, a golden palace comes into view. The entire ground beneath the airplane is covered with glistening lights. We are approaching LaGuardia Airport, and the airplane is finally descending. Although my heart still hangs in the air, the new attractions soon bring me back to earth.

We step out of a tunnel and into a wave of humanity. I notice different ethnic groups, dark skin, brown skin, yellow skin, white skin. Mustaches and beards. Some people hold signs like "V.I.P," "Koi Yamamoto," "Miaoxing Wang." Suddenly I am lost. I feel as though I have arrived at a space station on the moon. After we have pushed through the waiting crowd, we are confronted with a parade of cab drivers. They are overwhelming. They are irresistible. We are grabbed by a tall, handsome Iranian with a slightly crippled leg.

When we finally arrive at the hotel chosen by our travel agent, I look up and see a thirty-story building decorated with neon-lit letters as big as its windows. A Hispanic hotel clerk checks us in. Excited by the setting and atmosphere of the room—fancy by our standards—we cannot go to sleep. What a waste to sleep in this city. We flip through all seventeen channels on the TV, including one pornographic channel and one in Chinese. At three o'clock in the morning, we fall asleep.

Someone is pushing my shoulder.

"Ah...Don't push me! Don't push me!"

I am having a bad dream. I am still in the airplane when the ground beneath me opens. I fall into the sky, with one hand clinging to the airplane. Manny was also tossed out of the plane and has managed to grab my foot on his way down to the abyss. We hold onto each other; my grasp on the airplane is tenuous. A gust of wind whisks Manny away. I look down and find that the lower half of my body has gone with him. The upper half still hangs onto the airplane.

"Meihua, get up. It is eight o'clock. You should call your friend." Manny is shaking me awake.

"Yes, push me down, please," says my upper body. Then, I stretch and get up. I realize if I do not call Wang Ming right away, I will miss my chance to see him.

I pick up the telephone and dial a New Jersey phone number. The phone rings for a while.

"Hello, may I speak to Wang Ming?"

"Yes, this is he."

"This is Meihua. I am in New York."

"Hi! Why are you calling so early?"

"Why?"

"You have woken up everyone in the apartment!" Although he does not raise his voice, his words are strong and firm. I can tell he is angry.

"Oh, I'm sorry. I thought I'd better to get a hold of you before it was too late. Last night we didn't arrive until midnight."

"You should have called then."

I had forgotten the graduate student's lifestyle—going to bed after midnight and rising at noon. But he promises to pick me up in front of the hotel at 11 a.m.

I have two and a half hours to prepare, and I feel overwhelmed. When we met in New York three years ago, I wore a three-dollar T-shirt and cheap blue jeans, while he wore name brand clothing like Nike and Pierre Cardin. This time, I want to look expensive.

I spend a long time in the shower, shampooing and conditioning my hair, and washing my body with the hotel's scented body gel. Then, I gel my hair and spray it. I decide to wear a new pair of stockings and my favorite dress. Staring at my headbands, I have a hard time choosing the right one—the wide, black one or the narrow, black one?

The phone rings, and I rush from the bathroom to pick it up. I'm still only wearing my underwear.

"Hello!"

"Hi, this is Wang Ming."

"Oh, Wang Ming. Where are you?"

"I am downstairs in your hotel lobby."

"What? So fast! I'll be ready in five minutes."

I put on barrettes, my nylons, a dress, and a nice sweater. I grab my purse and run out the door.

168

At the front entrance, I look through rows of tourists at the front desk and can't find a trace of Wang Ming. I imagine his grin with dimples, his eyes turning into thin lines behind his glasses when he is happy, his sly smirk, and the way he doubled over with laughter once when he swept a tennis ball in front of my toes. I can also picture his apple-red face and the dreadful silence when he's angry. I do not know what kind of face I'll encounter today.

As I wander toward the door, a young man appears in front of me behind the revolving door. I am shocked. I back up a few steps before realizing he is the person I am looking for. Wang Ming wears a pair of faded blue jeans and a Princeton University sweatshirt. His hair is incredibly long, which makes his small face even smaller.

"Hi!" He seems numb and tired. He raises his right arm to shake my hand, but hesitates. It is me who grabs his hand before he pulls away. His hand is soft and bony.

"Hi, it has been quite a while." I am trying to be calm.

"Yes, several years. You look quite different this time." He says this quietly and in a serious tone. Like usual, he does not consume much energy while speaking.

"Thank you." I respond like an American. I do not know whether he means the appearance or the inner world.

"Let's go." He turns and walks into the revolving door. I follow him.

"Where are we going?" I ask.

"My car." He gestures to a Toyota Tercel parked on the street.

"Hi, Meihua! How are you?" A nice-looking fellow, wearing khaki pants and a tan jacket, jumps out of the car. He is also a former classmate, a popular guy named Zhang Li. He shakes my hands with a big grin.

As we greet each other outside the car, I notice another person in the car, a young Chinese woman.

"Who is she?" I ask.

"Who is she? Ha, ha…" Zhang Li laughs. Wang Ming, too, thinks this is funny. I'm relieved to see him smile. Okay, I think, I will figure it out myself. If she is Zhang Li's wife, she would have probably come out to greet me. Therefore, she must be Wang Ming's girlfriend.

"I know who she is."

"Of course, you know." Wang Ming says, looking at the street traffic.

We get into the car. Yumei, Wang Ming's girlfriend, and I sit in the backseat. We smile and nod at each other, which is enough greeting for Chinese people.

She is a shy woman. She has short hair, wears blue jeans and a cute black sweater with a pocket on her bosom. Like many other Chinese students, she also wears white-framed glasses.

I feel overly dressed, and sense that I've intimidated Yumei into silence.

"How have you been?" Zhang Li is the most talkative one.

"I'm fine. I heard you just finished your PhD degree. Congratulations!"

"Well, nowadays, a PhD is not worth much."

"Come on," Wang Ming joins in. "You are making three times as much as me, just because you have a PhD and I am still a graduate student."

"You could be a salesman, Zhang Li," Yumei says seriously "They make a lot of money, and I think you are qualified."

"Of course!" Zhang Li laughs. He does not mind being called a salesman.

I am glad Wang Ming and Yumei help me answer Zhang Li. I do not know what to say to him. My decision to quit graduate school was not based upon whether a PhD is worth something or not. I have just applied to a creative writing graduate program—a program, I'm certain, they will think is impractical. So, I keep quiet. Besides, I was never very good friends with Zhang Li. In college, he was a popular guy in a popular group in Class 2. I was an unpopular girl in Class 1. We were apples and oranges. Five years of separation has whisked away most of my memories about him, except for the superficial ones.

"Where are we going?" I change the topic.

"China Town," says Zhang Li.

"Zhang Li has invited us to lunch." Wang Ming tries to brighten everyone's spirit. I am glad to see he is getting cheerful.

"It is always nice to go to China Town," I comment, "especially for eating out."

In truth, I hate China Town. It only seems to invoke bad memories for me. I did not grow up with Kungfu movies. I did not enjoy much delicious food when I was young, living under the Chinese Communist regime. Things like superstitions and Confucius' sayings were criticized in my circle. And I had never encountered a single fortune cookie. The only familiarity I found in China Town was that the people all looked alike. And even that had changed after marrying Manny. Is it true that people tend to look alike after living together for a long time? My love of Chinese food still hasn't changed, but it is also fading due to Manny's simple tastes.

What should I do? I decide to relinquish control and let them choose what we do. I want to be a good guest, especially for Wang Ming. I let my visions of going to a ballet performance or concert slowly slip away.

Wang Ming is driving quietly. I can only see the back of his head. His dark, straight hair is like a curtain that divides us.

When he visited me in China four years earlier, his shoulder-length hair was long by Chinese standards. When we made love, his hair was always in the way, covering his face and his expressions.

"Your hair is pricking me," I complained. I never liked men with long hair.

"Would you hold it?" he said to me.

"No, I can't." I did not think that was something I should do during intercourse.

"Okay, okay!" He turned his head sideways, to avoid getting his hair in my face. This made things even more awkward, especially since this was our first time being intimate together.

Later, we met again in New York. His hair was well-trimmed, and he wore suits and ties, with a pair of Pierre Cardin leather shoes. After going to see a New York City Ballet performance, we made love.

Lying side by side on his apartment's bed, he asked, "What are you thinking about?"

"Nothing."

"How about getting married, since we already…" He left the sentence dangling, but I knew he meant that we had already made love.

"No, no, no!" I did not want to tell him how little I enjoyed what we had just done in bed. After being in the US for one year,

I had developed a different idea about what love should be. It should be crazy, passionate, and expressive. I was not used to the Chinese's subtle love dance. Looking at his wool suit and shiny leather shoes, I told him he was immature. I broke up with him.

He was shocked. In his mind, if a Chinese girl made love with a man, she was giving herself to him. Otherwise, she would make life difficult for herself—a non-virgin looking for a husband.

Now, he seems to have become a hard-working student again, with no time to cut his hair or buy new clothes. But I still do not know what is lying underneath the surface—a naïve heart or a mature one.

We have already arrived in China Town. It seems a lot larger and crowded than I remember.

"What is this?" I point to a store full of fancy magazines and costumes, with huge movie star portraits in the windows. The sign says "He Hua Wu," which means "Lotus House" in Chinese. This does not make sense to me.

"It means Hollywood." Yumei says.

"I see. I really need to come here more often; we do not have a China Town in Minnesota." I try to find an excuse for my ignorance.

We drive around the small streets between stores. It becomes even more cramped when cars line both sides of the streets. After twenty minutes of spinning around, Zhang Li spots a Volvo about to pull out of its parking space. Wang Ming parks the car, and everybody tries to put coins into the parking meter to share the cost. I am too slow to make a contribution.

We walk into a grocery store. The front stand is filled with roast pork, chicken, pig's feet, cooked pork intestines, and a roast whole pig on rotisserie. Looking at this familiar food, my mouth starts to salivate, but the feeling is pushed away by guilt. Since Manny and I maintain a low-fat diet, I have not had meat in months. I almost forget what it tastes like. Whenever I think of eating meat, it conjures images of being fat, unhealthy, and high in cholesterol. I do everything in my power to escape these temptations.

Wang Ming, Zhang Li, and Yumei seem to have much clearer objectives than I do. They run around, finding what they want among this enormous collection of food. I follow for a while, still unsure of what I want. It seems I want everything, and nothing. I still remember the good taste of this kind of food, but I do not remember how to put the ingredients together. The recipes I used to keep in my head have flown away. Growing up, we didn't have cookbooks—just recipes passed down through the generations.

I tell Yumei I'd like to buy some dried shrimp. She takes me to the dried shrimp and dried mushroom section. There are shrimp of all sizes, with or without shells. They are wrapped in fancy plastic bags of big, medium, and small sizes. Yumei tells me the small shrimp are good for making soups and dumplings, and the big ones are good for stir-fry. I do not tell her that I only need them to nibble on between meals.

"This is good, made in Taiwan." Yumei hands me a bag of medium-sized shrimp.

I take it and decide to stop seeking the perfect shrimp. Suddenly, I remember Manny hates dried shrimp. For him, it is a symbol of preservation without refrigeration. And he does not like the smell—he finds it stinky. I throw the shrimp back on the shelf. Yumei asks me why, and I say my husband doesn't like dried shrimp. Then, I tell her stories about how I sometimes frighten Manny with fermented soybean cakes, thousand-year eggs, pig ears, livers, and tongues whenever I come back from a Chinese market.

"Is it easy to teach him about Chinese food?" Yumei asks.

"It is not very easy, though I suppose I could try a little harder. But I don't like to cook. I am lucky he does not care for fancy Chinese food."

"I see." She seems to have a hard time comprehending how I can live without Chinese food and what Wang Ming would think if she did the same. I want to tell her that, since I'm so busy with other things, eating is no longer an important part of my life.

I then follow Zhang Li, who is looking for chive sauce. I have never heard of it, and he explains that it is important for hotpot cooking, and hard to find. Finally, he finds a bottle of greenish sauce and holds it triumphantly.

In a drug store, Wang Ming is looking for Ginseng. Ginseng is a root found only in the high mountains of Korea. He tosses me a package of tea.

"Are you still drinking tea? This is a very good tea. When you pour it out, it looks crystal green." I notice he avoids eye contact with me.

During the shopping, Wang Ming has kept his distance. When scanning the shelves, I sometimes found him staring at me from a distance, a look of desire on his white, smooth face. In college, we fell in love by eye contact. I can tell his fire is still there, but it needs some fuel. And Yumei is not going to provide it—maybe he needs someone with more experience.

"Not like this kind." He tosses another package to me. "It is called green tea, but it actually looks brown."

"Really? I never noticed the difference." I begin to wonder if he's referring to the changing color or my heart—my sudden betrayal of him and his failure to recognize it?

"It would be nice if you bought some for your husband," Yumei says innocently.

"He only drinks herbal tea," I say.

"Chinese medicine for tea, yuck!" Wang Ming comments.

We leave the drug store and stop at a Chinese restaurant for lunch.

"I thought we could go to a better restaurant than this one," Yumei complains when we walk in. "But I do not think Wang Ming will listen to me. He never listens."

"Really? I don't remember him being that way."

We dine on snails, beef dumplings, and thousand-year egg soup. The delectable food reminds us of the good old days in college. Again, Zhang Li talks too much. His self-assuredness makes it very hard for anyone else to speak.

"Wang Ming, do you remember our adventures in college, our mischief in the dormitory, and drinking and talking about women in the campus restaurant?" Nonsense flows nonstop from Zhang Li's mouth.

Wang Ming drinks a mouthful of wine and sighs. Then, he starts to devour his rice. In the middle of a bite, he says, "Ask Meihua."

Now everybody is staring at me, except Wang Ming. Did I have a good time in college? Under the circumstances, I guess I did. At least we had courage to love, to kiss, while many Chinese youths were afraid of it, enduring the torture of lonely hearts.

"I enjoyed reading Cheng Lili's diary," I say.

176

"What did you read?" Zhang Li asks anxiously. Chen Lili was Zhang Li's former girlfriend, a famous Chinese physicist's daughter, and my college roommate.

"A lot of bad things about you."

Everyone laughs. We're finding common ground in gossiping about others and talking about food.

"Americans don't know how to eat. They just cut a chunk of meat, cook it halfway, and eat it while it is still red and bloody. And it doesn't have any taste." Zhang Li asserts.

"They eat vegetables with a strange sauce," Yumei adds.

I sit, listening to them talk about our national pride. I agree with them. There are a lot of good things that emerged from China's five-thousand-year history. Cooking is just one accomplishment from our brilliant civilization. But I still believe we can learn from the West—things like freedom, liberty, and equality that can be incorporated into Chinese culture.

After lunch, we are back on the street. We visit several street vendors, with their supplies of fresh fish and vegetables that are favored by Chinese people. I try to avoid fish juice dropping onto my new shoes, which means I don't see much of the food.

"Do you like fish?" Yumei asks me.

"Yes, of course."

"Wang Ming and I eat fish for almost every meal."

"Who does the cooking?"

"Me. I have gotten used to it. I even cook fish for lunch."

I realize that no matter how plain she is, she really is an ideal girl for Wang Ming. She is a tolerant person and a hard worker. Compared with her, I am a lazy girl. I do not know how to clean fish, and I hate frying fish because it makes my clothes and my entire body smell like grease.

After our China Town tour, Wang Ming suggests that we stop by his apartment. It is in an old colonial building on a narrow New Jersey street. The apartment's wooden stairway reminds me of my great-grandmother's home in Shanghai. Like a lot of graduate students, they live in domestic chaos. Half-eaten food crowds for space on dishes, on top of the counter, and in pots and pans. Books, notebooks, and term papers occupy every corner of the room—the floor, couches, tables. Dirty clothes, clean clothes, and blankets embrace each other on the bed. Judging by the bedroom's double bed, I assume that Wang Ming and Yumei are living together. Chinese students are often very open about living together before marriage in the US. If it were China, they could be persecuted.

Wang Ming's space has not changed much since the last time I visited. Although, it seems he does not buy expensive art books anymore. Three years ago, he showed me a thick hardcover book about Impressionism. Now, I only see a few nondescript art and literary books on the shelf. I pull out a book called *Selected Poems by Woman Writers* and ask, "Why do you read poems written by woman writers?"

"It only cost three dollars. Besides, I like to understand women better."

It is apparent Yumei has changed Wang Ming's extravagant way of living. He has finally saved enough money to buy a car, instead of constantly borrowing money from friends. I am genuinely happy for him.

Zhang Li brings along pictures and videotapes of his son. When he turns on the TV, a pleasant three-year-old boy is playing in the grass with his grandmother. I do not pay much attention to the little boy. Like many American women, I have not decided

178

whether I will have children of my own. I'm not sure how to comment on the video, but Yumei does it naturally.

"What a cute boy! He looks just like his father. He will be a handsome man."

As Zhang Li puts away the tape and video camera, I apologize for my conduct.

"I'm sorry I was not paying much attention to your son. Maybe it is because I do not have any children of my own. Honestly, I'm not sure I could raise a dog."

Yumei is stunned. She looks at me, mouth agape. She holds a kettle in her hand, and hot water drips to the counter. She must think I am a witch or a monster.

Zhang Li takes my statement in stride.

"We did not plan on having him," he says. "It just happened, and we decided to keep him."

I do not reveal that I was once pregnant, too—a pregnancy I ultimately terminated. Chinese students do not know much about contraception, and premarital sex is considered a crime. Therefore, after these virgin Chinese girls come to US, they must often face the consequence of their ignorance: pregnancy.

Before we leave, Zhang Li looks through all the Chinese magazines and videotapes in the apartment. Wang Ming's apartment is a cultural center for all the Chinese students on campus. I stand, unsure of what to do. Since I've been away, I've immersed myself in the English language, reading as many books in English as possible. Chinese is becoming secondary to me and, as bad as my English is, at least it's improving. In the meantime, my Chinese is going downhill. When I write to my mother in Beijing every month, I often have trouble remembering words.

As the afternoon winds down, Wang Ming offers to take me back to the hotel. On our way there, I talk about my husband. Wang Ming just listens. As I am about to jump out of the car, I give him my hand.

"Please forgive me, Wang Ming. It appears you have found an ideal girl. I wish you well."

He keeps silent for a while, then says, "What does it matter anyway? I don't think you are Chinese anymore."

I do not know how I get out of his car. I am standing in front of the hotel, looking lost. People rush by me. The world starts turning and spinning. Wang Ming's words have hit me— hit me harder than anything else I experienced in China Town. A seagull flies by; the white feathers on his body look so pure. Yes, I am Chinese—pure Chinese without any other genes mixed in my blood. But I feel American now. I have transformed with the ease of the sun rising in the east and sinking in the west.

Cloud Nine

It was over. She knew that. She could feel it over the phone as he relayed, excited, that he was going to visit a former girlfriend. He was going to paint her portrait. Again. She knew that this wasn't just a painting.

On a hill next to a quiet highway, Ben and Meihua sat together and watched the grass wave under the summer breeze. Ben softly touched her, from her knees up her thighs, and from her thighs up to the edge of her summer shorts. With his fingers probing under her shorts, he told her this was why he liked summer. Ah, yes! She remembered that. Once, Ben told her he liked summer because it was easier to paint landscapes. Even then, she suspected it had more to do with bare skin.

Staring into the distance, Ben seemed attracted to the wavy, blanket-like lawn stretching alongside the highway. He truly didn't know what to think about this smart, unpredictable Chinese girl. She excited him tremendously, and he thought about her all the time. His desire was so strong, he feared he would say the wrong thing and frighten her away. Today's afternoon meeting was only the third time they had been alone together. They hardly knew each other, but Meihua felt a strange closeness to him, enough so that his intimate touch felt safe and comfortable. Still looking into the distance, Ben said in a quiet, intimate voice, "I want to paint you sometime to develop our intimacy. I have thought about it for a while."

Meihua's heart quivered. She could hardly catch her breath.

She wanted to open her arms, wrap Ben in a big hug, and whisper in his ear, "Yes, of course!" But she didn't. Meihua knew she had to play a little game to keep some mystery in their budding physical relationship.

"Don't you think that is dangerous?" she said.

"Dangerous? How can something as beautiful as art be dangerous?" Ben answered innocently.

"No. I meant intimacy," said Meihua.

Still looking in the distance, Ben didn't say anything. He moved his hand back down to her knee.

"I think intimacy is the one thing all humans want most," Meihua answered, hoping to subtly let Ben know she was still interested.

Ben sighed. He turned his head and kissed her. His tongue moved forcefully back and forth in her mouth, and she responded in kind. During the long kiss, he moved his hand up to her panties. She felt a soft wetness on the fabric surrounding his fingers and wondered if he could feel it, too.

She put her hand under his T-shirt rather awkwardly. She liked the thick patches of hair on his chest. Slowly, she moved her hand back and forth across his chest, feeling his stringy hair. Yet, she didn't venture below the belt because she was shy. After a while, Ben released her and sighed again.

"What's wrong?" Meihua asked.

"When you have a certain feeling about someone," he said, "you just know."

182

His words made Meihua happy. Beneath his blushing face, she could feel the sexual excitement rushing through his body. On the other hand, his speech seemed somewhat cold and confused today.

Why is he always looking at the stupid grass or off into the distance? Grass is beautiful, indeed, but did he bother to drive half an hour just to look at grass? Why is he so distant? Had she done something wrong? Does he think less of her for letting him touch her?

Ben popped a grass stem in his mouth and chewed.

"You look like a farm boy." Meihua couldn't think of any better words to describe him.

Ben had always been like a boy to her. This was the first time in her life she had felt love toward a "boy." Ben swiveled around and, for the first time that day, looked at her deeply.

"Why don't you touch me? I've touched you. Don't you think we should be equals?" Although his voice was timid, the invitation thrilled Meihua. He seemed to have resolved his internal agony or put it aside for a while. He pulled her hand over, placing it in his shorts. Now, Meihua's own blood rushed. Her stroking fingers made the warm mass of flesh slowly harden in her hand. He started kissing her passionately.

She felt like her whole body was melting, along with her soul. As they touched each other quietly and intimately, every part of her body began rising, rising toward the sky, floating around, above the beautiful city on this pleasant midsummer afternoon.

Occasional wind gusts brought floating curtains of dust past them. People passed by. About ten feet away, a group of students sat beneath a tree. Meihua ignored their presence, savoring the chance to be close to Ben. They were like two birds, enjoying the privileges of belonging to nature, neglecting the existence of human beings.

Meihua had spent days asking herself why she liked this handsome, passionate, but childish young man. Ben was eight years older than she, but he still sounded and acted like a kid. Maybe her distaste for immaturity was why she chose to marry old Manny, who was thirty years her senior. Ben often spoke without thinking, easily changed his mind, and sounded like a crying baby at times. He belonged to a newer generation than her husband—one that enjoyed talking about sex, writing about sex, and painting sexual themes. Ben often mentioned making love in public—thinking that sexual intercourse in an elevator or on the roof was an adventure, while Manny, who belonged to the Second World War generation, avoided even talking about sex. To Manny, sex was not a topic for polite conversation even, it seemed, with his wife.

Manny was the only avid bicyclist Meihua knew who refused to wear standard bicycle tights, because they made him feel almost naked, and he thought it was inappropriate attire in front of others. As an adventurer, he admired Jean Cousteau, Beebe, and Columbus, who had devoted their lives to exploring nature and the new world. Ben's heroes, on the other hand, were Sigmund Freud, Claude Monet, and Pablo Picasso, who were the greatest explorers of the human mind.

Though Ben was physically attractive, Meihua thought Manny was more masculine and she was determined to devote her life to him. What did she like about Ben? His sentimentality? His passion? His sexual obsession? Yes, all of the above. The thought of sex with Ben excited her.

184

Meihua grew up in Communist China, and coming to United States felt like landing on an alien planet. The blue eyes and blond hair, the supermarkets, ATMs, fast food joints, adult bookstores, and readily available porn movies—everything was new for her. Even driving a car down the highway reminded her of a fast-speed capitalistic lifestyle. Since landing in San Francisco four years ago, Meihua had become increasingly comfortable in this society. She had found a nice, albeit old, American husband, quickly adapted to her new culture, spoke fluent English, and could openly discuss any popular issue with Americans. Yes, she liked this country and the people in the western world.

But deep inside her, she still bore the scars of her traumatized childhood. She had always thought her mother's lifelong infidelity was rooted in her father's inability to satisfy her mother's emotional and sexual desires. Now, she wondered if her own desires were inherited or learned.

Her mother was a striking beauty with an overtly sexual presence. Her husband, a mathematics professor eighteen years her senior, couldn't love her the way she wanted him to. The old man had lost his sexual ability since returning from a labor camp during the Cultural Revolution in China. Because of prevalent economic and cultural taboos, they had avoided divorce, but Meihua's childhood was never peaceful. Her father, an introversive person by nature, drifted into alcoholism. Besides the constant fights and violence within her family, she also had to tolerate the neighbors' gossip and her classmates' curiosity about her mother's very public extramarital affairs. Meihua had suffered enough.

In the United States, she had never been happier. Not until she married Manny did she ever question her own future happiness. She always dreamt of finding a nice husband and having a peaceful life together. She had achieved some of this with Manny, but became painfully aware of the thirty-year gulf between them. What had made her agree to this impossible marriage? She did not know. She had choices at the time, but she willingly entered the union. Maybe, it was a form of fate— embracing, and perhaps enhancing, the genes she shared with her passionate, sex-driven mother. It was during this time of doubt that Ben entered her life.

"I can imagine kissing you, hugging you, and doing the most intimate things with you!" Those parting words from their afternoon rendezvous echoed in Meihua's head. She knew she would see him again. She and Manny were invited to a party he was hosting at this home and studio on Lake Minnetonka. In the meantime, their telephone conversations had become increasingly intimate.

"What if we were alone together right now?" Meihua had asked him on the phone last week. "I would want to kiss youuu! What about a step further? Let's verbally touch each other."

"I get hard just talking to you! Have you ever made love on the phone? No? Let's do it." Ben's passion poured over Meihua's body like a midsummer shower. Her heart pounded with anticipation.

"I want to make you very, very wet and then I want to fuck you. That's what I want to do with you!" During that call, Meihua sat quietly with her eyes closed and let Ben's voice probe the depths of her mind.

"I still remember my first glimpse of you." Ben's voice drilled deep within her. Yes, Meihua remembered that moment, too.

186

It was at Manny's college reunion party. After walking through the elegant doors of an exclusive golf club, Manny realized he was surrounded by many young, unfamiliar faces. "I really am an *old* alumnus," he said. Looking around, few people's nametags read '53 or '54.

"Manny, Manny Goodman!" someone called from behind us. We turned to find a tall man with a fringe of gray hair walking toward us.

"It's Bob, Bob Robinson," the man said, staring at Manny with eyes wide behind his thick glasses.

"Oh, my goodness! Bob, we haven't seen each other in almost twenty years." They hugged for a long time.

By now, most people were sitting at the many round tables.

"Would you like to join us at our table?" asked Bob.

"Sure, that'd be great."

After Manny and Meihua seated themselves at the table with Bob and his wife Nancy, a young man joined them.

He was introduced as Ben, a friend of Bob's. Bob served with Ben's father on the board of trustees of Amherst College. Meihua's first impression of Ben was that he was such a handsome thing. She liked his dark, slightly curly hair and passionate eyes. Ben stood between Meihua and Nancy, interrupting the start of their conversation.

"Hey, it is nice to be surrounded by women," Ben said, pulling a chair from the other table and sitting between them, which forced Nancy to scoot a few inches away.

"Hey, it's also nice for us to be surrounded by men," said Meihua, in frustration. Yet, despite herself, she thought, "Oh my God, who is this guy and why do I find him so fascinating?

"Ben, why don't you tell everybody about your adventures in New York City?" Bob's comment brought Meihua back to the present. Ben started telling everyone about his capers in New York as an artist, a performing artist, a party promoter, and a videographer.

"I used to have a Chinese lover," said Ben, looking intently at Meihua.

"Really?" Her interest was piqued.

"Which part of China are you from?"

"Mainland China, Beijing. I came here as a grad student a few years ago."

"Oh, really? My girlfriend was from Taiwan, but she thought her roots were in Mainland China." He said that with a certain kind of emotion that made Meihua feel that this former lover had been something special to him. But she did not want to pry. Ben turned around and chatted with Nancy for a while.

The lull gave Meihua a chance to finally talk with Manny.

"You've had a very interesting conversation," said Manny with a smile.

"Oh, well." Meihua felt a bit embarrassed but did not want to show it.

"Sometimes I create art just to please myself." Ben's voice suddenly dominated the table.

"Personal pleasure?" Meihua did not agree. "I think art is something you do to express yourself to the world."

"Yes, that's right. I use my art to express my emotions to others all the time," said Ben, staring at Meihua with a strange glow in his eyes.

Yes, art is a language, and Ben and Meihua had suddenly found a common language between them. She did not remember exactly what she talked about with Ben later that evening. He was not an engaging conversationalist, but from his warmth toward her and his willingness to talk, she felt at home with him. And, he seemed to like her.

It was a long party, half of which was spent listening to a speech. While sitting between her husband and Ben, uneasiness nipped at Meihua. Pretending to look toward the speaker and her husband, she imagined Ben's eyes staring at her—eyes full of desire and passion like two, hot laser beams. She could feel the penetration of those eyes, through her skin, into her heart, but she didn't look back. After dinner, Meihua and Ben shook hands and said goodbye. She yearned to get to know him better.

Ben was looking at the other side of highway now, where yellow and pink wildflowers waved under the wind.

"It is so beautiful," said Ben, still playfully touching Meihua. She enjoyed his touch intensely and tried not to swoon.

"That flowery landscape is just like the farm fields in China."

"She is a beautiful girl," said Ben.

"Who are you talking about?" Meihua asked.

"You." Ben turned and looked at Meihua.

"I don't believe it." She pushed his hand away from her shorts. "You must be talking about another girl."

"No, I mean you. You really are a beautiful girl—a nice girl." Ben stroked Meihua's hair.

How could he say that? Meihua's appearance had apparently reminded him of his former Chinese lover, Linlin. She was also an attractive girl and an extraordinarily talented one. Ben and Linlin had been involved in an intense love affair. How could he forget about those exciting days with Linlin? Linlin's courageous nude modeling in front of the Trump Tower, his first taste of Chinese Gongfu under Linlin's instruction. Now, that was all over. He was married with a three-year-old son. He had tried to use hard work to suppress his desire for outside excitement and adventures, but meeting Meihua seemed to erase his efforts. Long forgotten images of Linlin had popped up in his mind, and he started drawing her from memory. His artist's instincts told him Meihua was somebody he could create a great artistic experience with. His eagerness and desire for adventure were enough to let him cross the boundary of his marriage to pursue something with Meihua. Yet, he was not sure how Meihua would handle the situation. He was not even sure if he could handle it himself. He was confused, out of control.

"Do you remember our first date?" Ben pulled his mind back to the present.

"Of course," answered Meihua. "But it wasn't really a date!"

While reading a book about Vincent van Gogh, Meihua waited for Ben at a table in a public library. She was early and didn't know why. Maybe it was because she had been so eager to see him. It had been more than a month since they first met at Manny's college reunion. After ten minutes of desperate waiting, at five past eleven, she noticed a young man wearing a heavy black woolen coat moving up the escalator. Ben walked directly to her table, sat, and set a can of watercolor pens on the table.

"Hi!" He shook her hand and put some papers and a drawing book on the table. Out of intense curiosity, Meihua opened the drawing book. The first drawing was a portrait of a disintegrated body with two large eyes and a big mouth splayed beneath a huge sea wave.

"The wave is passion," Ben explained. "Sometimes you feel overwhelmed and hopeless in front of it."

"Really? I think I am different. I ride the top of the wave and keep everything under control," said Meihua proudly.

"Really?" Ben looked at her face and smiled wickedly.

"Yes, that is me," said Meihua.

"I see. But, then, what are you doing here today with me?"

"I don't know," said Meihua. She suddenly felt embarrassed and dropped her head. She could feel her face burning.

The next drawing surprised Meihua.

"A naked Chinese girl?" She protested softly, pretending this body had nothing to do with her, but noticing the overall size of the figure, the hips, and the breasts closely resembled her image.

"Yes. I just did it yesterday. What do you think?" Ben stared at her with his expressive eyes.

"Pretty good," answered Meihua. They both laughed and didn't say anything more specific.

"How about doing some drawings together?" Ben suggested.

"Okay. That sounds fun."

On a piece of paper, Ben drew a random, curled blue line—God knows what it was. He handed the paper to Meihua. She was puzzled. Although she had studied random, abstract drawing during college and did quite well, Meihua had never shared her drawing with anyone else. It was too private. During the random drawing exercises, she would relax, open her imagination, and cleanse her mind to embrace the vastness of the universe.

"Come on, do whatever you want." Ben encouraged her.

Still nervous, Meihua chose a yellow marker and drew a barely visible line. Then, Ben did something, too. After a while, the increasing complexity of the drawing became interesting and Meihua began to relax. Ben drew an arm like curve, and she drew a mirror image on the other side.

"Oh, good! The curves are matching," said Ben.

The two curves were very different, but they interlocked with each other. What did that mean? Meihua asked herself.

"Do you think there should be a head?" Ben woke her from her thoughts—thoughts of a physical, and not just an artistic union.

"Oh, yes," said Meihua. She was still wondering what she thought about the interlocking lines.

In a while, a lovely fat doll evolved on the page in front of her.

"What a lovely thing!" exclaimed Meihua.

She really did love it. She loved it because it was like a newborn baby, created by them both.

"Why do you like to draw?" Ben asked, seriously.

"I like to draw because I am attracted to it recently," said Meihua, a little embarrassed.

"For me, it's more than an interest. I am an addict," said Ben happily.

Meihua didn't know how to respond.

They started talking about art, each other's dreams, the mystery of the double helix, and the universe. Meihua told Ben about her sometimes romantic, but also chaotic family. Ben talked about his dream of exploring frontiers, becoming a great businessman, but also an accomplished artist. Although they continued to draw while they talked, they found the talking more interesting. Ben looked at Meihua more attentively now, which Meihua liked.

An attraction bloomed between them, and time passed quickly. Ben had already fed the parking meter four additional quarters.

"I have to return to my office. Before I leave, I want to kiss you. I feel the need to touch you." Ben looked into Meihua's eyes with an irresistible force. Although his words excited her, she didn't know how to respond.

"Kiss in public?" she whispered.

"Yes." Ben stared at her even more zealously. Meihua could hear his heavy breathing.

Meihua offered Ben her lips. Their mouths touched and merged. They held each other in a long, passionate kiss.

During that endless kiss, Ben's tongue explored every nuance of her willing mouth. Meihua was so excited, she hardly could breathe.

One of Ben's hands touched Meihua's left breast—a wild move that made Meihua jump, but was not unwelcome. That simple touch made her feel like she was lying on top of the open sea, her body rocking back and forth, up and down by the waves.

"No, No! I can't do this in public!" Meihua tried to push Ben away. She had spotted a lady sitting next to them who was watching intently. Yet, her passion would not allow the closeness to end. She didn't even remember when she finally left the library.

She didn't do anything else for the rest of the day. At home, she could think of nothing but him—his kiss, his touch, and the drawing of the Chinese girl, which she imagined to be her, naked and waiting for him.

Ben and Meihua kissed and groped for each other amid the waving grasses. Her heart beat fast. Ben's hand was probing deeper into the folds of skin beneath her panties. She longed for him to pull the panties aside, to feel his skin against hers, but he maintained that thin fabric barrier—a threshold they had silently agreed not to cross.

"How would you feel if we made love here?" Ben asked. He pulled Meihua to his chest and kissed her passionately.

"That would be wonderful," Meihua said, wrapping her arms around Ben's neck and pulling him in for another kiss. She pushed the narrow bridge of her panties aside, so he could penetrate beyond the wetness and probe deep inside her. With his other hand, he again guided Meihua to touch him. She felt the full force of his manhood and stroked it gently, almost in rhythm with his touches, falling into an unspoken closeness.

After a while, Ben gently pushed Meihua aside and sighed once more. Startled from her place of contentment, she asked what was wrong.

"Life is too powerful!" Ben said, looking away. What else could he say? Things were developing between them at a pace beyond expectation. What could they do? To become consummate lovers seemed to be their only choice. The other alternatives were even more out of the question. Could she handle it? Could he? He wasn't sure. She was still young, with no experience in relationships of this complexity.

Meihua nodded and seemed to understand the meaning behind Ben's words. Yes, life was too powerful sometimes. And life didn't always provide easy choices. On the one hand, she felt she loved Ben. Everyone would understand their relationship when they saw how much they had in common and how many things they could do together—creating art, making films, writing poems. Meihua had wanted to do these things her entire life. On the other hand, she loved Manny, too. Manny was smart and nice. She loved their intimacy and how he made her feel. They had a peaceful, happy marriage together and, compared with her sad, tumultuous childhood, she couldn't ask for more in life than what she had with Manny. Besides, he needed her, and she could never think of leaving him. Since they had married, he had been so much happier. She could not think of cheating on him either, because she was too inherently honest and sincere. Thinking of what she did at Ben's lake party, with Manny there, she felt a deep, lingering guilt.

The party had been at Ben's home about a month earlier. Meihua and Manny arrived late, because sensitive Manny was uneasy about it.

After driving up a long, narrow driveway, they arrived at the Minnetonka Peninsula. In the distance, they saw a black, wooden house by the lakeshore and a young man with wide shoulders and narrow hips wearing only a bright red, French-cut swimming suit.

"That's Ben!" Meihua said proudly.

"Really?" Manny could hardly recognize him, having seen him only once before, at the reunion.

They disembarked from the car, and Ben came over and carefully shook everyone's hands. He had obviously been waiting for them, because everyone else had already gone to the beach.

Looking Meihua up and down a few times, Ben said cunningly, "I hope you guys brought your swimming suits."

"Not me," Manny answered.

"Of course!" Meihua looked at Ben and smiled before running into the house to change.

Ben's home and studio was contained in a black carriage house. The first floor comprised a two-car garage; the second floor held two bedrooms and a living room. The rooms were simply decorated, except for the walls. Meihua could see Ben's artistic talent displayed everywhere. Here was a painting in his three-year-old son's room, displaying two little ghosts jumping around a dark purple background. Here, a funny face with a red nose made of a salad bowl and a screwdriver.

The bathroom was strange, containing a toilet, a shower, and a desk. A few books were scattered on top of the desk, with a sketchpad in the center. Out of curiosity, she opened the sketchpad. Oh! There were lots of drawings and writings in it, some of which were bizarre. For example, one was a lower body self-portrait of him, emphasizing the sexual organ.

No wonder this book had to be in the bathroom—he could start drawing right after a shower! Meihua quickly closed the drawing book, changed into her swimsuit, hung her street clothes over the shower rod, and ran out of the house.

It was a nice early-summer day. The sun was getting tired and hanging low in the afternoon sky. About ten people lingered at the beach, most of whom sat on the dock. She shook hands with Ben's wife Gretta, who sat in a lawn chair on the dock with her son on her lap.

Ben, she discovered, was windsurfing on the water. He was so far from shore that Meihua could barely make him out, save for his bright red swimsuit. Standing on the windsurfing board, Ben's body was straight and beautiful like a Greek god. Meihua didn't want to show too much admiration for Ben, so she began playing with Ben's son, Vincent. She was always curious about kids. Vincent was a strange child with big, dark, sad-looking eyes who liked to dig around in the dirt. He spoke broken English, intermingled with French, which was his mother's native tongue.

Every guest took turns with Ben on the windsurfing board, while Meihua stayed behind and played with Vincent. She didn't want to seem too friendly. Just standing there, looking at him was already a treat.

"Hi! You must enjoy playing in the sand."

Meihua raised her head. It was Ben.

"No. I just wanted to play with your son, which is a real challenge because we don't really share the same language."

"Yes. It is hard, right? But it can be done. I speak practically no French, but we are doing okay." Ben looked at her wickedly. Meihua wanted to laugh, but she didn't. She could not imagine what would happen between them if she *only* spoke Chinese.

"Do you want a ride on the windsurfer?" asked Ben.

"Okay," she said. She had been waiting patiently, hoping her chance would come before it grew too dark.

"Fantastic!" said Ben. He jumped up and walked to the surfboard. Meihua followed.

First, Meihua knelt on one end of the surfboard while Ben steered away from shore. Then, he asked her to ride on top of the board, sitting forward.

"I forgot to shave," Meihua said, looking down to her thighs. Some hairs poked out of the swimming suit.

"They look lovely," said Ben.

Meihua thought briefly about the afternoon he had spent touching her. With the stiff summer wind, the board flew across the water. After five minutes, the beach was already out of the sight.

"Come and stand in front of me," said Ben.

Meihua looked at him with some skepticism. But she trusted him and carefully moved forward. She was an accomplished swimmer and didn't fear the water.

So close to Ben, Meihua could hardly contain her excitement.

"Lower your knees like you are sitting on a chair," ordered Ben. "Yes. That's right."

The wind grew stronger. Their little surfboard sailed through the waves like a shark, breaking the waves as it moved. Suddenly, Meihua felt a strange current shooting through her body. The current was so strong, she almost lost her balance. She grabbed the sail tightly.

"Let me control the sail!" Ben commanded.

Meihua started to feel something pressing against her body from behind. Ben was pushing against her, his swimsuit pounding against her hips. Meihua could feel he was very hard and eager to attack her. She turned her head, watching his eyes glowing with bliss. Turning her body completely, she gave him a kiss. The sudden shift in weight overturned the surfboard and they fell into the water together. Holding each other tightly, they started to sink. They had forgotten about the surfboard, the guests, and the beach. In the clear water, Meihua looked at Ben's body closely and clearly. His chest and back were full of dark hair. So were his arms and legs. His short-cut swimming suit was now around his neck, and Meihua could see his naked body. There was a lot of hair around "there" too, framing a thick, strong organ, in full strength and ready to go. She couldn't look away.

Ben began removing Meihua's swimming suit. Already immersed in love and affection, Meihua let Ben do whatever he wanted. In a big hurry, Ben came quickly. Between tight

198

embraces, they occasionally rose up for gulps of air. Since they were intently kissing, the oxygen did not make much difference. She did not know how much time had passed before they paddled back to the surfboard and headed back to shore.

People were already starting to eat the food that Gretta had brought out. Changing out of her swimsuit in the bathroom, Meihua was irresistibly drawn to the sketchbook once more. She found the sketch of his lower body and stared at it with a new appreciation. With a long sigh, she quickly changed and joined the group. Although Manny seemed to sense something between her and Ben, he remained gracious. Meihua talked with some people, searching for Ben occasionally and meeting his still-passionate eyes. After they were done eating, Ben showed Meihua his paintings in the storage area. Manny and the others followed. She listened silently as Ben described many of the individual works. Soon after, she and Manny drove home mostly in silence. She did not sleep all night.

About a week later, Ben and Meihua rendezvoused again at a park a short distance from Meihua's lab. They lay close together, feeling intimacy blooming between them. "Did you enjoy that the other day?" Ben asked.

"Yes, but I can't say it was my favorite way to make love. Though, it was very exciting." Meihua looked at him with a timid smile.

Ben gazed at the parked cars on the street and sighed. This time Meihua didn't ask why. She knew better.

"I have to go back to my office and get some work done." Ben caressed her hair.

"That's fine. I'd better return to the lab." Meihua looked into his eyes eagerly, trying to find something more. Yet, she saw nothing except distance and frustration. Ben gave her a final squeeze and a kiss. They got up and walked down the hill.

"Do you want a ride?" Ben asked.

Meihua hesitated. She was torn between spending a few extra minutes with Ben and prolonging both their frustrations. She mumbled a few sentences, then said no. At the intersection, they parted.

"It was nice to see you," Ben shook Meihua's hand. This time, his grip was so tight, she was afraid he would crush her fingers. Then, he ran across the street to his car before the light changed. Meihua wished she could have followed him, but it was too late.

At ten o'clock that evening, Meihua lay in bed, waiting for Manny to return home from work. She had just talked with Ben on the phone, and the conversation resulted in sadness, which morphed into grief, then despair.

"I made love with a man the other day," he had said. "It was an accident. Gretta was still in Europe, and I was so bored that I decided to go out one night. I just happened to sit beside this guy and a group of his friends, men and women."

"Oh, my God! How do you feel?" Meihua was shocked. She had never thought of Ben being a gay man.

"It was okay, not particularly sexy or enjoyable. I thought it might be better for me to make love with a man, so I could find release and Gretta wouldn't be too jealous," Ben said matter-of-factly.

"Really? Are you going to see him again?" asked Meihua. She was beginning to hate him.

"No, I don't think so, because his long-time lover just died of AIDS. Don't worry. He said he tested negative."

"What? Are you crazy? You must be desperate. You can die from AIDS, you know!"

"I know, but who cares? I don't really like my life now." Ben's voice tapered off.

Meihua was deeply shocked. She now realized how bad his situation was. She felt sorry for him and wanted to help, but what could she do? They were both married.

"I'd better go eat my pizza. It must be cold by now." Ben paused. "I know I can't control myself. I should cut my penis off, so it won't cause any more trouble for me or anyone else. I can chop it into pieces and put them on top of my pizza like pepperonis." He was attempting humor, but it fell flat.

Meihua's heart was tangled. She felt sorry for him and wanted to cry, but she also despised him. It seemed everything with him came down to one thing: sex. That was all he wanted, not the art or the writing. It apparently didn't make any difference whether he lay with a man or a woman. Part of her understood why he needed it, but she still couldn't accept his idea of casual sex. She needed to think seriously about the remains of their relationship. Maybe it was time to put it on hold, because things were getting dangerous now. She didn't want to expose herself or Manny to AIDS.

Lying there, she stared at the wall. The portrait of Manny's grandmother, looking solemn and graceful, stared back. She heard the door and knew Manny was coming back from work. Like always, he walked in with a big smile and opened his arms to give her a hug. She bounced out of bed and hugged him tightly, appreciating what she had and what she could lose.

"Let me see your new haircut. You must be excited about it," Manny said, pulling back, but still holding her hands.

"Yes, of course. I hope you will like it this time," said Meihua quietly.

"Oh, of course. It looks nice on you." Manny gave a big smile and they hugged again.

Manny undressed and came to bed. They made long, passionate love. That night, Meihua had a nightmare. She imagined a beast chasing her in the rain. She was running like mad, shouting and trying to get away from it. Finally, she ran out of strength and fell. The beast sauntered over, flipped her body, and sat on it for a long time. When she awoke the next morning, her body felt wet all over. She sighed.

Wildfire

The fire started shortly after dawn. Black smoke blows over the Mississippi from the boathouse, hovering just above the river. Red flames shoot up like vicious devils declaring their power, as the precious wooden boats burn to ashes.

Riding my bicycle along the river, seeing the boathouse burn, rekindles the flame in my heart. The rowing season is over. So is my little interlude with Ray. The place that had been filled with beautiful moments with Ray is about to become debris and cinders. Looking at the black smoke in the distance, I cannot ignore the lingering heat in my heart. Is that what I am seeing? The still-smoldering fire in my heart?

Those long-ignored smoldering embers, nearly forgotten, have enkindled a renewed fiery passion. Through the smoke, past the blackened wooden A-frame, I can still feel Ray's wild kisses. I feel his gentle touches. In a dark corner of that boathouse, while everyone else was rowing on the river, we shared our private time together. As I watch the smoke and flames licking the sky, I feel him rubbing my hair while I licked him. I hear him whispering in my ear as his warmth swells inside me. The excitement returns, but only for a brief second, as I watch our special place burn in the distance.

I met Ray briefly several years earlier, when he was funding one of my husband Manny's research projects. We met again when he started lessons at the Minneapolis Rowing Club. To my surprise, he remembered me.

Ray had never tried rowing or any other active sport, for that matter. He did not even know how to swim. Since he owned a house on Lake Minnetonka, he thought it would be fun to learn rowing. He had seen people out in kayaks and sculls, and he admired their dedication and envied their apparent joy and tranquility. I broke the news that, unfortunately, not knowing how to swim disqualified him from rowing. However, since he was so sincere *and* could become a financial contributor to the club, the leadership decided to accept him anyway as a new student. They had him sign an agreement that released the club from any liability, should he end up drowning.

He took a turn rowing in a crew—a standard introductory exercise—but he did not like it. It was hard for him to follow other people, stroke by stroke. "Too much teamwork," he said. The other option was to learn solo sculling.

Since I was also one of those odd people who didn't like crew rowing, I became his personal sculling teacher. He was certainly not the athletic type. He was six feet, six inches tall with a prominent beer belly. He was so over-sized, he looked like an alien from a different planet. As a successful venture capitalist, he was not used to taking directions from others and was not easy to coach.

"At work, I am the commander in chief, and perhaps, the benevolent dictator to some people. But my wife, Alice, is the boss at home. You know why? She controls the cash flow." He enjoyed talking about the work that had been his life for the past twenty years—backing startup companies, financing deals, playing on Wall Street. He was financially quite successful, yet he could not stop working. He wanted to drive a Rolls-Royce someday.

Though he was not conventionally handsome, I found him attractive right away.

He reintroduced himself on the first day with, "Call me Ray." He did not even shake my hand, but I felt instantly at ease. "So, this is what you do? Just rowing up and down the Mississippi River?" He was not impressed. "I saw Ben-Hur, and it seems like a miniature version of that. I can handle it."

"It's a lot of work." I tried to convince him.

"Work? This is recreation. I have worked hard for twenty years. I know what work is like."

Beginning rowing was boring. New rowers are not allowed to row on the water initially and have to practice everything on the ergometer (rowing machine) before moving to a docked boat. Only once they've mastered these two steps can they take to the water. Because of his financial contribution, Ray was allowed to nearly bypass the docked boat step.

Ray turned out to be more athletic than he seemed. He had two strong arms with muscles shaped like dinosaur eggs, and his long legs were quite strong. However, he had no patience with the sport.

"If you think I am going to row on this stupid machine for forty minutes, you're crazy."

"That's what the training program prescribes." I was new at teaching and was just following the book.

"I think you need to apply the rules intelligently. For extra-talented students like me, you should cut practice time to ten minutes."

"Okay, but you still need to practice your patience." Somehow, I knew I was going to lose any argument with him.

"Patience? I have a lot of patience when it is worthwhile. If I didn't have twenty years of practice with my wife, I would never put up with this kind of absurdity."

Now I knew who forced him to take up rowing at the club. Later, I did find out he could be very patient with a certain kind of activity.

By bending the rules a bit, we made it onto the water during his second week. We rowed a double. I was the actual rower, demonstrating the technique. He sat in the bow as the coxswain, navigating as we rowed. Since rowing moves the boat backwards, the bow position is extremely important. But he was an older man with a responsible position in his business, and I trusted him to not crash us into anything or anyone.

During our second lesson a couple of weeks later, the weather turned humid. He dressed in a pair of jean shorts and a strange T-shirt that resembled a Twins baseball uniform.

"I left my water bottle in the Jag." He ran back to get it.

He didn't run but walked very fast. Because his legs were so long, he walked faster than most people.

"How are you doing today?" he asked.

"Bad." I liked to tease him.

"Let's see if I can cheer you up. Can cheering you up count as my tuition to the Club?"

I was beginning to understand how he had made so much money. He knew how to charm and bargain.

"Most people work for money, not fun," he said. I wondered whether I was teaching him for fun.

"So, what's on the agenda today?"

"We will try to row to the seven-mile marker—the Showboat."

"How do you know it's seven miles?" he asked.

"I was told so."

"Are you an engineer?"

"Yes."

"I thought so. A guy engineer can measure things without a ruler, but a girl engineer can never measure anything without a ruler. You know why?" He squinted his eyes and held his fingers about three inches apart. "They're always told something this long is six inches."

It was s sex joke and I got it, but I was not used to it. Manny never joked about sex or even talked about it. I blushed and was silent for a long time. Then, I decided to hit him on the shoulder, not once, but twice.

He seemed to like that.

Once, he made me so mad that I threatened to push him into the water. He was unperturbed, saying, "Think about that for a minute. If you push me into the water, you will get wet, too. You'd have to jump in to save me."

"Who said I have to save you?"

"You're legally liable."

I wanted to remind him of the liability agreement he signed a few weeks back, but I demurred. Of course, I would save him. Sometime later, I told him I would have to become very strong if I needed to pull him—a 300-pound fish—out of the water.

On a Saturday morning a couple of weeks later, the water was mirror smooth. On the edge of the dock, pockets of foam from the distant dam floated by. The water nearest the shore was covered with green moss and assorted debris where trees had fallen.

Ray and I were the only rowers at eight a.m. Getting to the boathouse by eight in the morning was a considerable challenge for him. I was glad he made it. Maybe his wife had awakened him, or maybe he made it on time because he was enjoying our time together. I hoped for the latter.

We put the boat on the water. Just before jumping in, he pointed to the floating foam by the dock, cradled his chin in his hands, and started talking in a squeaky voice, "I hate getting my clothes dirty." Sometimes he talked in an effeminate voice, which was funny, considering how masculine he was.

I ignored his sarcastic comment and we assumed our places in the boat. I pushed off from the dock and we started to row.

Even though I was the better rower, he was doing most of the work. He was the epitome of a *real man,* with muscles bulging. Rowing down the foggy river, my body seemed to levitate. I felt like I was carried up to the trees, up to the clouds, gliding in the sky.

"Way-enough." He said, giving me the command to stop. He enjoyed giving commands, which was the bow-rower's job.

I knew he had to stop to wipe his sweat. He sweated a lot, yet I enjoyed the smell of it. He handed me the water bottle, and I caught him looking at me. I had the sudden urge to embrace him, but that would be dangerous in this narrow boat.

On the way back, I saw a blue heron on the shore, hard to pick out with its color blending with the trees. "Look, a blue heron taking off. So graceful."

He did not say anything.

When we returned to shore, he said to me, "You sounded like a poet on the water."

"Besides an engineer, I am also a romantic poet. I am full of contradictions."

"Sorry, I'm not a romantic person. I decided to become an accountant when I was very young. First, public accounting, then brokerage, then venture capitalism. It's been my whole life. It's so consuming that I've never had a hobby, and my wife decided I needed one."

"I bet you can be very romantic." I did not know why I said that, and my cheeks flushed, embarrassed. But I was proven right later.

The river was a beautiful place, especially when the stars came out and the streetlights turned on. Reflections from the streetlights looked like giant candles in the river, creating another world in its depths—a heavenly world.

On one of those beautiful evenings, Ray and I finished rowing. We put the boat away and stood side by side on the grass, staring at the river.

I was not in the best of moods. Ever since Manny hurt himself skiing last winter, my life had been miserable. He could not row any more, and he considered that the worst possible thing that could happen to him. Rowing was his only real passion. Even his work did not interest him as much as it used to. Not rowing made him moody for months. Sometimes he ventured to the boathouse to watch me row, but even that was too painful for him. Instead, he spent most of his time watching TV. I thought about him and thought he must be watching *The William Buckley Show.*

Since he was a devoted conservative, that was Manny's favorite show. I could not stand staying in a house that had hour after hour of news and political debates flowing through the air. Teaching Ray twice a week became an escape—a treat. Ray was easy going and open-minded, not stuffy like Manny. I had a lot of fun with Ray, even though we were very different creatures. He was a big football fan, even holding season tickets at the Metrodome to watch the Vikings play. I couldn't care less about the sport. He was a big fan of the Beatles, a band with which I was only vaguely familiar. Born and raised in China, I had missed a whole era of modern music. I had become a classical music fan, because that was the music I grew up with. We were like apples and oranges, yet I was very much attracted to him. I liked his big round belly and small, but sharp, deep blue eyes. It took me a while to realize why I was attracted to him.

"The river is beautiful," said Ray, waking me from my deep thinking.

"I thought you lived on the water."

"I do, but lakes and rivers are very different. I never really appreciated that until now. It's different, too, in a motorboat. You're usually just watching for traffic. On the river, you see the bank, the trees, the houses, and all the reflections. Gee, I'm even starting to appreciate nature."

"Write a poem for me." I was challenging him, which was always fun for me.

210

"Hey, don't push the envelope. But keep trying—maybe after ten years, you will get a few lines out of me."

Then he turned around. "By the way, I will be on a business trip next week. I can't take lessons for a week." His two small eyes glowed like a river flowed through them.

I stepped over and hugged him.

"I will miss you." The words slipped out of my mouth.

He was silent a long time. Then, he started kissing me. His tongue forcefully filled my mouth. With the Milky Way stars as witnesses, his passionate kisses made me feel otherworldly. When was the last time I had such an experience? I could not remember.

He held my face with his big, rough hands. His face glowed under the stars and the reflections of the streetlamps.

"Meihua, what we have just done could damage both our reputations and could be dangerous."

Silence. A cold breeze made me shiver.

"It is worth it with you," I said. He showered me with more kisses. I felt tiny and cozy between his muscular arms.

I don't quite remember how I got home that night.

In the morning, he left a message on my machine at work. He said that was the most exciting thing to happen to him in an awfully long time. He wanted to have a picnic together when he returned.

On the day of the picnic, I felt young in my Hawaiian dress. Ray knew a wild section of the shoreline, just south of an old iron bridge. As we walked along the river, I teased him. "Since you haven't dated anyone in twenty years, do you know where to start?"

He turned around and kissed me. "How's that?" he asked.

We spread our blanket and listened to the birds singing in the bushes. My face grew hot, but not just from the humidity on that August afternoon.

Sitting on the blanket, we drank wine and ate fruit. At least that was the plan. Before we came here, he had said, "We could find a place where we could just touch each other for hours, but I think talking is more important."

We soon discovered kissing was our preferred way to communicate. Our tongues poked in and out of each other's mouths. Our faces rubbed against each other. We were like two birds, enjoying a freedom unavailable to human beings.

His belly was a good place to rest my head. Lying there, I could feel the warmth of his chest. His hands rubbed my head, as though I were his pet. What else could I be, his mistress? I thought a pet sounded better. Once I told him if I could be his lapdog, I would be happy.

"I dated a married man before I got married myself," I told him. "He was a talented artist, eighteen years older than me. He had a hard life in China during the Cultural Revolution, because his father was a famous poet."

"Eighteen years older! I feel like a young stud." Ray was ten years older than I was.

"I thought he would understand me since I also had a hard life in China. Somehow, it didn't work out that way. When I was not married, I always wished he could marry me, but he didn't intend to."

"You think differently now?" he asked.

"Yes. I love talented people. I love to share experiences with them. I think you are very smart and charming." I buried my head in his chest. "I want to experience things with you."

212

"I had an affair twenty years ago. I met her at work when I was at Dean Witter. We spent a lot of time talking about what was wrong with the company and the market, in general. Then, we went on business trips together. I liked the intensity."

"Intensity." I repeated. "I like that too."

We kissed and kissed, our hearts echoing along with those wet kisses. It seemed so right. Maybe we both had this uncontrollable wildfire burning in our hearts.

The first regatta of the year was the Minnesota Boat House Regatta on Lake Phalen. It was early May, and the weather was pleasant—not a rain cloud in sight. Rowers hated rain, since it usually meant a wet ride and turbulent water. The rowing shells, especially the single shells, could not take on many waves.

It was a cool, sunny day. Ray and his wife, Alice, sat on a blanket alongside Manny and me. Alice was small and compact, with short, blonde, curly hair. She had high cheekbones, deep-set eyes, and a long nose. Chinese people always notice the size of people's noses because we typically have small noses. We have nose inferiority.

People always want what they don't have. Curly-haired people want straight hair. Small-nosed people want large noses. Alice had a few things I did not have—her curly hair, her big nose, her wealth. But I had a few things she did not have. I was an engineer and a novelist; I was Chinese. I felt good about my assets and understood that nobody is perfect. I often said if you wanted a perfect man, you needed to have several. That sentiment might sound perverted, but it reflected what I genuinely felt. Besides, I came by this way of thinking honestly.

Ray was quiet in front of Alice, because Alice was such a fast talker. "I didn't know rowing was so much work," she said, talking with her hands. "I can't believe Ray ever put up with such a thing." She shot Ray a disdainful look.

I know exactly why he puts up with this hard work, I said to myself, smiling inwardly.

"Oh, so much work," she continued. "I am sorry, Ray. I pushed you so hard to try this, but you should really thank me. Look at what great shape you're in!"

She was exaggerating a little. Even though Ray had lost some weight and was developing bulging shoulder muscles, his prominent belly had not diminished. But I did not mind at all.

"Rowing makes you feel good," Manny said. "I am not surprised Ray has become addicted to it." Manny had been a true rowing addict before he injured his back on the ski slope. The injury almost killed him—and his spirit, too.

"Yeah. It's better than orgasms." I teased him.

"Sometimes that's true, although it's better to have both." Manny smiled. The trouble was Manny couldn't do either very well now. It was not fun having an injured, moody husband.

"I always think people do sports because they don't get to have sex," said Ray.

"Lay off, Ray." Alice patted his shoulder, embarrassed.

"What do you think about rowing now, Ray?" I asked.

"I haven't done enough to find out yet."

"I hope you don't strain yourself." said Alice. "I don't want you hurting yourself."

Ray and Alice seemed comfortable together, and I became a little jealous. But the feeling soon passed. That was life, I told myself.

214

One of the Minneapolis crews finally won a race against the St. Paul Rowing Club, which was very rare. I joined the other Minneapolis Rowing Club members, waving and yelling.

"Go green! Go green!"

Ray and Alice were excellent cheerleaders, probably well accustomed to cheering at football games. Yet, Manny's deep baritone was the loudest.

Most people in the Minneapolis Rowing Club were laid-back types (Manny was an exception), so we tended to win few races. It was still fun, though, and if we won, we cheered much more passionately than the St. Paul Rowing Club. The woman's crew, in particular, would kiss and hug each other. Rumor had it, some were lovers. Their excitement was so uncontrollable, they even threw people into the water.

"Everyone looks like they're having so much fun," said Alice. "I want to go to a regatta out of town. Who wants to join me?"

"They have regattas all through the summer," said Manny. "I recommend the one in August in Duluth. It's one of the best organized events."

I turned to Ray and said, "Maybe we should sign up for a race."

Before Ray had a chance to answer, Manny cut in. "Oh, sure. Doing a race would be good for you. It's great experience. I would if I could."

I went along with the idea. At the very least, it would be interesting to go with them, since I did not have many friends at the Rowing Club.

It turned out, Alice had other plans that weekend, and Manny had a meeting in Washington DC. Ray and I would go together, since we had signed up for a race.

"We have to go." I said at the end of practice one day.

He gave me a whole-hearted smile. "So, we can finally touch each other for hours."

"I guess we might be too busy to win any races."

"If we don't fall out of the boat, I'll be very happy." He stepped over, grabbed my butt, and pulled me toward him. "It will be exciting to go with you."

That night, we made love for the first time in a dark corner of the clubhouse after everyone had left. Our evening ended with more passionate, wet kisses in his car. He would not let me go. We both knew we had to go back to our own homes and spouses. Our wild moment had to end for the day. It was hard to imagine that such intensity could last, yet life often surprised me.

Friday before the Duluth regatta, Ray met me at the boathouse. It would be an exciting, comfortable drive to Duluth in his Jaguar. We loaded the boats onto the Club's trailer. First, we unrigged the boats with a wrench. Then, we lifted the boats onto the trailer shelf and tied the riggers and oars onto the side of the trailer. After the boats were hauled to Duluth, they would be unloaded and re-rigged to prep them for the races. This process was repeated twice during each regatta. People can be very patient when working on their favorite pastime.

We were on the road now. After we left the Twin Cities, I felt safe enough to kiss him. I held his arm with both hands and cuddled next to him. I kissed him on his big chin. For a long while, I stared at him, studying the face I was so attracted to.

216

He gazed into distance, looking unusually serious. His face was rosy and slightly sunburned from rowing. He had a salt-and-pepper beard, yet his hair remained its original dark color. His eyes were not large, especially compared with his large, hooked nose. I never liked large-eyed men, because they looked too innocent. My ideal man was older, mature, and a little mysterious.

His rough, radiant face and sharp eyes brought me back seventeen years, when I was a college student in Beijing. I stood at the Beijing Ping-An-Li subway station, waiting to meet my "uncle" Weiming. He was Mother's former lover, and I loved him like a father. But, seven years earlier, he had abruptly stopped visiting our home. I missed him ever since and realized I might have been secretly in love with him. Since I had not seen him in seven years, I wondered what he looked like. Finally, he appeared at the entrance of the subway station. His face was rough and radiant. He had sharp, small eyes and a big nose. His belly bulged a little, typical of a man reaching middle age. I ran toward him, wanting to give him a hug. Instead, I hesitated, and we shook hands. I had searched for him for seven years and, when he was finally in front of me, I did not know what to say.

In America, thousands and thousands of miles from Beijing, I had found a man who resembled my long-lost father figure and fantasy lover back in China. This explained why I had been so attracted to him right away.

"Want to have dinner?" Ray asked, bringing me back to reality.

We ate pizza at Toby's Restaurant. I did not tell him he resembled my long-lost father. I was afraid he would be offended. Instead, I told him about an enthralling affair story I had read in the New Yorker.

"Armand Hammer married a very rich woman. After he built his empire with her money, he fell in love with another woman. That woman became his long-time girlfriend and travel companion. Before he appointed her as head of the Armand Hammer Collection of artwork, he asked her to undergo plastic surgery to change her identity, so his wife would not be suspicious."

He listened silently, then remarked, "Maybe you have to do the same thing."

I smiled and did not believe him for a second. I was proud of my appearance, and Ray certainly found me attractive.

By the time we arrived in Duluth, it was already dark. Having made the last-minute decision to attend the race without Manny and Alice, we had left without hotel reservations. We tried a few local hotels, but the ones that met Ray's high standards were all booked.

"Looks like we have to sleep by the lake," I said, half-joking. "We could borrow sleeping bags and a tent from the Club's supply trailer. They always bring camping equipment, just in case."

"Sleeping outside? No way!"

I knew that would be a radical change for him, but we had no choice.

"Come on. You have spent your life in hotels. This will be a new experience for you."

We picked up the camping gear. He remained skeptical, until we drove past Grandma's Restaurant, approached the High Bridge, and parked by the North Shore of Lake Superior.

It was unbelievably beautiful. The lake was showered with reflections of bright stars. Waves washing over the shore sounded like Mother Nature breathing. Crickets chirped everywhere, announcing the beginning of a nocturnal party.

Standing in front of this vast lake, I thought about things beyond my everyday existence. What might life be like on another planet like Mars? What kind of society would we have? Could Ray and I solve our problems by flying to the moon and living happily ever after?

At the campground, we set up the tent on a small hill with a clear view of the lake. The only other tent in sight was maybe thirty yards away. The breeze off the lake made us both shiver, and we scurried into the tent and lay down on our unrolled sleeping bags. He kissed me. It was so intense, my breath caught in my throat. I tried pushing him away just to tease him, but he held me tighter.

We sat up and started drinking wine: a red, dry variety for him, and a sweet, white one for me. He was a wine connoisseur, and I knew nothing about wine.

The screen window of our tent looked over the sky and the lake. "The stars are our witnesses," I said. "They are watching us here."

"Better stars than people."

"If she found out, what would she do?" I was curious and did not think about the seriousness of the question.

"We wouldn't know because we'd both be dead," he said in a serious voice.

Although his tone and the answer scared me, I did not want to spoil the moment.

"If our spouses had watched us tonight, they both would have been very jealous," I said.

Our relationship was not about sex. It was about sensuality. It was about unearthing the passion inside an unromantic person like Ray. It was about a young woman who had never truly connected with her father and spent her entire life searching for older men to compensate for her father's absent love. It was about hungering for something natural in this materialistic society, something that touched our hearts, despite it violating societal norms.

After an active and sleepless night, we still managed to make our race. There were three boats in our division. We won the bronze medal, despite coming in last place.

Many people cheered us on. Being in the beginners' class, our boat was the last one in the last race. By the time we finished, everybody was hungry.

The celebration dinner was held in the Duluth Rowing Club. It was a potluck, with local rowers providing a variety of food. People sat around in sweat-soaked tights and T-shirts, eating spaghetti and salad. Toward the end of the dinner, somebody announced that the awards ceremony was about to start. Ray and I stepped up to accept our medals. We were proud, even though it was almost a joke. This was the first athletic award Ray had ever won. Before rowing, the closest thing to a sport he had tried was the debate team.

"You should thank me for this," I said, as we high-fived.

"Thank you for what?"

"Aren't you glad you tried the race?"

"Absolutely. How about you?" He stared at me with his magical eyes. Each one contained an entire galaxy, reflecting the inner world whose existence he often denied.

"Of course." What else could I say? I hugged him, in a friendly, publicly-acceptable way.

Soon, loud rock and roll music started playing. The crowd drifted upstairs and began drinking and dancing. We found a dark corner on the upstairs balcony. Standing close, we each nursed a bottle of beer.

A few young rowers got drunk. They took off their pants and mooned each other. Then, they tried to throw each other off the balcony.

Watching, Ray laughed and laughed.

"You probably haven't seen this kind of activity since high school," I commented.

"I went to Catholic high school. We didn't do things like that. The nuns pretty much kept us in step."

"You went to Catholic high school?" I feigned surprise.

"So?"

"What do you say about us in confession?"

"I'm not a practicing Catholic anymore. But I bet those horny priests are dying to hear a juicy love story."

More dancers joined the crowd. The upstairs balcony started shaking up and down along with the music's rhythm.

It felt dangerous. It felt chaotic. It felt dynamic. The building could collapse at any moment, it seemed. Yet, everyone was drunk and nobody cared.

Ray and I stared at the star-filled sky. Northern lights shot up from the horizon and lit the sky, so bright it scarcely seemed like night. We turned and looked at each other silently, communicating with our eyes. Someone once said that was how people fell in love—they saw each other's souls through their eyes.

That night we were able to find a hotel room. Once, he told me if I ever wrote about him, the sex part would have to be good, since he had a reputation to protect.

That night, he lived up to his reputation.

We drove back in the morning. It was sad, and we didn't talk much. I just cuddled next to him, holding his arm. We both knew we would probably no longer see each other much, since the rowing season was almost over.

When I returned home, Manny told me he knew Ray and I were having an affair. He would forgive me if I promised not to see him anymore. He also met privately with Ray and made him promise the same thing.

Ray and I saw each other one more time. It was at Seafood Palace, a Chinese restaurant. Like many other Chinese restaurants, you could smell it before you could see it. Fryer oil mixed with garlic, onion, and ginger rushed to my nose and filled the surrounding air. People either liked the smell and immediately craved Chinese food or hated the smell and ran away. The place was mysterious, with only one grease-covered window letting in a modicum of light and sheltering the interior from prying eyes. Yet, when we walked in, the small wooden tables and tiny chairs were filled with happy diners. They sat next to each other, elbow to elbow.

Ray and I sat across from each other. We both knew that if we sat elbow to elbow, the attraction between us would be uncontrollable. We would end up on top of each other, kissing, hugging, and everything else, right in public.

Instead, we stared at each other. Our feet touched. His staring was so intense, I felt his invisible touch. We tried and tried to reach out to each other, but we had a wall between us. That wall was so high, neither of us dared to scale it.

"I promised your husband I would keep my hands off you. I have no choice." Ray's voice was sad and a little weak.

"Maybe we could have a platonic relationship," I murmured.

"Platonic? We have already done it. It's not platonic anymore."

He was right. Like many questions in life, we did not have an answer for this one. Maybe after a while, we would figure out an answer. Maybe time itself would solve it. I knew in this moment how much we wished to reach out to each other and start everything all over again.

The fire from the boathouse still burned. Smoke filled the sky, making it dark. Sirens wailed everywhere, as firefighters attempted to save a few surrounding trees. Not much remained, except for the boathouse's blackened wooden frame. I wondered what else had been destroyed by the fire.

"Waves"

Waves hit the shoreline, generating thousands of bubbles and pushing up millions of seashells. The air was salty and moist. He, sitting in his usual chair, stared at the ocean. I, just returning from body surfing, was wet and happy. Hugging him from behind, I gave him a wet kiss.

"Are you having fun?" he asked.

"Yes. How about you?"

"I fell asleep for a while."

"You old man, what else can you do?"

We had been going to the beach every day for the past year. Even though he hardly could walk, he seemed happy to have my company. The heart attack and subsequent heart failure had nearly paralyzed him, and his wife had left, so I—his former lover—decided to take care of him. I had somehow always looked forward to this day. When my father was dying, I hated him so much that I never went to see him. Now that someone I loved was in decline, I felt the need to be there—to be the caretaker I couldn't be for my dad. But how wicked the idea was. When we had first met, neither of us were free. Yet, I had always thought I would be of some use to him in the future. Fifteen years later, he needed me. Even though I was not free when he needed my care, I decided to do it anyway. I told my husband what I was doing, and somehow, he understood.

Here I was. A week after he called, I flew to see him. He and his wife met me at the airport. Seeing him in a wheelchair made me cry. I rushed over and kissed him passionately right in front of his wife. *She is leaving*, I figured. His kisses were still very forceful.

After we arrived at his oceanside house, we could not wait to take each other's clothes off. After I helped him into bed, he touched me all over and I enjoyed sucking his long, rounded private part. The familiar intimacy returned to us.

From then on, we were together day after day. Usually, we spent the whole morning in bed, kissing and touching each other. Then, we'd go to a restaurant for wine and lunch. After that, we'd have the ocean all to ourselves. Sometimes, we would read a book together. Sometimes, I would sketch a portrait of him. Sometimes, he even sketched mine. In the evening, we would snuggle in our little home theater, watching an old movie until we fell asleep. We rarely had outside contact. We never felt we needed the company.

Staring at the ocean, I heard a little voice.

"Here is the 'Li-mama.' This is the 'Big-daddy.' I am the 'Little-piggy.' We are such a happy family."

Three of us sat on the swinging chair outside of our oceanfront motel in Cocoa Beach. We swung back and forth, back and forth, following the wind and the rhythm of the sea. Occasionally "Little-piggy," who was four years old, climbed to the top of a chair while holding onto a rope.

"Where is my little robot?"

"Here it is."

I, the "Li-mama," picked up a can-opener (robot) from the sand and gave it to Little-piggy.

The robot had two legs, one with a feeler and one without, two wings on an axle that went around and around, and two mouths, one for eating and one for speaking.

"The robot is dead," said Little-piggy.

"Robots can't be dead. It can be fixed. They are not like people."

"People can be fixed, too. That is what doctors do."

I was surprised at how smart Little-piggy had become. He used to think doctors poured water on people's heads to make them feel better. He confused them with barbers.

"You are right. When people are injured, doctors can usually fix them."

"Let's take the robot to the hospital to give him an operation."

We ran back to the motel room. The Jiminy Cricket jumped down from the shelf.

"Jiminy Cricket is the doctor," said Little-piggy.

A loud, grinding sound filled the air. Jiminy Cricket covered the robot with seashells. The operation began.

"The robot is fixed."

"It's time for bedtime stories! What are we going to tell this time?"

"The story of Mistry and Blink," said Little-piggy.

"One day, the magician Mistry was in his study, planning a new show." Big-daddy started the story. "Meanwhile, the kitty Blink was bored and went up to the rooftop to look around. He spotted a smokestack emitting puffs of smoke. Being a curious kitty as always, he looked directly into the chimney. His eyes were sensitive, so the smoke burned them as soon as he peered over the edge. Before he could turn his head away, another puff of smoke drifted out. He became so dizzy, he fell right down the chimney. Inside the house, Mistry was very hungry and was cooking a big pot of soup in a fire beneath the chimney. Stirring the soup with a ladle, Mistry was just about to spoon some into his bowl when down came the kitty Blink. Blink fell right into the soup.

I had been crying for three days. It was time for me to go, to return to my own family. But I was not ready. Every day I snuggled next to him, crying. He rarely said anything. We ate, and I helped him to the bathroom in silence. On the third day, we decided to go to the beach.

The sky was cloudy, and the sea wild. I asked him if he was cold. He shook his head. We approached our usual spot.

"Keep pushing!" he yelled, just before I stopped.

I did, but had to stop as we came to the wet sand.

"Keep pushing!"

I stopped and he tried to keep the wheelchair moving towards the surf.

"Stop!"

"You will be free if I go."

I had to run fast to stop him from spilling into the ocean and getting swallowed by the violent waves.

I pulled him back. Shaking his head, he was furious. I had rarely seen him so angry with me.

"I can't believe you want to die like this. Aren't you happy with me? Aren't you?" I was angry, too. Deep inside, I wanted to stay with him. He needed me, and I loved his company. Yet, there was the other part of my life—the family who also needed me. Sometimes, I was not sure which part of my life had a stronger attraction.

I pushed him home in silence. I had to wake him up to get him out of the wheelchair. Leaning against the pillows, he turned on the TV with the remote control. I jumped next to him. I kissed him on the cheek. He turned around and started kissing me passionately.

"Should we watch some football?"

I nodded and rested one hand comfortably on his belly, occasionally on his privates. He liked it. I leaned against his big body for a long time, only getting up briefly to order Chinese food. After dinner, we watched *Cider House Rules* in our own little theater. The movie was about an old doctor who worked in an orphanage. Among the many unwanted babies he delivered, a precocious child named Homer caught his attention. Homer grew into an intelligent young man and mastered the skills the old doctor had taught him. He became the protégé of the doctor, who intended for him to take over his practice. Yet, Homer had different ideas. After spending his life in the orphanage, he wanted to travel the world. So, he left. The old doctor, who loved him like a son, was extremely sad and did everything he could to get Homer back. But he was not successful. Later, the doctor died of an ether overdose. After hearing this sad news, and with his brief love affair coming to an end, Homer decided to return to the orphanage and take over the doctor's job.

The movie brought me to tears. I felt like Homer—so very much like Homer. I didn't want to leave my old lover, who needed me. He looked at my tear-filled eyes with understanding. Then, he kissed me passionately.

"I have seen the world. I don't have to leave."

He nodded and kissed me more.

"Let's go swimming," said Little-piggy. It was the morning of our second day in Orlando, and we had not yet tried the heated swimming pool.

"What a good idea," said Big-daddy.

"I want to play 'Crab,'" said Little-piggy.

"Crab" was a game Little-piggy had invented that summer at the University Club's swimming pool. During the game, I was the Crab—the evil being who tried to capture the good guys, Little-piggy and Big-daddy.

When we arrived at the swimming pool, Little-piggy grabbed a lifesaver.

"So I don't get drowned," he said in a mature tone.

We started chasing each other around the warm pool. Whenever they cornered me at the edge of the pool (this was the only way they could catch me), Little-piggy would use his hands as sharp claws to scare me. I would, of course, escape. Sometimes I would try to grab his legs, and he would cry for help.

"Big-daddy, save me!"

He found another lifesaver floating in the water. "Use this to catch the Crab and put her in jail," he said.

"Good idea."

Soon, I found my head buried within three lifesavers. I could hardly breathe. Little-piggy and Big-daddy sat on the swimming pool steps, laughing.

"Crab is in jail. Crab is in jail," they chanted.

We were getting ready for supper. He was cooking his specialty, nachos supreme. I was making Chinese dumplings. The phone rang.

"Hello!"

"Hi, Li-mama!"

"Oh, this must be Little-piggy."

"Oink, oink!"

"Are you and Big-daddy having fun?"

"Yeah, but we are wondering when you're coming home."

"Oh, as soon as I'm done here."

"Okay. Bye, Li-mama! Here is the Big-daddy."

"Hi."

"Hi."

"Em… you think you'll be home soon?"

"I don't know yet."

"Little-piggy and I are lonely without you."

"I will try to come home soon."

"We will be waiting patiently for you."

"Bye."

We ate our dinner in silence, each of us waiting for the other to start a conversation. No one opened their mouth, except to bring food to it. After dinner, he made a point of doing the dishes, which was usually my job. I let him do it. Then, we sat on the couch, as he channel surfed with the remote.

"You should go home." He let the words sneak between his teeth.

"Who is going to take care of you?"

"Don't you realize I can live without you? You have only been here two months and you think I can't live without you? I could hire a maid."

His voice grew louder and louder.

"A maid would be cheaper."

"How could you say that?" I collapsed on his lap and started sobbing.

"This is my house. I can say anything I want. You get out tomorrow."

"I am leaving right now." I got up and wiped my tears. I rushed out the door.

What a jerk, I told myself. I had wasted my love on him.

Music played on the beach, and a bonfire glowed in the distance. Like an adventurer finding a new continent, I ran toward it.

The next-door neighbor, an artist, was hosting a beach party. African drummers beat a constant rhythm. Dancers circled the fire, their hair wreathed with flowers.

"Hi, welcome to the party." Andy, the artist neighbor, greeted me. He wore a pair of natural-colored, drawstring pants and no shirt. His crewcut made him look younger than his forty-five years. His eyes glowed with life.

"Come, join the dance."

"Okay."

"You have to take off your top."

I looked around and realized that most of men wore no tops and most of women wore only bras. I took off my T-shirt and joined the dancers.

The breeze, warmed by the fire, blew my hair and encircled my body. I wanted to sing, to yell. I felt life. I felt energy.

232

I danced until my hair was matted down and my body was drenched with sweat.

"Come tomorrow. An interesting model is going to pose for us," Andy said, as I was putting on my top.

When I returned home, I found him waiting in his wheelchair outside.

"What's the ruckus out there?"

"It was the craziest party I have ever been to."

"Had sex?"

"No, only innocent spirituality."

"Yeah?"

We went to bed in silence.

In the morning, I cooked his favorite breakfast—sausage and eggs.

"Now you've found our next-door neighbor sexy. Don't you want to go over there?" That was the only thing he said during the whole breakfast.

"Maybe you should go with me," I said. "Then, you can see the beautiful model."

"Are you sure you want me to go?"

"Sure. Who said I don't love you anymore?"

"I hugged him from behind and kissed his cheek. He turned and gave me a long, wet kiss.

It was obvious this was an artist's house. Instead of displaying real flowers, the two giant bronze flowerpots by the front pillars held flowers sculpted of bronze. They were abstract flowers, with small, naked human bodies engraved on them.

"Hi, I'm glad you made it." Andy came over and gave me a hug and a kiss on the cheek.

I could tell Ray was a little jealous. I pushed him forward and said, "This is my dear friend, Ray."

"How do you do?" Andy shook hands with him. "I have seen you two on the beach a lot."

"Just about all the time," said Ray.

"Yes. I really like the fresh air. He has been trying to ditch the wheelchair, jump into the ocean, and take a long swim to China."

"Yes," Ray said. "That seems to bother somebody."

"Of course, a lot!" I could not help yelling at him.

"Okay. Let's have some fun here before you two decide whether it's better to die or not." Andy cut in casually, as though he had to deal with life and death every day.

"This is Cash. She is going to be our model today. He introduced a green-haired, African-American lady who looked about eighteen. She wore a red tank top over her bra and a pair of black tights. Her smile radiated from her dark-brown skin.

Each of us was given a piece of clay to work with. I had never known that kneading clay was such an emotional process. My emotions passed directly from my heart, through my fingers, to the clay. One could mold a piece of clay into their lover and make love to it. Although not as involved as I was, Ray did a good job sculpting the model's body. But the face was blank.

"Ray, I can tell you got all the important parts right," I teased.

"I have studied women's anatomy."

"How about the face? Why is it blank?"

"I'm not done yet. I had to get her vital parts ready first."

He liked to sound like a regular guy. Actually, he was a regular guy. I still could not figure out why I was so madly in love with him. When it comes to love, one does not need to know why, at least for me.

"You two are natural artists," said Andy, looking at Ray's life-sized sculpture.

"I think it looks a bit like Meihua."

"Yeah. She is the only woman I have now."

"You should come here more often. We have a lot of women you can meet," said Andy slyly.

Cash wandered over, and Andy gave her a big kiss in front of everyone. He turned to me while still cradling Cash.

"Yours is more like Matisse with the disproportional long limbs. It is beautiful."

"I had never thought I would enjoy sculpturing so much."

"You should come for my class."

Twice a week, Ray and I went to Andy's house for art class. Occasionally, we invited everyone back to Ray's house for dinner. Ray entertained them with his cooking skills, with me as his assistant. Time passed quickly. Ray's wife, Alice, called and said she wanted to visit.

"Should I leave?" I stared at him with my big eyes, imaging them so transparent he could see right through me.

"No. I don't want you to go." He shook his head. "I want her to see I can live happily without her. And we should rent a sailboat and have a yacht party with Andy and the gang. We should ask Little-piggy and Big-daddy to come too."

I dove into his chest, eyes moist.

"Ray, I didn't know you adopted a family," said Alice.

"Does that bother you?"

"If it's okay with them, I don't care."

Five of us sat around the dining table: Ray, Alice, Little-piggy, Big-daddy, and me.

"We are here to have a beach vacation," said Big-daddy, matter-of-factly.

"Yeah. We are doing bodysurfing tomorrow, aren't we?" Little-piggy chirped.

"How about tonight?" said "Big-daddy. "Once, I saw a squid on the bottom of the sea during night snorkeling."

"Not here," said Ray. "The sea turns into a monster at night and could swallow you."

"Ouch!"

After dinner, I showed Little-piggy and Big-daddy the guest bedroom.

"Are you going to stay?" Big-daddy asked.

I nodded.

"Let's tell each other a story," said Little-piggy.

"That's a good idea." I sprawled across one double bed, while Big-daddy and Little-piggy shared the other.

Big-daddy started the story. "Once upon a time, there was a dog named 'Five-hands.' Instead of feet, he had five hands and five pockets."

"The villagers thought he was a magic dog," continued Little-piggy, "since every time he put one of his hands into his pockets, a treasure came out. Once, he took out a golden ring, another time a giant ruby. He became the most popular dog in the village."

"Then one day," Big-daddy tagged on, "he lost his magic. He put one of his hands in a pocket and nothing came out. He put another hand in a pocket, nothing again. When he put his last hand in the last pocket, he only found a little silver ring and a little egg."

I lay on the bed, listening, not wanting to say anything.

"The villagers were disappointed," said Little-piggy. "They wanted Five-hands to leave the village. Then, a little boy came along. 'An egg is a treasure,' said the boy. He took the ring and egg and offered them both to a legless man, who was sitting in a wheelchair. As soon as the ring touched the man, wings grew from his back and he flew away. The end."

Everyone gathered at the harbor when it was time to set sail. The sky was blue, the sea violent, as usual.

"There is a 50 percent chance of a storm. Should we go?" The bearded captain asked Ray.

Ray contemplated the captain's words. "Let's do it. I don't have parties like this often. We don't have to go far, just anchor somewhere offshore. Besides, a storm will make it more exciting."

"What, are you thinking about a long swim to China again?" I asked.

"And taking twenty people with me," said Ray. He was in a good mood.

"Yes, sir."

At first, it was a fun ride. Everyone took turns sailing the boat for a while, even seven-year-old Little-piggy. Nobody sailed the boat badly enough to cause sea sickness. Upbeat salsa music played, and Andy encouraged everyone to dance, no matter how young, old, or disabled. Even Ray danced with his hands, which became easier after a few drinks.

Then, the wind picked up. Big waves crashed against our fifty-foot boat, and we started rolling up and down, like a roller coaster. Everyone was soaked. Some passengers began to vomit.

"Try bailing out the water," said the captain. "We're sailing back!"

"Andy, steady the sail. Meihua, help take down the spinnaker."

Everyone worked in unison under this wind, under this storm, against these huge waves.

Fog

I drove frantically in the rain, in the dark, in the fog. Rain splattered my windshield. The wipers worked hard, but couldn't clear the fog rolling up from the Mississippi. They couldn't clear the darkness I drove into.

I was talking to Ray on a cell phone through my Bluetooth headset. He was out of town again in New York, schmoozing on Wall Street. He was at his hotel, working. It was 8:30 p.m. there.

"Hi, Ray!"

"Hi." He was not surprised to hear from me any time of day.

"Are you still working?"

"Yeah. I actually *do* work here. It's not all power lunches and expensive dinners."

"We all think you're just living the high life."

"It's a common misconception."

"Lots of pretty secretaries?"

"I wish."

"Right. You specialize in office romance."

"Got a PhD in it."

"Hey, do you have time to hear about a movie I just watched?"

"Okay." He didn't sound excited—his excitement was only reserved for sex.

"It's called *Le Divorce*, a French movie."

"A chick flick."

"Of course."

He was a macho man. He didn't like chick flicks, yet he loved chicks. He couldn't live without them.

"The main character's sister is in her early twenties and she decides to have an affair with an aging politician who is fifty-five years old."

"He's old!" Ray laughed. He was only one year younger.

"The affair was pleasant, but heartless. It was supposed to be secret, because he was married."

"That's why it's called an affair! Duh."

"On the day after their first meeting, she received a package delivery. Inside the package was a big, red purse.

'An expensive gift from an admirer,' her sister commented. The purse was called Kelly, after actress Grace Kelly.

'Don't accept expensive gifts from a man,' her sister advised.

'Why?' she asked.

'Because then you will be obliged to do things for him,' said her sister.

'I'll do *things* anyway,' the young woman replied." I couldn't help but laugh. Ray didn't give me purses, but I did things with him anyway.

"Why didn't you ever give me a purse?" I asked Ray, even though I knew it was a stupid question.

"Because I really need to keep our relationship a secret."

"You're right. As soon as the young woman carried her new purse on the street, people knew who her lover was. A lot of other girls had been given the same purse by this man."

240

Ray joked, "I would have to buy them wholesale and give them away one at a time."

"Where is mine?"

"I ran out. You think I just sit on the couch alone every night?"

"I know. At least you should give me a scarf to end our affair gracefully."

"I don't want to end it. You are my Minneapolis girlfriend."

We could go on like this forever. The truth was, I didn't actually know what he did in New York, Boston, Chicago, and all his other travel destinations. I only saw him when he was in town.

I hadn't seen him in a while, almost two years. We had met several years ago when he was funding my first husband's medical research ventures. Later, when I was ready to go back to work after my baby, he got me a job at one of the medical companies he had helped to found. He wasn't around the building much. Typically, he only stopped by for board meetings, which were usually in the evening. Two months ago, we ran into each other in the basement.

I was putting away old files in the storage room, when he walked into the room to search for some old financial papers. We looked at each other. His eyes were like hooks that pulled me right into his chest. He closed and locked the door.

"I've missed you!" His hands were on my breasts.

I closed my eyes and kissed him.

When I opened my eyes, my surroundings changed. We were lying together on a white-sand beach. A multi-colored beach towel spread beneath us. The ocean was blue and filled with parasailing boats, their colorful parachutes in the air.

We did meet in Florida once. He had arranged a financial meeting at one of his companies where I needed to do some equipment testing. We traveled separately. When I got there, he was waiting for me at the airport with a big grin. After calling home and telling Tom I had arrived at Miami safely, I followed him to the parking garage where his rented Mercedes convertible waited. After sliding into the seat, I gave him a kiss.

"Are we going to a restaurant?" I asked.

"Are you hungry?" He sounded like he had no dinner plans at all.

"Starving. I need nourishment."

"Yes, of course. You have some hard work ahead of you."

We stopped at a dark strip mall with a storefront French Bistro and a Subway sandwich shop.

He threatened to take me to Subway, but after my repeated protests, agreed to take me to the fancy French restaurant next door. I knew he would never go to a Subway anyway. He reveled in luxury. Staying at anything less than a Four Seasons Hotel was considered a camping trip. I didn't know what had happened to him today. *He must be anxious to see me.* I was telling myself.

The French Bistro was dark. Candles on the tables simulated a romantic environment. A bottle of French red wine arrived first, followed by olives and bread. The wine was supposed to be good and expensive, yet I didn't enjoy it. The best wine I had ever tasted outside of China was Croatian wine. The French wine was so new, it still had a hint of grape flavor.

My sea bass entrée was small and over-cooked. The mashed potatoes were fine, but the asparagus was soft and tasteless, even in season.

"The lamb chop was excellent," commented Ray. But I had no interest in lamb.

We didn't say much. He commended the French restaurant on its fare.

"I guess the best part was the wine," I said, trying to be agreeable.

"Yeah. Wine can be great, but only if you match it to your meal."

"In my opinion, French food is usually overpriced and has small portions. But for someone who doesn't even appreciate wine, I don't have a right to comment on the French food." I was not used to expensive French restaurants and drinking expensive wine.

"It's too bad. I'm trying to get you drunk, you know."

"Come on. You should know better. I can act drunk without drinking." I tried to lighten up a little.

We left the restaurant, and half the bottle of wine.

The hotel was a typical Westin. As the clerk behind the shining wooden counter checked me in, Ray sat on a couch and checked his cell phone messages. He tried to stay as invisible as possible.

When I finished checking in, he followed me to the elevator and then to my room. He was quiet. We both knew what was coming. We kissed each other on the lips for a while, then I let go.

"I have to make a phone call," I said.

"Sure, take your time. You are worth waiting for." He understood my situation.

I wandered outside to the heated pool. The water was empty, as usual. It was amazing how much energy the hotel wasted on heating the largely unutilized pool. I usually made good use of it, though. Every time I stayed at a hotel with a heated pool, I would try to swim. But this time, I wouldn't have the time.

I scanned the wall for windows to see if he was watching me, but our room appeared to be on the opposite side.

Sitting on one of the plastic chairs and putting my feet on another, I called home.

"Hello." My son, Little-piggy, picked up the phone.

"What are you up to?" I said.

"Doing homework."

"Are you almost done? It's almost bedtime."

"Yeah. I also played piano."

"You are a good boy."

"Of course. Do you want to talk to Daddy?"

"Yes."

My husband, Tom, came on the line. "How are you?"

"Good." I answered and wasn't really lying.

"Where are you staying?"

"The Westin."

"Where is it?"

"A little way from the airport, near Transmedics, where I'm going tomorrow. The outdoor pool looks great and it's empty."

"Are you going to swim?"

"Yeah, very soon."

I returned to the room. Seeing me coming back, Ray turned off the TV. He stared at me with a magnetic glow in his eyes—it grabbed me and pulled. Our lips touched; his hands were on my breasts. His touch was magical, and I became lost in ecstasy. He licked me as though I were a delicious entrée. I let out quiet a moan. He then moved on to his dessert, which was liquid. He finished the last course with a bang.

We lay naked on the bed. He sipped red wine from the minibar; I was half asleep and feeling unsettled. I wanted to tell him I was not totally committed. I wished I could be more for him, but I was not ready. When you are married with a child, affairs are least destructive if they're kept secret from family. I remembered my rules with Ray: It's only sex and it can't get in the way of either of our work or home lives.

I woke up in the morning and noticed he was gone. I called his cell.

"Why did you leave?"

"I had to go out and get something."

"I have never had a boyfriend walk out on me like that."

"I'm sorry. Next time I will be more attentive. Should I come and get you at 7 a.m.?"

"Ok, I'll try to get ready by then."

At 7 a.m. sharp, I waited outside in the sun. After about ten minutes, he drove up in his convertible. We had talked about the risk of driving to Transmedics together, but few people knew us there, so we decided it was safe.

I jumped in. He drove silently during the short trip. The wind blew my hair into octopus tentacles, and I remembered why I don't like convertibles.

"Make sure you act professional in there," he said. He sounded cold and distant. He had already switched into business mode, which I could never get used to.

"When have you ever seen me behaving unprofessionally?" I grinned. "Maybe a little last night."

We arrived at a green office building; morning sunlight danced off its windows. I had forgotten how much earlier the sun rises on the East Coast. I looked around and saw nothing but tall office buildings and sprawling industrial warehouses. I wondered if there were any sidewalks where I could stretch my legs during lunch.

We walked through the marble entrance and took the elevator to the second floor. No receptionist greeted us, and instead, we had to call someone to let us into the secure office area. The spacious room was illuminated by sunshine streaming through the enormous windows. Once inside, we each called our contacts and set about our separate tasks. Ray went to the large conference room with the company President, and I went to the lab with the head of Test Engineering.

I began my calibration procedure by running through the series of tests. I had done this dozens of times and could probably perform the procedure blindfolded. My boss would often complain that the company could run the calibration procedure themselves, but they felt more comfortable having me do it, since I was part of the group who had originally designed the tester. The office suite was large, but with all the glass, I could see Ray through the conference room's side window. He appeared to be deep in a serious conversation. Watching him, my mind drifted to the night before. I felt dazed. How could we work in the same office and pretend nothing had happened?

As lunchtime neared, Ray entered the lab with a man I recognized as the company president. He was tall and skinny, with a crew cut, a hooked nose, and a slightly protruding chin. "Jack, this is Meihua from Minneapolis. I've known her for years." Ray turned to me. "Working hard, Meihua?" He said it in that sarcastic way of his. This time, it didn't sound as funny.

"When do you ever see me *not* working hard?"

"How do you do, Meihua?" Jack shook my hand. His gaze lingered on me, as though I were naked, which was my own fault. I was wearing a low-cut top and a pair of pants that were especially tight around the hips. The trip was a surprise, and I had packed in a hurry, thinking about Florida and warm weather, not about my professional image. I was dressed like a loose woman and felt like one, too. Still staring, he seemed to be mentally undressing me, as though I were emitting a special scent that aroused all men's instincts. It surely worked last night. Could he sense what Ray and I had done the night before? He took his eyes off me before I started screaming.

But part of me was flattered by Jack's attention. I had first met him last year, while running the same calibration test during an all-company meeting. He was terribly rude to me that day, maybe because I was an outsider. What had made Jack change his attitude toward me? I mulled this over for the next hour or so, not paying much attention to my work. We didn't break for lunch until 1 p.m., because Ray was stuck on a lengthy phone call. I had long finished my testing by then and was ready to leave.

I suggested Cuban food, and Jack drove us to a nearby Cuban restaurant in his big Lexus. Besides the chips and salsa, we each ordered a plate of saffron rice and some smoked pork. Enjoying such interesting food made this trip worthwhile. During lunch, Ray didn't say much. Jack talked about his hobbies, one of which was surfing.

"I saw some surfers when I was here last year," I said, trying to keep the conversation flowing. "It looks fun and addictive, but I don't think I could handle it."

"You look like you could do it," said Jack. He was no longer visually undressing me, which made it easier to converse with him. "The surf's much better up north, but we make do down here."

"Yeah, I think she could do a certain kind of surfing," said Ray in his usual deadpan voice.

"I have tried body surfing in the Caribbean," I said innocently.

"Body surfing? That's a little different," said Jack.

After lunch, Jack dropped us off by Ray's convertible. I wondered if Ray had told him about us.

"When are you coming back?" he asked, directed at both of us, but mostly at Ray.

"When duty calls," said Ray. For someone who had never served in the military, it was amazing how many military terms he used in conversation. I kept my mouth shut.

Ray drove his convertible under the hot Florida sun. I glanced at the clock. "Oh, we have extra time."

"Yeah, are you surprised?"

"No."

He winked at me.

We took a short walk by the ocean, watching people fishing and kids playing under the sun. The ocean was vivid blue and the sun bright—what else did we need? But we both wanted something more.

After the walk, we drove back to the Westin. We grabbed our bags, Ray quickly re-checked us in, and we proceeded to the room. As soon as the door closed behind us, we kissed. I headed to the bathroom to change into the lingerie I had brought to surprise him. When I emerged, he was standing in front of the work desk, buck-naked. He was typing on his laptop. I jumped behind him and touched his groin. He turned his head. Before he could kiss me, I ran away toward the windows. He chased after me. We both fell onto the couch. We kissed each other. His hands touched my breasts through the silky lingerie, gently rubbing back and forth. I loved it. I screamed with joy and grew wet. Then, he flopped back on the couch, his right hand clutching his chest.

"Take my pulse," he said.

Looking at my watch, I felt his throbbing wrist for fifteen seconds. I was amazed by how fast it was going.

"Two hundred and five." Stunned, I mentally ran the calculations.

"Drive me to the emergency room." At least he was calm enough to think.

"Okay."

I darted to his laptop, ran a Google search, and found a university hospital nearby. We dressed swiftly but silently. I grabbed my purse and his car keys off the desk. We went downstairs and he slid into the passenger seat. The leather seats were hot, but I didn't mind. I rolled out of the parking lot, surprised by how easily the car handled compared to my old Audi.

Speeding the few short blocks to the hospital, I parked the car and checked him into the emergency room. He already had his insurance card out and handed it to me while he sat nervously in a nearby chair

"Are you his wife?" asked the nurse.

"No, a co-worker. This happened at work and we are from out of town." I quickly concocted the lie.

"I see."

I waited outside while they examined him. It was excruciating. I thought about calling his wife, Alice, but decided to wait for the results before calling. I worried and felt partially responsible for his condition.

After about an hour, a nurse came up to me and said, "He is doing well. He had a bout of atrial fibrillation. Pretty common. We had to give him a shock. Before we can discharge him, we'll have to keep him under observation for another three hours."

"Okay. Can I see him?"

"You may."

She led me back to a curtained cubicle. He was sitting up on a wheeled bed with just a hospital gown on. Wires ran from his arm to the cardiac monitor and EKG. Despite what had happened, he looked calm. A nurse buzzed around, taking a blood sample and checking his vital signs—blood pressure, heart rate, blood oxygen level. "I'll come back in half an hour," she said.

"Should I call Alice?" I asked.

"I'll take care of it." He dialed his cell. "Hello, Alice? There is a complication here. I had a little heart problem earlier. A-fib. It's very common. I'm fine now. Yes, I'm at the hospital. I'll be out in a couple of hours. Yes, they shocked me. Meihua took me here. I won't be able to come home until tomorrow."

"Is she worried?" I asked.

"Yes. She is concerned," said Ray calmly.

"Is she going to fly down?"

"No."

I nodded. He grinned and put his hand on my head, as one would do to a pet. Another day. *I have to break the news to Tom and Little-piggy,* I said to myself. I felt awkward, but I couldn't leave Ray at the hospital by himself.

After a couple of hours, a nurse entered the room with a clipboard containing a stack of forms—insurance information, discharge instructions, prescriptions. She gave the clipboard to Ray, and he signed the necessary forms.

"You can go now," said the nurse.

The sky was darkening when we left. He walked to the driver's side of the car and got in. I didn't argue. I sat in the passenger seat and handed over the keys.

"Are you feeling good?" I asked.

"Like new." He turned and winked at me. Then he started the engine.

"I wouldn't risk it." I couldn't believe what he had in mind. I was still shaking from this afternoon.

As though he sensed my feeling, Ray drove us to a restaurant, a fancy place overlooking the ocean. We were seated outside. Listening to the waves pounding the shore and smelling the salty sea, I finally felt at peace. A waiter with a chic haircut and crisp uniform served us wine and a few dishes of raw tuna, pot stickers, and sushi. Everything was delicious.

"I guess we've got the whole day off tomorrow," I said, happy again.

"Until our flight at 6:30."

"Should we go to South Beach?"

"Sure, but only if I survive the night."

"If you don't, I'll just have to leave you there and go myself."

251

After dinner, we took a walk along the beach. The moon was high, the air breezy. The ocean stretched out on one side, a string of fancy hotels and condos on the other. Peering at the gaps between the taller buildings, I saw brightly lit houses shining like diamonds.

"What a beautiful view."

"Living here is nice, until hurricane season. You're right about the view."

Despite his comment, I began to envision living in one of those condos with Ray. Every morning, I would get up to a vast view of ocean. I would sit on the veranda, sipping tea, reading or writing. When I got hungry, Ray and I would walk along the beach to an oceanfront café for lunch. It seemed worthwhile, even if a hurricane destroyed the beach and our lifestyle after only a year or two.

That night, we huddled together and slept. I enjoyed the break from sex. Sometimes, it seemed that was all we ever did together, along with eating. In the morning, he woke me by touching my breasts. Then, he rolled on top of me and kissed me.

"Are you okay?" I said, finally awake.

"Fresh and new."

His touch got me so excited, I forgot about yesterday's crisis. Sex was living up to its reputation as a dangerous game.

He moved further on top of me and started kissing me from my breasts down to my bushy private. He licked the juice. Then, he flipped me around, put a pillow under my stomach, and entered me. I came over and over, howling like a wolf. He wrapped me between his arms and legs, as though I were a chick in his shell. With a push, he came and fell back next to me. With eyes closed, he looked as relaxed as a baby. Lying next to him, I wondered whether he was okay. I took his pulse and estimated about eighty beats per minutes. *I guess he has survived this one*, I said to myself.

After showering, I put on my swimsuit and romper, and we drove the few short blocks to the inland waterway, over the causeway. At the beach, we found a partially shaded spot behind a lifeguard stand and set down our things. I ventured to the water and body surfed, while Ray sat and watched. Afterwards, I snuggled next to him for a while, before sitting up and making a sandcastle. He was so relaxed, he fell asleep. Our morning activities had probably been too much for a guy with a heart condition. After a while, I nudged him awake.

"Look, Ray. Look at that beautiful kite."

Down the beach, a group of people were flying kites. One resembled a giant lobster.

"Ray, get up." He didn't move. "Ray, are you all right?" I pushed him hard and pulled his head up. His face was red and sweaty. His arms seemed limp. Panicked, I retrieved my phone to call the paramedics, when he suddenly sat up.

"It must be a dream. We are sitting together on a beach." He started kissing me. His hands were on my breasts, ready to take off my swimsuit.

"Stop, this is a public place." I pushed him away. "Are you in any shape to do it again?" He put my hand inside his trousers, and there was no doubt he was ready. We drove back to the Westin. This time I was on top. He nibbled my breasts, while I thrashed back and forth. Even though I was a little sore, I came multiple times. That night, we ate a big meal in an upscale Chinese restaurant. I enjoyed the stir-fried sea bass and the crab with garlic sauce. Best of all were the giant sea cucumbers.

When he dropped me off at the airport, he lifted my bag from the back seat. Stepping forward, he kissed me on the lips.

"Thanks for coming."

I looked into his small, but penetrating eyes. "I'll come again," I said with my eyes.

***

The rain stopped, and the fog lifted. My vision was much clearer now. As I drove forward, I put Ray in my history compartment, trying not to look back.

Doors in Paris

In Paris, they don't have doorknobs. Doors are controlled by buttons, latches, and keypads that are nearly impossible to decipher. On top of that, the first floor is called "zero," and the second floor is called "one." What an incredible incongruity that is. I ring the doorbell on the third (second) floor for ten minutes. No answer. In a moment of wisdom, I look up and see the shining brass number two. My heart jolts. Please don't tell me my apartment is farther upstairs. I don't want to lug my suitcase up one more step.

Five minutes and another flight of stairs later, a tall, blonde woman—my landlady—steps out of a door on the fourth (third) floor. She wraps me in a big hug and smothers me with kisses, which lifts my mood. If not for my upcoming agent consultation, I probably would have collapsed onto the comfortable bed in the bright living room. Instead, I must perk up for my agent consultation appointment.

I'm here to attend the Paris Writer's Workshop—something I had dreamed of doing for sixteen years, when I was awarded second prize in the short story competition organized by WICE (a nonprofit Anglophone volunteer-run culture association). At the time, I was unable to attend the workshop and have thought about it periodically ever since.

I embark on the forty-minute walk to the WICE offices, where the Paris Writer's Workshop will take place. The walk is pleasant, and I only get lost three times at two street corners. When I finally find the entrance, it seems to be an apartment building, not the office of an elite non-profit. Desperate, I press my face against the tall glass door, trying to see through. The word WICE is visible on a small door across a courtyard. The office appears to be closed and empty, showing no signs of humanity inside or nearby.

"Come on. I have crossed the Atlantic for this conference. Let me in!" I yell, while violently pushing against the door.

I see a petite old lady inside. "I need to get in!" I shout. She shuffles over, mumbles something in French, and opens the door. I run straight to the WICE office. As it seemed, it is closed and dark inside. There is no notice of the Paris Writer's Workshop on the door or window. Disappointed, I turn just in time to see the old lady walking away. If I don't hurry up, I realize, I may be locked in here forever. I chase after her, yelling, "Open the door!"

After I leave the building, I find myself alone again with nowhere to go. I'm feeling discouraged. If I can't find my agent consultation, I may as well go home. Then, I remember something. The conference brochure lists another site, only about five minutes away. I open the map and navigate to the venue.

When I arrive, I'm not surprised to find that door locked as well. I go to the Catholic church next door to consult with God. "Push the button, then pull!" says the priest (who must represent God). I obey and walk into a paradise.

After I register in the office, the organizer tells me everyone is socializing in the garden. I follow the light and run straight into the garden. Shrubs and vines border the wall. A large pond sits in the middle, surrounded by many kinds of flowers—pansies, dahlias, daisies, cosmos, lilies. Peering into the water, I see tropical fish swimming and a couple of frogs hopping around. Of course, in France, the frogs are food.

An assortment of tea and decadent chocolate chip cookies are arranged on a table. It occurs to me I'm in Paris, so the food must be good! I trot to the bountiful table and wolf down three cookies before circling back and attempting to engage in literary conversation with the other workshop participants.

Making the rounds, I learn that quite a few participants are from Paris. A skinny lady with dark skin begins talking with me. She is a volunteer for WICE and a writer. She has moved to Paris from Indonesia and her English is good, but she is still struggling with French.

"I entered the 'Paris Prize' and didn't win. I'm discouraged," she tells me.

I don't know what to say. I'm too embarrassed to tell her, "Do you know how many competitions I have lost?" Yet, I'm still writing. I'm still trying to pass through the door. Though I have finally figured out how to get through physical doors, I'm struggling to enter this invisible world for writers. I have spent almost $4,000 to participate in this workshop. I'm still not sure why I'm here. Yes, I won second prize for my short fiction sixteen years ago. In the intervening years, I have written a few more works (five short stories and a partial manuscript for a novel) and have hardly published anything more. Now, I'm making one last attempt before I become old and gray—well, old, anyway. The gray hairs have already begun to take over.

"Are you meeting the agents?" The lady from Indonesia asks.

"Yes," I say seriously. That is why I'm still there, fighting jetlag.

"You will meet with the one you have chosen at 2:30 p.m."

"Okay." I look at my left wrist. To my horror, I have forgotten to bring my watch, and my cell phone doesn't work in Europe. I have no way to tell time. I could try using the sundial in the courtyard, but I don't know how. I have failed my first survival test.

"I will come and get you," she promises me. "Are you tired? I can show you where to take a nap."

"That sounds like heaven." I follow her.

She shows me a table where several chairs are partially hidden under a grapevine by the pond. I sit and put my feet up on the chair in front of me, trying to nap. But, I'm feeling unsettled. Occasionally, I get up and walk up to a stranger to ask for the time. That is how I meet Brenda, a beautiful African-French woman from Jamaica who volunteers for WICE.

"What brought you here?" She smiles at me, showing her perfect white teeth. Her short hair is curly, her silver dress fits her shapely body.

"I have a novel I would like to show the publisher." I mumble a little. I always have trouble demonstrating my talent.

"Oh, you have written a novel." She sounds impressed.

"I have also written a book of short stories and a book for young adults." I manage to show off some more, but that is really my limit for the day.

"You have written three books and you haven't done anything with them yet?" She looks very surprised, and I'm flattered.

"Hi." The lady from Indonesia comes over. It is obvious she knows Brenda.

"What time is it? Is it my turn?" I ask anxiously.

"No. Don't worry. You should go and sleep. I will come and get you."

"Okay." I rush back to the hidden table and chairs under the grapevine and try to sleep. Of course, I don't feel sleepy anymore. My head is spinning, and I realize I haven't brushed my teeth or changed my clothes for two days. *I'm in no condition to meet with a literary agent or a publisher,* I tell myself. Why didn't I think of this before? Why didn't I arrive a day earlier? Everything is too late, and I must get it over with.

I alternate between blaming myself and being in a daze. Finally, the Indonesian woman comes over and announces, "It's 2 p.m. and you should get ready."

I follow her inside to a waiting area just outside the room where the publishers and agents are camped. Here, I join a group of writers comprised of gray-haired older men, middle-aged ladies, and skinny athletic women. They are sitting, pretending to read newspapers or magazines, or standing and brooding. Feeling tired, I look for a seat, but cannot find one. I decide to stand among the crowd and attempt to read a book to kill time.

"Meihua Zhang." Brenda calls my name with a big smile. A little startled, I feel unprepared. I think of my odor-filled mouth and unchanged clothes as I follow Brenda to a big empty room where three agents/publishers sit behind a desk. Patrick Jackson, a tall, handsome publisher from HarperCollins UK stands and shakes my hand. He's wearing a tailored tan suit and wire-framed glasses. We both sit. Still worrying about my bad breath, I sit sideways so I don't face Patrick directly.

"Do you want to get published?" He leans forward and speaks earnestly. His eyes seemed huge behind his wire-framed glasses.

Of course, I want to get published. What sort of question is that? I nod. I only get fifteen minutes, so I'd better talk fast. I start telling him about my childhood in Beijing, my mother's affairs, and my great-grandmother's brothel in Shanghai. He listens and occasionally nods. When I start talking about my complicated childhood, I see fear in his eyes. Am I too much for this publisher? Yet, I don't stop talking.

"I'm addicted to crazy people. My first husband was a medical device inventor and a trained thoracic surgeon. He was thirty years older than me. Life with him was fun—like a fairytale."

Now, he seems impressed. "You should write a memoir," he says in his lilting British accent. "Your life up to now sounds fascinating."

When our conversation is just getting interesting, Brenda comes in to tell us our time is up. But we continue.

"I have also written a novel. Have you read the sample pages?" I point to a few pages of writing on the table.

"Yes. Not bad, not bad," he says, which sounds like a compliment to me. "I will write down a list of agents in the US for you to contact."

Now it sounds like a rejection.

"You are a publisher! Why can't you take my manuscript?" This is my last chance. I must be brave!

"I'm just getting started." He leans back to create distance between us. "I need to read a little more. It is hard to tell where the story is going in only three pages." He extends his hand to me.

At that moment, I wish I could put fifty manuscript pages in his hand. But I can't. This is the only copy I have brought for the Master Class in Novel Writing with Catherine Dumas, a French-American writer.

"I...I can't. I need my copy for my class," I say, downtrodden. "Would you like to read some of my short stories?" I pull three stories from my bag and try to dump all three in his hands.

"Just one," he says softly. "I want one that is autobiographic." I'm sure he is used to this kind of situation.

"This one is autobiographic. It's about my first husband." How can anyone invent a story like that—a young girl marrying an old doctor and having a lot of fun? "This one is my best story, according to friends." I stuff another story into his hands. "This one won the second prize in a WICE short story competition." I give him another one.

Brenda comes over for the third time and insists our time is up. Patrick walks me to the door. As I walk away, he bends and gives a bow, as though to usher me through the door—the door to the literary world, which I'm so desperate to enter.

A Moment of Freedom

The cat Xiaohua was in heat again. Meiling held her against her chest, shaking and rubbing, trying to calm her down. Suddenly, the front door flung open. Her daughter Mingming came in.

"Gee, Xiaohua is in heat again? How come she is this way so often?"

"Come on, don't scorn her. My poor little Xiaohua. How pitiful." Meiling tapped Xiaohua's white nose.

"Aarh, Aarh…" Xiaohua was howling again.

"Oh my god, she is in despair."

"Stop, would you! You have complained enough. Xiaohua is nice. She just gets that way occasionally. She can't help it. In fact, she is nicer than you are."

Mingming wrinkled her nose at her mother's words and slid past her room. A young man, pale and slender, wearing a polyester white shirt and navy-blue cotton pants, followed Mingming into the room next to Meiling's.

"Pong!" The door slammed shut.

Silence. Everything was back to normal again. Meiling sat on her bed, still embracing Xiaohua. She gazed at Xiaohua's sad, clear green eyes.

Outside, it was autumn again. Dead leaves rolled down the street. They fell into ravines and gathered at corners. They would stay there, wet and rotten, and eventually turn into fertilizer.

People walked back and forth, shopping or returning home from work. Everybody had a goal in life. What was hers?

Her husband, Professor Chen, had passed away last year. He had never been a good companion. They lived together as enemies for thirty years.

The things she grew accustomed to—the cursing, the drunken howling, the crash of breaking dishes, the sad violin tone—had all disappeared.

Meiling's bedroom sat half-empty for months. Nobody bothered to visit. Nobody was eager to jump into her bed. Where were the men she used to feed, take care of, and love—the men who would stay in her apartment and were impossible to push away? They were all gone. It was not that they didn't need her anymore. It was that she didn't want them. She was old. Her face had grown wrinkles and pimples. Her skin was loose, hair gray. It did not look good anymore to go out with young men. She was terribly tired, like a mountain climber who, drained of energy, couldn't climb a step higher.

"Ha, no, no, ha, ha…" The noise issued from Mingming's room.

Is it she? Meiling asked herself. She used to take those guys in, close the door, and have all the fun in the world. She was a wild and beautiful woman whom every man desired and loved.

"Ha, ha. Again, again. Ha…"

Meiling was glad Mingming had closed the door. She wished the wall was better at insolating the sounds she didn't want to hear. What could she do? She was happy for Mingming. It was her time. She was young, and youth was worth a thousand yen.

"Oh, oh. That's enough. Oh, oh…"

Meiling used to be a loud girl, louder than Mingming. Her husband, Professor Chen, could even hear it when he played the violin. He had to knock on the door to tell them to be quiet. She told him she was not bothered by his violin, so why did he care about her playing?

"Hi, Mom. Are you still here? Wow, it's so cold."

The door opened. Mingming ran out, shivering under her pajamas. "Oh, I need to go to the bathroom so bad," she said.

That was her, Meiling said to herself. The reddish, shiny face, the red lips—she used to be like that after having fun. She would wrap her sweaty body with a towel and sweep through the apartment to the bathroom, happy and excited. She would light a cigarette and sit for a while to cool down.

"Ha, ha, let me see yours. Ha, ha…"

Meiling couldn't stand it anymore. It was dark outside and already 5:30 p.m. She had to go to work. Putting on her work pants and shoes, she walked out the door.

The street was very busy. Waves of people poured from different directions, converging on the street. Some were heading home, some were hurrying out to buy groceries, some, like Meiling, were going to work.

She wore a pair of tinted glasses and a scarf to cover her face. She did not want to be seen. Bicycle bells rang around her. That annoyed her. She used to be a tall, sexy young woman, attracting eyes wherever she went. Now, there was no point showing off her old, fat body. Now, she was tired of hearing people talk about her love affairs at street corners. She knew they were jealous. She walked rapidly and took shortcuts through a park and an athletic field to stay away from the busy streets. Finally, she arrived at the gate of the Beijing Institute of Aeronautics and Astronomy's main campus. Two guards in green uniforms stood watch, wearing their quilted coats and leather hats. The younger-looking guard stopped her with his palm. She had started working there just three months earlier.

"Hi, don't you remember me?" Meiling shook his hands. He stared at her but did not react.

"Arya, you are probably too young to remember me." She walked toward the older guard.

"You should remember me. My name is Chen Meiling. I used to teach here five years ago." She moved even closer, her two big breasts pointing directly toward him, wobbling slightly. The guard smiled.

"Sure, I remember you. But you know this is our new policy. Everyone has to show an ID."

"Come on. Have a cigarette. You young men work too hard, I would say." She put a hand in her pocket and tried to pull out a cigarette packet. The guard stopped her with his palm.

"That's okay. That's okay." He waved her in.

"Thank you! Sweet young man. Take care." She slipped in.

God, that was easy. Her old tricks were working. She should chase down the bureaucrats to get herself an ID soon. She was self-employed, so there was no reason they had to check her background (going back three generations) to issue her an ID. This encounter stirred up the bitterness in her life. She slowed and walked into the bushes. Finding a large rock, she sat and started smoking.

266

A year earlier, her husband had died of cancer and her business partner was absent for two weeks.

"Hi, Mom. How are you?" Mingming had just come back from work.

"Don't bother me. Mom doesn't feel well today."

"What's going on? Has Uncle Zhang shown up yet?"

Silence.

"Mom, you lost your job."

"Stop! I never worked for him. He was working for me."

That was when Meiling decided to find a new occupation. But what would she do? Leaning on her six years of entrepreneurial experience, she decided to start a cleaning business. She would begin cleaning classrooms for the university—a handy occupation that she knew was sorely needed. This work used to be done by students themselves—that was how it was when she was a student thirty years earlier—but now students were unmotivated and did a slipshod job of cleaning up after themselves. They no longer believed in the Communist slogan: "Serve your people whole heartily." Now, students were more concerned about themselves than anything else. But their lack of attentiveness provided an opportunity for her. So, she began her cleaning business.

It was completely dark now. The campus' spherical streetlights shined, reminding her of full moons. She stood and walked back to the street. She had to start working. She cleaned two buildings each day. It took her ten days to finish the campus' twenty buildings.

She walked into the "Fifth Department" building. As a military research institute, any work performed on campus was confidential. Therefore, the buildings were named by numbers instead of their specialties. Every room in this empty building was lit with fluorescent lights, bright and empty. Ready to be cleaned. The students had been told to stay away.

She made her way to the back of a classroom and began sweeping the concrete floor. It was a large classroom with more than twenty rows of desks arched around a podium. Life was a strange dream. Thirty years ago, she had met her husband, Professor Chen, in this room. He had been a professor, and she was his student. Three months later, they married. She quit her college studies to become his housewife.

It was so quiet here; one could hear a needle drop to the ground. She could not remember any other time in her life when she had worked alone. She always had partners or colleagues. She used to love people and could not live without them. Now, she enjoyed silence. She could fall into the past while sweeping the floor or picking up bottles, candy wrappers, and sunflower seed shells.

When was that evening? She had danced with Premier Zhou at a party during her freshman year. She was so young and beautiful, with a head of long, fluffy hair, big charming eyes, and a knockout body. He was so handsome. Under the light, his big eyes, thick eyebrows, straight nose, and cleanshaven dark chin were unbearably attractive, his voice so tender.

"You've come from Shanghai? Have you grown accustomed to our Beijing lifestyle?"

"Oh, yes. It's not too bad." She was too nervous to say anything more.

She put her hands on his shoulders and he held her waist. The romantic waltz took them swinging, turning, swinging…She almost lost conscious.

When had she met Weiming? He was a twenty-year-old playboy with unusually curly hair and a big nose. He did not look Chinese at all. They met when she was thirty-five, still beautiful and sexy.

"Have you heard of a book called *Jane Eyre*, college graduate?" He asked her while they were working on the factory floor.

"Of course," she said. "My major was airplane engine design, but I also studied literature. I would even compare myself with Jane Eyre. We have so much in common."

"I don't think you are Jane Eyre. You are beautiful and innocent. She was plain and mature."

"Come on, I'm thirty-five years old—fifteen years older than you are. Don't pretend to be mature."

"I like innocent girls better. Have you read *Madame Bovary*, a French novel?"

"Yes."

"That's you, an unsatisfied doctor's wife."

"How do you know?" She was surprised that this young man understood her so well.

After that, they spent endless evenings together, strolling on the street, sitting on park benches, and playing piano in his apartment. One day, he showed her a piece of a drawing.

"I designed the interior of our future home. What do you think?"

Silence.

"Don't you like it?"

Silence. She did not know how to tell this young man her husband didn't want a divorce. She had two young children to take care of. However, they continued as lovers for eight years, until one day she decided to let him go. He needed to find his own life, and she realized she wanted the same. The end was messy.

He had sneaked over to her bedroom as usual, even though her husband was long accustomed to his presence. He knocked, and she stepped out of her bedroom shutting the door behind her. Clearly, she was with somebody else.

They moved into the kitchen. He threw his bag on the table and sat down in a chair, silent. He sensed something was wrong.

"What are you doing here?" Meiling said firmly, arms akimbo. "You'd better go back to your pretty, young girlfriend. I have found out everything!"

"I'm not serious with her."

"Not serious? Who are you serious with?" Meiling threw some old photos of them at his face. He stood and rushed out. He never returned.

When did she meet this kid—the twenty-one-year-old? He had small, round eyes, a flat nose, and a dark, brushy mustache. He played the guitar, violin, and cello. She recalled his politeness and how, as her apprentice, he called her "master." Somehow, he found his forty-five-year-old "master" attractive and romantically exciting. She was both a mother and lover to him for many years.

This young man had a deep feeling toward life and art. They would sit, playing his guitar and singing every day after work, and she would forget all the unpleasantness in her life. They rode their bicycles on the street, carrying instruments on their backs and attracting a lot of attention.

"Gee, someone is cleaning the classroom. We have to go somewhere else."

"Why does the school let these people clean at such a late hour?"

Two students walked by the door. Meiling's heart beat faster. Her face reddened. Sometimes, she wondered why she had become a janitor in old age. She had been a professor's wife, a mother, a factory worker, and the head of her own construction business. Maybe she had had too much fun earlier in life. This was what she deserved.

She knew these students, the top 10 percent of Chinese youths. Having been one of them, she knew how privileged they were. Yet, she felt like shouting at them.

"Hey, kids! Don't feel too proud of yourselves. You are still young. You don't know what the future will bring for you!" She chased them out the door.

The students disappeared in the dark. She was back in the empty classroom and wanted to cry.

At ten o'clock, Meiling was home. Mingming was already sound asleep, resting before work in the morning.

Meiling quickly washed herself with heated water before slipping into bed. Wide awake, her head felt inflated and heavy. She hoped that was not a sign of an impending migraine—her migraines often made her delirious for a week. She thought about meeting with the public housing officials tomorrow and asking to keep this apartment. After her husband passed away, they had wanted to take away her three-bedroom apartment. This kind of privilege was only for professors and their family members. But she wanted to keep it. Now that she worked at the institute, she had a legitimate reason to live here. She also wanted Mingming to have a place to live when she married. That was all she could provide for her daughter.

Gradually, she fell asleep. She dreamed how she might have lived her life differently. She might have studied harder and become an engineer. She could have taught here in the institute, just like her husband. She might have a head of snow-white hair by now, but that wouldn't matter. People would respect her. She might have lived with her mother-in law and her several younger children in a small apartment. She might have cooked for and taken care of them after work, then graded students' papers until midnight.

She was awakened by construction noise outside. Looking out the window, another building was going up. She knew how it was done. She used to share a construction business with her partner, Lao Zhang. She sweated a lot and had fun.

Meiling turned on a tape recorder. It played a sad song.

Please have a cup of tea,
Please have a bottle of wine.
Youth is like morning dew,
Pretty soon will be overdue.

Despite her recent melancholy thoughts, Meiling had been enjoying herself lately. The tranquility in her house pleased her.

"De, de, de…"

Whose motorcycle? She did not remember anyone owning a motorcycle in this neighborhood. She glanced out the window.

"Oh my god. What is he doing here?"

A tall, strong, sharp-looking man around forty-five years old parked his motorcycle in front of the building. He wore a leather jacket and a pair of black, woolen pants. Turning off the engine, he did not bother to lock the motorcycle.

Meiling heard a knock on her door. She opened it a crack.

"Hey, how are you?" said the man. He small eyes flashed with affection.

"Why are you here?" Meiling answered in an unpleasant tone. "I told you not to bother me anymore. We are through. My husband has just died, and it's not good to be involved with someone right away."

"I thought you might need a job." He pushed her aside and barged in. He put his big buttocks on the bed in Meiling's bedroom, as though he were a family member.

"Come on. This is not your home." She sat on the bed, looking out the window.

"It was my home," he said slyly. His fierce eyes stared at her irresistibly.

"What do you want?" asked Meiling.

"I just found a new business opportunity for us. I met with people in the northwest who would like to contract with us to build some structures for them. We could leave Beijing for a while, make some money, and come back."

"I have my own business," said Meiling firmly.

"What? Say it again."

"I HAVE MY OWN BUSINESS," she yelled.

"Your own business! Come on. I know you can't live without me." He put one hand on Meiling's shoulder and stuck another under her thin, almost transparent polyester shirt. He started kissing her.

Meiling immersed herself in it for a while. She could feel his thick, hot lips, his tongue, and the hands that fondled her breasts. She loved it. But she pushed him away and moved a few inches from him.

"I have lived alone for six months," said Meiling bitterly.

"I'm sorry." He edged a few inches toward her and put his hand back on her shoulder. "I was looking for business opportunities for us. Since your husband just died, I thought it might not be a good idea for me to bother you too soon."

Meiling started to cry.

"Hey, don't cry. I'm here now." He passed her a handkerchief. Then, he took off his shoes and jumped into the bed. Lying by her, he put his hands on her thighs and grinned at her affectionately.

"Go. I want to be left alone for a while," said Meiling.

"Okay." He got off the bed and stood up. "I'm leaving now. You'd better prepare to leave here in thirty days."

"No, I'm not going with you."

"What? You must be out of your mind." He stamped his feet.

"I have my own business to take care of," said Meiling calmly.

"What, your cleaning service? What a joke! You won't last ten days."

"I have been doing it for a month."

"Okay, okay. I'm leaving. I'm leaving. Don't tell me I never offered you anything!"

He stormed out, grabbing a tape recorder that had belonged to him as he left.

Meiling sat, staring at the wall and empty table where the tape recorder used to be. A wave of sadness and grief hit her. She wanted to cry, to wail.

That was the first time in her life she had ever stood up for herself.

"Aaeh, Aaeh!" The cat Xiaohua sauntered in and jumped onto her lap. She nestled comfortably against her chest.

Looking out the window, a gust of wind blew dead leaves up into the sky. They flew around and clashed against each other. They soared like many butterflies. She felt a sudden sense of relief. Yes, this was what she wanted. No matter where she ended up—rotten in a ravine, abandoned in a ditch, buried underground—this was what she wanted. A moment of freedom.

Nice, My Dream

I have been living in Nice, France for a month. Sitting in the balcony of my seafront apartment, I can see the calm blue Mediterranean Sea and pebble beach. Except for its light blue color, the water might have been a lake. Striped umbrellas of various shades of blue decorate the beach—a signature feature of Nice. I miss the summer atmosphere—the music and spontaneous dancing on the Promenade.

I had decided to move to Nice after a quarrel with my husband. I told him I needed a break. He said he'd give me one month to think things over, and I readily agreed. One month in Nice! It was a dream for me.

It is rather quiet now. Five years ago, I had visited this place for the first time with my family.

My husband Jason and I first came to Nice after we missed our train to Provence. Drawn in by the city's beauty, we decided to stay for five days. After booking an apartment through Airbnb, we went for a walk. The temperature was 21°C, perfect. We walked by giant sculptures made of steel and wood. Children climbed freely on wooden fish, lobsters, and octopuses in the park. Birds left their droppings on top of David's head—a different and less famous David statue.

We wanted to go to the beach but took a wrong turn. Instead, we found ourselves in front of a small restaurant with a cute floral name. Construction outside the restaurant forced us to cross a temporary bridge to reach the door. We walked in and found it completely empty. A man with salt and pepper hair greeted us and asked if we had reservations. We said no. He ushered us out the door, saying, "We are totally sold out tonight." We walked out in disbelief. Only later did we discover this was a Michelin-starred restaurant.

Nearby, we found another restaurant with outdoor seating. We drank wine, soaking in the scent of orange shrubs and the fragrance of the rosemary plant on the table. We enjoyed tomato salads with fresh mozzarella cheese accompanied by caramelized orange peels in everything. Our seafood entrées tasted fresh from the water, only two blocks away. We were jet-lagged but happy.

The second day, after eating fresh croissants and rich coffee for breakfast, we headed toward the beach. Before we arrived, we were seduced by the colorful fresh produce market with its bright red, plump tomatoes, dark purple figs, juicy strawberries, succulent peaches, and my favorite: luscious apricots. It was hard to resist buying a huge box of these natural treasures.

Our day had scarcely begun when we decided to walk the famous Promenade des Anglais, a one-mile walkway along the beach. The boardwalk ended at the famous hotel Negresco, which was built by a Russian Czar as his summer palace. As we enjoyed the area's many shades of blue, romantic music flowed into our ears. A saxophone played "Ava Maria," the smooth melodies floating like an elixir from my ears to my heart. The moving music made me tremble, and I knew I was falling in love with Nice.

After indulging in decadent ice chocolate, we decided to climb Castle Hill. As we walked along the ancient pathway, history and amazing views met us at every turn. When we arrived at the top, the Nice skyline spread at our feet. We asked a young Chinese student from London to take our picture. As the night drew to a close, we dined on broiled octopus and a tuna niçoise salad.

The third day, we couldn't wait to pick up our son, Sam. The temperature had shot up to 32°C, so we spent the morning swimming in the soft blue sea and sitting beneath two blue and white striped umbrellas.

Afterward, we took the bus to the Nice airport and picked up Sam. He waved to us, carrying a heavy duffel bag on one shoulder and looking happy and healthy. We checked into the apartment I had rented—a quaint place that was even closer to the beach than our previous hotel. The apartment sat on the fourth floor, meaning we had to climb five flights of stairs every day at least once. In Europe, the ground floor is considered the zeroth floor. But, our walk to the beach was shorter, and we didn't have to take the trolley bus far.

The fourth day, we cooked breakfast after shopping at a nearby market. My caprese sandwich tasted better than any sandwich I had ever eaten. Nothing could beat the freshness of Nice ingredients.

"We should visit Saint Paul De Vance," said Jason. "It is a magical place."

"Why, Dad?" Sam asked.

"Great artists like Matisse, Braque, Calder, Miro, and Picasso created many iconic works of art there."

"Sure. Let's go," said Sam. As a professional media artist, Sam understood art's magic.

We took a taxi to the center of France's best-preserved medieval village. There, we enjoyed expansive views of olive groves, fig trees, and vineyards that stretched as far as the eye could see. A group of Chinese tourists exited their tour bus; I was surprised to see them this far off the beaten path.

Looking around, everything was made of stone—stone walls, stone steps, stone buildings. Hidden behind the stone walls were galleries, restaurants, gift shops, and even restrooms. We found a stone landing that stood at least six feet high. Jason and Sam climbed onto it and I followed, a little scared. But I was willing to sacrifice my safety for a little fun.

After a challenging walk, we found a restaurant on the hill with stunning views and tasty fish sandwiches, accompanied by fresh tomatoes and mozzarella cheese. Looking at the rolling hills full of grape vines and fig trees, I prayed for this moment to last forever.

That night, I dreamed I was in Saint Paul De Vance. I strolled through an opening in a stone wall marked "Toilette" and noticed a young Chinese man in a suit and black glasses. He stood at the bathroom entrance, struggling to put coins in the slot. I showed him he was using a one-Euro coin, when he only needed twenty cents. From his open palms, I fished out the correct change from a collection of coins. As I touched the coins, I felt tiny electrical shocks—static electricity?

"Where are you from?" he asked in Asian-accented English.

"Minnesota," I said. "Which city are you from in China?" I asked in Chinese.

"Shenzhen, where I work for a medical device company," he replied.

I told him I also worked for a medical device company, and we started talking about the industry. We had a lot in common. Over the past twenty years, I had worked on about ten different medical devices, and he understood each one. At some point, I mentioned I was a big Elon Musk fan. He said he was, too. He owned a Tesla Model X. I stared at the blue sky over Saint Paul De Vance and asked, "Is this real?"

"Do you want to visit my company in Shenzhen?" he asked earnestly.

"Sure. I can probably come next year." I couldn't believe I had agreed to visit a stranger in China. *This can't be real.*

"Let's go." He grabbed my hand.

"Now?"

"Yes. We will be there in no time."

I stared at him and nodded.

After an eternity, we stepped off a bus in a Chinese city, which I assumed was Shenzhen. Waves of humid air hit me, welcoming me into this south China city. He held my hand, and it felt natural. Guiding me down a narrow street, we stepped through the grand entrance of a tall skyscraper, the tallest among many in this new industrial city. As soon as we stepped inside, light from a bright chandelier blinded me, and I struggled to see my surroundings. When I could finally see, I didn't recognize my reflection in the mirror. I looked like a young woman in her late twenties, wearing a formal, olive-green woolen suit jacket, a matching woolen skirt, and a maroon silk blouse. We walked into a conference room, and a group of people stood and clapped.

"Welcome back, Mr. Cheng."

So, his last name was Cheng, but that was all I knew. I wanted to learn more about the man I had followed from Nice, France. Was I awake? I tried to pinch myself. I felt something, but not pain, so I decided to follow along. *I like what I've seen so far*, I told myself.

"Sit down." Cheng motioned for everyone to sit.

In the middle of the table, Cheng and I sat next to each other in two empty chairs.

Everyone was quiet. It was obvious Cheng was their boss. I looked around and noticed a delicious lunch spread—huge lobsters in ginger scallion sauce, jumbo shrimp and scallops in a noodle bird's nest, red cooked pork with hard boiled eggs, Sichuan eggplant, and the most provocative dish of all: stir-fried cockroaches.

"This is comrade Zhang." Cheng turned toward me. "We met in Nice, France. Since she is an expert in the medical device industry in America, I immediately recruited her. Let's give her a warm welcome." Cheng stood and applauded, and everyone followed suit.

They started singing a song that sounded familiar. It must be their company song, I told myself. I felt moved. I didn't remember Cheng hiring me. It had all happened so fast, I didn't have time to think or refuse. But I was glad I had followed Cheng here. These people were obviously very happy workers. They seemed driven by ideology instead of money, which was the culture I had grown up with and tried to run away from. Now, it was a breath of fresh air. After living in the US for over thirty years, I missed this mentality.

Everyone began eating, and I joined in.

"What do you think?" asked Cheng.

282

"Good, great," I said while trying to put a fried cockroach into my mouth.

"Ha, ha." Cheng noticed my wrinkled nose. "You don't have to eat it. It is just for decoration, or something to scare the foreigners."

"Why didn't you tell me earlier?" I spat it out.

"I thought you knew." He laughed again, delighting in my mistake.

We made eye contact, and I felt the ground underneath me shake again. The room blurred, the wall drew nearer, spinning in a checkerboard of different colors—red, green, blue, purple. It morphed into a tunnel, and I couldn't help but wander inside. Cheng followed, grabbing my hand again.

As I was about to fall asleep, we landed on a beach—an empty and vast stretch of shore. It was evening and a full moon illuminated the sky. We stood on the wet, soft sand, listening to waves pound the shore and seagulls squawking. I stared at him questioningly.

"This is my hometown," he explained. "I grew up in a small fishing village called Hainan. Are you surprised?"

I shook my head repeatedly. "No. If you told me you were a merman, I wouldn't be surprised." I leaned closer and stared at him, eye to eye. "Are you?"

He moved away and laughed loudly. "Does that mean you are a mermaid?"

"Wow, I'm honored." I gave him a hug.

He grabbed my hand and said, "Let me show you something."

We came to a giant sailboat. Cheng walked up to the deck, and a couple of seamen stood and saluted him.

I followed him to the ship bridge at the stern. He turned a key and started the engine. "We will motor for a while before opening the sails."

"I take it you're the captain?" I asked, admiring this man who had enough confidence to run this huge vessel in the dark.

"Of course. I've been a captain since I turned fifteen years old." He turned the steering wheel slowly. "But we never had a boat this big when I was young. Only after I made my own fortune in new China, did I have the opportunity to drive such a colossal boat." Something flickered in his eyes, and I could tell he was bothered by his past. He brushed it away.

"I see," I said. "You have worked your way up. You started young and achieved much—enough to obtain a big, handsome boat. You could invite your whole village to party here." I teased.

"Work my way up? You have no idea how poor I was. We didn't even have enough food to eat. I have taken many leaps to get here."

"I'm not good at high jumps. I only passed the high jump in gym class because my legs were long." I held his shoulders and leaned toward him. "Sorry. I didn't mean to trivialize your achievements. The American government tends to accuse China of stealing intellectual property, attributing that to China's success. But I think it's not that simple. Stealing, alone, does not guarantee success. Chinese people work hard and have a greater desire to succeed, which contributes to its enormous economic achievements."

"What a lecture!" He smiled.

I smiled back, relieved I hadn't bored him. "The 9/9/6 schedule[1] will definitely make China the superpower of the world."

"What do you know about 9/9/6?" He asked.

"Not much. I know I can't do it, which is why I live in the US. But I did 9/9/6 while I was trying to get into Peking University."

"Are you saying that studying is the same as working? I was loading and unloading fish when I was ten, while you were sitting around studying."

"Okay, you win!" I turned to him and hit him lightly on the arm. "Now I understand why I instantly trusted and followed you. It is because you seemed reliable and remarkable. I could sense it."

He looked at me and asked, "Are you sleepy?"

I nodded.

Cheng asked one of the seamen to take the steering wheel, and we walked together to the ship's cabin. What happened next is forever engraved in my mind. As soon as we were downstairs, Cheng picked me up and threw me on the bed. He invaded my vessel like a violent storm, and we rocked in unison with the sea. I yelled and yelled, sounding like a loud crow. Passion poured from me like a waterfall, engulfing Cheng. He echoed my passion, equally loud. It ended in a gentle lullaby that drew me into a deep slumber.

I was awakened by a loud noise. Cheng's side of the bed was empty. I moved toward the door and put my ear against the

---

[1] 9/9/6 is how Chinese people describe their long work hours which stretch from 9 a.m. to 9 p.m., 6 days per week.

wood. A man was speaking Cantonese. "We want cash, not digital currency. We don't want to leave any trace."

"I can pay you in crypto currency, a privacy coin that's impossible to track," said Cheng.

"No, I don't trust you. Call your company and tell them to bring us cash. In the meantime, you're coming with us."

I heard a small boat motoring away. Gradually, the sound faded. My heard sank. How would I survive on this gigantic boat without a captain? I ventured to the deck and gazed at the full moon. Tilting my head toward the brightly lit sky, I sang a sad song.

I opened my eyes and saw sunshine streaming down from the sky. I looked down and found I was lying on the sand in front of a blue ocean with seagulls soaring through the sky. Mr. Cheng sat next to me, staring at the ocean.

"Merman, thank you for bringing me back to Nice," I said sweetly. "Are you going to start a fishing company?"

"No. No more work. I want to enjoy life in this fabulous city." He turned and gave me a kiss.

While still enjoying the sweet taste of Mr. Cheng's kiss, I awoke and found myself back on the beachfront balcony of our rented apartment. The fresh sea breeze must have addled my dreams. My gaze drifted from the vast Mediterranean Sea to the handful of cheerful beachgoers in colorful pastel clothing. Loneliness swept over me. I longed for a companion with whom I could converse and share this beautiful view of Nice. Someone tapped my shoulder. I turned and saw my husband standing behind me.

"Jason! I'm so glad you're here." I turned to him and gave him a hug. "Are you going to stay a while?" I asked.

"Sure, if you want me to."

"That would be lovely," I said, not bothering to conceal my joy.

"Should we go for a swim?" he asked.

"Sure." I stretched my stiff arms. "You've read my mind."

Walking to the beach hand in hand, a thought drifted through my head. *Life is getting better already in Nice. And I'm glad Jason is here to share it with me.*

Home, sweet home. Now I miss it. With all these beautiful memories in my mind, I think I'm ready to go back. After giving the blue ocean one more look, I walk inside the apartment and book a flight home.

About Lisa

Photo by Eric Wharton

Born and raised in Beijing, China, Lisa Zhang Wharton is a graduate of Peking University and the University of Minnesota. She is an engineer by education and an author by avocation. Her short story "My Uncle" won second prize in the WICE-sponsored Paris Writer's Workshop. *Chinese Lolita* is her second work of fiction. Her novel, *Last Kiss in Tiananmen Square*, was published in 2011.

Lisa strives to enlighten readers about cultural differences between the West and China, showing not only differences but also similarities, to foster global thinking and create a path to a more peaceful world.

She currently works at Medtronic, Inc. and lives in St. Paul, Minnesota with her husband.

Made in the USA
Las Vegas, NV
14 December 2021